Acclaim for Radcly*ff*e's Fiction

Lambda Literary Award winner "…*Stolen Moments* is a collection of steamy stories about women who just couldn't wait. It's sex when desire overrides reason, and it's incredibly hot!"—*On Our Backs*

Lambda Literary Award winner "…*Distant Shores, Silent Thunder* weaves an intricate tapestry about passion and commitment between lovers. The story explores the fragile nature of trust and the sanctuary provided by loving relationships."—*Sapphic Reader*

"Lambda Literary and Benjamin Franklin Award finalist *The Lonely Hearts Club* "…is an ensemble piece that follows the lives [and loves] of three women, with a plot as carefully woven as a fine piece of cloth."—*Midwest Book Review*

ForeWord's Book of the Year finalist *Night Call* features "…gripping medical drama, characters drawn with depth and compassion, and incredibly hot [love] scenes."—*Just About Write*

Lambda Literary Award finalist *Justice Served* delivers a "…crisply written, fast-paced story with twists and turns and keeps us guessing until the final explosive ending."—*Independent Gay Writer*

Shield of Justice is a "…well-plotted…lovely romance…I couldn't turn the pages fast enough!"—Ann Bannon, author of *The Beebo Brinker Chronicles*

Lambda Literary Award finalist *Turn Back Time* is filled with…"wonderful love scenes, which are both tender and hot." —*MegaScene*

Lambda Literary Award finalist *When Dreams Tremble*'s "...focus on character development is meticulous and comprehensive, filled with angst, regret, and longing, building to the ultimate climax." —*Just About Write*

A Matter of Trust is a "...sexy, powerful love story filled with angst, discovery and passion that captures the uncertainty of first love and its discovery."—*Just About Write*

"The author's brisk mix of political intrigue, fast-paced action, and frequent interludes of lesbian sex and love...in *Honor Reclaimed*...sure does make for great escapist reading." – *Q Syndicate*

Change of Pace is "...contemporary, yet timeless, not only about sex, but also about love, longing, lust, surprises, chance meetings, planned meetings, fulfilling wild fantasies, and trust."—*Midwest Book Review*

"Radclyffe has once again pulled together all the ingredients of a genuine page-turner, this time adding some new spices into the mix. *shadowland* is sure to please—in part because Radclyffe never loses sight of the fact that she is telling a love story, and a compelling one at that."—Cameron Abbott, author of *To The Edge* and *An Inexpressible State of Grace*

"*Innocent Hearts*...illustrates that our struggles for acceptance of women loving women is as old as time—only the setting changes. The romance is sweet, sensual, and touching."—*Just About Write*

"*Sweet No More*...snarls, teases and toes the line between pleasure and pain."—*Best Lesbian Erotica 2008*

"*Word of Honor* takes the reader on a great ride. The sex scenes are incredible...and the story builds to an exciting climax that is as chilling as it is rewarding."—*Midwest Book Review*

By the Author

Romances

Innocent Hearts

Love's Melody Lost

Love's Tender Warriors

Tomorrow's Promise

Passion's Bright Fury

Love's Masquerade

shadowland

Fated Love

Turn Back Time

Promising Hearts

When Dreams Tremble

The Lonely Hearts Club

Night Call

Secrets in the Stone

The Provincetown Tales

Safe Harbor

Beyond the Breakwater

Distant Shores, Silent Thunder

Storms of Change

Winds of Fortune

Returning Tides

Honor Series

Above All, Honor

Honor Bound

Love & Honor

Honor Guards

Honor Reclaimed

Honor Under Siege

Word of Honor

Justice Series

A Matter of Trust (prequel)

Shield of Justice

In Pursuit of Justice

Justice in the Shadows

Justice Served

Justice for All

Erotic Interludes: *Change Of Pace*
(A Short Story Collection)
Radical Encounters
(An Erotic Short Story Collection)

Stacia Seaman and Radclyffe, eds.:
Erotic Interludes 2: *Stolen Moments*
Erotic Interludes 3: *Lessons in Love*
Erotic Interludes 4: *Extreme Passions*
Erotic Interludes 5: *Road Games*
Romantic Interludes 1: *Discovery*
Romantic Interludes 2: *Secrets*

Visit us at www.boldstrokesbooks.com

RETURNING TIDES

by

RADCLYFFE

2009

RETURNING TIDES

ISBN 10: 1-60282-123-2
ISBN 13: 978-1-60282-123-1

This Trade Paperback Original Is Published By
Bold Strokes Books, Inc.
P.O. Box 249
Valley Falls, NY 12185

First Edition: November 2009

CREDITS
Editors: Ruth Sternglantz and Stacia Seaman
Production Design: Stacia Seaman
Cover Art: Barb Kiwak (www.kiwak.com)
Cover Design By Sheri (graphicartist2020@hotmail.com)

Acknowledgments

Writing about a beloved place is an unparalleled pleasure. The characters in this series never live and breathe for me more than they do when I am actually in Provincetown, walking the narrow streets, catching glimpses of sailboats in the harbor, and feeling the hot sun reflected off the sweeping dunes. I am ever so grateful to all the readers who give me a reason to continue to write these stories. Deepest thanks.

Thanks also to first readers Connie, Eva, Jenny, Paula, and Tina; to editors Ruth Sternglantz and Stacia Seaman and the proofreaders who work so tirelessly making me look good; to artist Barb Kiwak for translating my half-described vision into the perfect cover painting; and to Sheri for a brilliant cover design. Deepest gratitude.

And to Lee, for always being the final destination. *Amo te.*

Radclyffe 2009

Dedication

For Lee
On Every Shore

The two figures on the deck were easily visible by the light of the three-quarter moon. From his spot on the deserted, storm-ravaged beach, he could make out the way their arms entwined and their mouths met in a long, passionate kiss. He watched *her* press herself against the other woman, pretending she was excited. Pretending she could be satisfied by someone like that. He knew better. He knew who she really wanted, what she really needed. He imagined her rubbing her hard-nippled breasts against him with the same abandon, her pelvis rocking on him, inviting him to fuck her. He heard her moans and whimpers, felt his cock gliding through hot swollen flesh. He heard her panting, begging, crying out for release. He smelled her excitement, tasted her arousal in the back of his throat. His cock twitched at the thought of her tightening around him as she came. Begging *him* to fuck her the way she needed to be fucked. Screaming when she came. Screaming for *him*.

With shaking hands, he raised the Rigel 2500 night binocs. The images came into focus, so large and so clear he might have been standing on the deck with them. He could make out her eyelids fluttering as the interloper kissed her and fondled her breasts, long fingers plucking at her nipples through her partly open robe. Her face contorted with pleasure and she let her head fall back, offering her throat—a sacrifice to the unworthy. Her mouth opened in a silent sigh as the other woman kissed her neck and slid a hand inside her robe to cup her breast. Her lids lifted, her expression languid and ripe as she flattened her palms against the other woman's chest and pushed her away, laughing. She tilted her head toward the glass doors behind them. He knew what she was saying. Saying to him.

Take me to bed. I want you to fuck me. I want you to make me scream. Make me scream. Make me scream.

"I will, soon," he muttered as she disappeared inside and closed the blinds. His head pounded with a mixture of rage and resentment, the pain a muted echo of the insistent throbbing of the erection that strained against his pants. He gripped himself and squeezed so hard tears blurred his vision. "I'll give you just what you deserve. I promise."

CHAPTER ONE

At the sound of a knock on her office door just after nine a.m. on a crisp, sunny September morning, Acting Sheriff Reese Conlon happily shoved aside a pile of paperwork. In the past six months she'd gone from commanding Marines on the ground in Iraq to manning a chair for twelve hours a day. Even the recent hurricane had only given her an excuse to leave the office during the height of the catastrophe— she'd been back behind her desk coordinating the cleanup efforts ever since. The transition back to civilian life after having been deployed in wartime was harder than leaving active duty the first time, five years ago. Right about now, almost any interruption was welcome.

"Come in," Reese said, easing her nearly six-foot frame back in the swivel chair.

The door opened and Carter Wayne, an ex-cop turned small-town attorney, walked in. She wasn't wearing the designer suit Reese had seen her in a few days before at Provincetown City Hall. Today she was dressed in faded blue jeans, an open-collared, rust-colored silk shirt, and brown boots the same color as her dark chestnut hair. A wide belt with a flat silver buckle circled her sleekly muscled waist. Hazel eyes met Reese's across the desk.

"Sheriff."

"Carter," Reese said, waving to one of the two wooden fold-up chairs in front of her desk. "Have a seat." When Carter sat down, Reese pushed back from the desk and crossed one ankle over her knee. "What can I do for you?"

"How about a job?"

"Lawyering starting to wear on you, huh?"

Carter smiled. "I seem to recall you've been there yourself. Didn't you do a stint as a JAG in the Corps?"

"A short one. I still can't quite remember what made me think I'd rather practice law than drag drunk recruits back to base on a Saturday night," Reese said with a shake of her head. "Of course, military policing is different than civilian law enforcement. An MP has a fair amount of leeway to interpret the rules and regs. We go by the book here, even when it's less expedient."

Reese watched Carter's eyes as she spoke, but didn't expect to see anything in them. Carter Wayne was an experienced undercover state police officer, at least she had been until her involvement with the daughter of a reputed mob boss cost Carter her career. Carter had come close to abandoning her duty while undercover investigating Boston crime boss Alfonse Pareto. She'd fallen in love with Pareto's daughter, Rica Grechi, and run afoul of the FBI. Reese understood risking everything for the woman she loved. There was nothing she wouldn't do, nothing she wouldn't sacrifice, to protect Tory or their daughter. But she couldn't have an officer serve under her who she couldn't trust.

"I served twelve years, five of them undercover. If I told you I never bent the rules, you wouldn't believe me," Carter said, meeting Reese's deep blue eyes squarely. She'd expected Conlon to lay her past on the line. Carter had spent her entire life working with men and women who believed that the distinction between right and wrong was clear, and who were willing to risk their lives in the name of justice. She'd been one of them, although the years she'd spent undercover working drug and organized crime cases had dulled the blacks and whites to shades of gray more and more often recently. She'd never met anyone with a stronger code of ethics or greater sense of duty and responsibility than Reese Conlon. She half expected Reese to tell her she didn't measure up, and maybe by Reese's standards, she didn't. But she'd been a good cop, *was* a good cop. "You can trust me to hold the line. You have my word."

"What I want," Reese said, "is your promise that if anything comes up that might make you choose between honoring the badge and protecting your family, you tell me."

Carter stiffened. "Rica has nothing to do with this."

"Rica has everything to do with it. We both know who she is, and just because her father's kept a low profile and stayed out of her life for the past six months doesn't mean he's going to continue."

"I won't let him drag her back into his world," Carter said. "And I won't let him contaminate this one."

"And if he tries?"

Carter set her jaw, knowing the answer would determine Reese's decision. "If Rica were physically threatened, I'd do anything I had to do to protect her. Short of that, I'd deal with problems through channels."

"Meaning advise me," Reese said flatly.

"Right." Carter sat forward. "Look, we live here. This is our community too. I want to do my part, and that isn't filing paperwork for a living."

"Tell me about it." Reese looked at her desk and winced. Carter laughed. "The hurricane has chewed this place up, and we've got more work than we can handle, and will have for half a year or more. I can use you."

Carter let out a breath. "Good. I'm ready to work."

Reese nodded. "There's a bunch of paperwork—in your case, all of it a formality. Fill it out, and I'll push it through." She riffled through a stack of papers and pulled out the duty roster, giving it a quick look. "You'll have the midnight-to-eight shift for the rest of the week. Starting tonight."

"Riding graveyard." Carter grinned ruefully. "Always great to be the rookie."

"We both know you're not, but—"

Carter held up a hand. "Hey, I get it. I'm the new kid on the block. I don't have a problem with that."

Reese stood and extended her hand across the desk. "Then welcome aboard, Officer Wayne."

Once Carter left to fill out the necessary forms in the front office, Reese went back to sorting through the incident reports from the previous shift, most of which were the ordinary run-of-the-mill occurrences common in any community—traffic accidents, drunk and disorderlies, assault and batteries, domestic complaints, thefts. The bulk of the work facing her department resulted from the hurricane that had devastated the entire Cape a week before. In its wake, the storm had left washed-out roads, untold property damage, injured and displaced civilians, and dozens of reports of thefts and suspicious fires, all of which needed to be investigated. Most of the Provincetown residents who had evacuated were just trickling back into town. As the community repopulated, Reese expected to receive more reports of vandalism and theft.

She rubbed her eyes, her headache firmly in place even though it was only midmorning. She hadn't slept much in the ten days leading up to and following the storm, and although she was resting better than she had been immediately after her return from Iraq, she was still dreaming. Still remembering. When she felt the edges of her consciousness start to darken and a tightness settle in her chest, she reached for the phone.

"East End Health Clinic," a melodious male voice answered.

"Is she free?" Reese asked.

"Is she ever?" Randy, the clinic's receptionist, responded with a dramatic sigh.

"Two minutes."

"I'll be timing you."

Reese listened to the silence for a few seconds, and then the voice she'd been waiting to hear came on the line.

"Hello, darling," Dr. Tory King said. "This is a nice surprise."

"How's your day going?" Reese asked.

"The town may still be half empty, but we've got a full schedule. How about you?"

"I'm drowning in paper." Tory laughed, and Reese pictured her leaning against the front of her desk, the phone tucked between her shoulder and her ear, signing off on charts while they talked. She'd be wearing pressed jeans and a cotton shirt under her white lab coat. Her wavy, shoulder-length auburn hair would be loose, her sparkling eyes shifting between blue and green with her mood. Listening to her, remembering waking up beside her that morning, Reese's disquiet along with the band of tension around her chest eased. She took a deep breath and let it out, feeling the memories of death and horror slide away.

"What else is going on?" Tory asked gently.

"I just hired Carter Wayne."

"Good. You can use the help, and Carter is a pro."

"Agreed. Did you hear from Kate? Are they on their way back?" Reese was thankful for more reasons than she could count that she'd reconnected with her mother after years of estrangement, and that they lived in the same town now. Kate and her partner Jean were not only family and wonderful friends, they provided childcare for Reese and Tory's one-year-old daughter Reggie.

"Apparently the extended family isn't done spoiling Reggie quite yet. They're leaving tomorrow and will be back midday."

"Good. I miss her," Reese said. "Do you think she misses us?"

"I think she would, if she weren't with Kate and Jean. But she spends as much time with them as she does with us, so she feels safe and secure. I'm certain she'll be very glad to see us."

"Same here. Well, I should let you go, I promised Randy—"

"Are you okay?"

Reese sighed, embarrassed that she had disrupted Tory's always busy schedule because she couldn't deal with her own ghosts. "Am I that obvious?"

"Not at all, sweetheart. But you don't usually call me in the middle of the day."

"I'm okay. I just needed to hear your voice." And she knew if she shut Tory out the way she had done right after she'd returned, they'd both suffer. She'd promised she would try to reach out when she needed help, even though it went against her every instinct.

"I love you," Tory said. "I'm done at seven. Dinner?"

"I'll give it my best shot."

Tory chuckled. "You're an expert marksman, Reese. I consider that a sure thing."

❖

"So what do you think that's all about?" Officer Allie Tremont whispered to her partner, Bri Parker.

"Huh?"

Allie was struck again how much Bri looked like a younger, slimmer version of Reese—thick, coal black hair cut long in the front and short around the ears, indigo eyes, and a break-your-heart smile. Aware that Bri was staring at her with a confused expression, Allie tilted her head slightly and Bri followed her gaze. "Check it out."

Carter Wayne leaned against the waist-high counter that separated the work area, where Bri's desk and three others were pushed together, from the real heart of the department—the communications center presided over for the past twenty-five years by Gladys Martin, a civilian aide. Gladys screened incoming calls, relayed dispatch orders and information, and pretty much controlled everything else that kept the department running smoothly. Carter, a dozen years older and thirty pounds of muscle heavier than Bri, looked relaxed and casually self-confident as she rested an elbow on the counter and filled out forms. Bri knew as much of her story as anyone, but she didn't really know her. Carter was a lot like Reese—a seasoned cop, about the same age, and they'd both reached the top by being tough, and by being the best. Carter was Reese's equal in a way that Bri hoped to be one day. Secretly, she was a little bit jealous of Carter, even though she knew that was crazy. She couldn't help the way she felt.

"It looks to me like she's coming on board," Bri said tightly.

"Yeah," Allie said contemplatively, her soft Southern accent becoming more accentuated. "That's how I read it too. So, you think she'll end up partnering with one of us?"

Bri stiffened. "Why? You and I are partners. Reese won't split us up."

"I don't know. We're still the rookies, even if we have been doing this for a year. And Carter—well, Carter's gonna have rank on us."

"I guess it would be up to Reese." Bri stood abruptly. "Come on, let's get out of here. Take a tour around town."

"Hey, fine by me. I'll tell Gladys."

Bri watched Allie saunter over to the counter, knowing without being able to see her face that she would be cruising Carter. Allie cruised every woman, gay, straight, single, or married. With Allie's statuesque physique, her wavy mahogany hair, and her deep dark soulful eyes that promised fantasies come true, Allie generally got cruised back. Bri had only ever been in love with one girl, but for a few crazy weeks a year or so ago when her head was all turned around, she'd almost given in to Allie's charms. That was behind them now, and she and Allie were partners at work and tight friends. She was probably one of the only people who really knew that Allie was a lot more than just a beautiful flirt. Allie *was* both beautiful and a flirt, that was for sure, but she was also loyal and tender and, underneath her bad girl image, lonely.

Carter looked up when Allie approached, smiled and said a few words Bri couldn't hear, and then went back to her paperwork. From where Bri was standing, Carter seemed to be immune to Allie's charms. But then, Carter was rock-solid married. Like Reese. Like her.

"All set," Allie said when she returned to collect her gun from her desk drawer.

"Learn anything?" Bri settled her hat low over her brows and slid her weapon into her holster. She held the door open for Allie as they walked out the side door into the small parking lot.

"Nope," Allie said, passing Bri and starting down the stairs.

Bri was right on her heels and when Allie abruptly stopped on the last step, she plowed into her and almost bowled her over. "What the fuck, Al."

"What the fuck is right!" Allie sounded both shocked and angry.

"Uh-oh," Bri muttered, finally noticing the redhead standing on the blacktop path ten feet in front of them, her face set and her eyes riveted on Allie. Bri hadn't seen Ashley Walker for the better part of a year, not since Allie and Ash had split up. Ash looked thinner than she remembered, the lines around her eyes a little deeper, her body pared down to tight muscle and bone. She'd cut her thick, slightly curly crimson hair to just above her collar, and the sleeker look accentuated the tight planes of her cheekbones and jaw. Ash's blue eyes flickered over Allie's body and then resettled on her face.

"Hello, Allie. Bri," Ash said in a low, throaty alto.

"Walker," Allie said coldly. "What are you doing here?"

"Working a couple of dozen cases down this end of the Cape." Ash slid her hands into the pockets of her khakis and swallowed around the dry, hard knot in her throat. She had known this first meeting would be tough, and she'd thought she was prepared for it, but she'd been wrong. She'd underestimated just how hard it would be to see the anger in Allie's eyes and hear the loathing in her voice. In the eight months since she'd seen her, Allie had changed. She'd cut her long, dark hair to collar length, but that wasn't it. She'd lost the sheen of innocence that had shimmered beneath the sexual allure that was as natural to Allie as breathing. She was still beautiful, even more so now because of the edge in the sculpted planes of her face, but she also seemed remote, untouchable. And that was right, wasn't it. Ash had been the one to walk away.

"That doesn't answer my question," Allie snapped.

"Courtesy call." Ash tried not to wince when Allie snorted rudely. "I'll just head in to see Nelson."

"My dad's out on indefinite sick leave," Bri said. "Reese is chief now."

"Oh, damn, I'm sorry," Ash said. "Is Nelson okay?"

"He's doing better." Bri's mouth thinned. "He had heart surgery about a month or so ago."

"I'm sorry to hear that. I didn't know."

Allie strode down the path directly toward Ash, forcing Ash to sidestep hurriedly or risk getting knocked on her ass.

"Why should you know?" Allie said as she passed, a slight hint of DKNY's Be Delicious trailing in her wake. "You're not part of anything around here."

"Tell Nelson I said hello," Ash said quietly as Bri hurried after Allie.

"Sure. Thanks," Bri mumbled.

Ash heard a car door slam, then another, and forced herself not to turn around and watch Allie drive away. She'd already seen her walking out of her life every day for the last eight months, and she heard what Allie didn't say. *You're not welcome around here.*

❖

"I can't believe she just showed up like that. Like she could just walk right in," Allie fumed.

Bri wheeled the cruiser out onto Shank Painter Road and headed toward Bradford, carefully keeping her eyes on the road although she could have driven it blindfolded. Allie sounded mad, but underneath the mad was a little bit of quaver that sounded like tears. Tears just ripped Bri up. "She said she was here on business."

"Of course she is. When isn't she?" Allie folded her arms across her chest. "That's the only thing that matters to her."

"She definitely screwed up when she—" Bri caught herself just before she said *dumped you.* Allie was usually the one breaking hearts, and she'd taken it hard when Ashley Walker had called things off between them. Like a good friend, she said, "She didn't know how lucky she was."

"Old news," Allie said dismissively. "Ancient history. Hell, I would've been out of there in a few more weeks anyhow." She stretched her legs beneath the dash and tilted her head back, staring at the ceiling of the cruiser. "I like variety. I'm not like you and Reese, Parker."

Bri glanced over at her. "How's that?"

"Pussy-whipped. Not my style."

"Jesus," Bri choked out. "You better not let Reese hear you say that."

"I didn't hear you denying it, though." Allie tilted her head toward Bri and grinned. "Of course, you probably don't have all that much imagination, seeing as you've been sleeping with the same girl for what—six years? God."

"Don't go there," Bri said good-naturedly. Allie never passed up the opportunity to tease her about the fact that she'd only ever slept with one girl. She and Caroline Clark had been together since they were sixteen, and she knew she would never ever get tired of Carre's kisses, or the sexy glint she got in her eyes when she woke Bri up in the morning wanting sex, or the way she cuddled in Bri's arms after she came, sighing with contentment. Carre filled Bri's heart with wonder. She made sense out of a crazy world. She was the one.

"Don't worry. I'm not going to pick on the afflicted." Allie poked Bri's arm. "Swing by the rescue squad station."

"Why?"

"No reason. Just a friendly visit," Allie said nonchalantly.

"Uh-huh. No reason like the new EMT in town? What's her name?"

"Flynn."

"So what's her story?"

"Dunno." Allie grinned at Bri. "Yet. She only got here a couple of days before the hurricane hit, and then we were all so busy with the casualties I barely had a chance to say hello. She did say we should drop by sometime, so I just thought it was time we got properly introduced."

"Sure." Bri headed over to Conwell. They worked frequently with all of the emergency personnel in town, and it wasn't a bad idea to touch base with the new EMT, but she doubted that was the only reason Allie wanted to see the good-looking blonde. "Good idea."

"Thanks." Allie appreciated Bri not giving her a hard time just then. She wanted to flirt with a woman, laugh with a woman, feel the heat of a woman's appreciative gaze on her skin. She wanted to *not* think about what Ashley Walker was doing in town. Or how long she would stay.

CHAPTER TWO

"You've got another visitor, Sheriff," Gladys said when Reese picked up the phone. "Mighty popular today."

"Anyone I want to see?"

"Oh, I think so. It's Ashley Walker."

"Send her in." Reese walked around her desk and extended a hand as Ash tapped on the door, pushed it open, and entered. Reese liked the insurance investigator. They'd worked together before, had drawn fire together, and Ash had handled herself well. "Good to see you."

"Same here," Ash said. "Sorry it has to be under these circumstances. Route Six looked like a war zone driving in. You hit hard?"

"Hard enough." Reese sat in one of the wooden chairs and motioned Ash to the other. The hurricane that had trekked up the coast and savaged the Cape was the kind of natural disaster that occurred every few decades, and they'd had precious little warning. Their emergency response system had worked, and they'd managed to evacuate most of the visitors and many of the residents before the worst of the wind and surge had flooded the roads and most of the town of three thousand residents. In the week since the storm had blown out to sea, every law enforcement agent, volunteer firefighter, rescue worker, and public servant had worked eighteen-hour-days on the recovery effort. "Three casualties—one MI, one vehicular fatality, and one drowning. All storm related, but considering the amount of property damage we've got, it could've been a lot worse."

"What's the situation in town?"

"We've managed to restore most basic functions—pretty much the whole town has electricity again," Reese said. "We've got problems with sewage containment—a public health consultant is coming in tomorrow to test our water and liaise with our public works department. I imagine you're here about the property damage?"

"Property and personal losses," Ash said wearily. "Mostly corporate claims, though."

Reese noted the dark circles beneath the remnants of Ash's summer tan. "You look like you're running on fumes."

Ash grinned ruefully and flicked a crimson strand off her cheek, automatically raking a hand through her hair. "My biggest client happens to insure ninety percent of the businesses on the Cape, which means we've got claims pouring in by the hour as people return and start assessing the damage."

"I imagine along with the legitimate claims you'll get some bogus ones too."

"That's pretty much my specialty these days—insurance fraud. My job is to screen the claims on-site and hand off the straightforward ones to under-agents. Anything that looks questionable…" Ash shrugged. These days insurance fraud often involved organized crime networks, since purchasing real estate was a popular way to launder money. So was destroying property and picking up the clean insurance payouts. "I get to dig around until I'm satisfied that the claim is valid."

"What do you need from me?"

"I'd appreciate it if I could have a look at your incident reports to cross-reference with my claims."

Reese pulled a pad off her desk and made a note. "Done."

"And it would be helpful if you let your officers know that I'll be poking around pretty much everywhere in town for the next few weeks."

"Poking around." Reese raised an eyebrow. "We had quite a few fires, at least one major. The fire marshal hasn't even cleared half the damaged buildings yet. The town engineer has a list as long as his arm of public structures and businesses to be assessed for structural damage. I don't want a building coming down on your head."

"I've got a pretty good eye for structural integrity," Ash said mildly, not bothering to mention she'd been an arson investigator with the Massachusetts State Police before going private. Reese knew her creds.

"I know you can handle yourself, but while you're in my town, you're my responsibility." Reese tapped her pen on the pad. "I'll need a list of properties you intend to inspect and your schedule."

"I don't mind giving you the addresses of the claims, but my schedule changes constantly, depending on what I find." Ash shook her head. "There's no way I can provide you with any kind of itinerary."

"Then I'll need you to check in regularly."

"Reese," Ash protested, "I know what I'm doing."

"Don't doubt it." Reese spread her hands and said calmly, "The town is a mess, Ash. Parts of the West End aren't even habitable yet. Hell, even some of the big places up on Pilgrim Heights got hit. I don't want any more casualties, and I don't think you should be working alone. I'll have one of my officers accompany you as much as possible."

Ash's face lost all expression. "That's not necessary."

"There you go, trying to tell me how to do my job again." Reese stood. "You've worked with my people before. We won't get in your way."

"I don't suppose I can change your mind?" Ash said, getting to her feet.

Reese knew Ash didn't expect an answer to her question. "Where are you staying?"

"At the Crown Inn."

"Leave your cell number with Gladys. I'll have one of our officers contact you later this morning."

"Thanks, Sheriff."

"Be careful, Ash."

"Not to worry," Ash called over her shoulder as she left. "Careful. That's my middle name."

❖

Rica Grechi finished taping up the padded wrapper on a small oil painting and smiled as she handed it across the counter to a customer. "This is a wonderful gift. I'm sure your sister will love it."

"Thank you so much," the middle-aged woman said. "I was so worried I wouldn't be able to get here, what with all the mess out on the roads."

"I really appreciate you braving the chaos to come in."

"Oh, it was worth it. I just love your gallery." The customer gathered up the painting along with a voluminous purse and several other packages. "I'll be sure to tell all my friends to stop by—as soon as things get back to normal. Whenever *that* is!"

"Thank you," Rica called.

The bell over the door chimed just as the woman reached it, and Rica prepared to welcome another customer. Then her pleasant anticipation changed to a quick thrum of excitement when she recognized Carter holding the door open for the customer to exit. She hurried around the counter just as Carter shut the door, and flipped the store sign to *Closed*.

"Come on in the back," Rica said, grasping Carter's hand and pulling her through the gallery.

"Glad to see me?" Carter inquired with a suggestive chuckle.

"Nope. Had enough of you last night." Rica smiled to herself, remembering how hungry she'd been for Carter and just how many delicious ways Carter had made her come. When they reached her office, out of sight of the front windows and the people walking by on Commercial Street, Rica threaded her arms around Carter's neck and kissed her. Carter made a low, growling sound in her throat and tugged Rica's silk shirt free of her pants.

"We'll see about that," Carter muttered.

"Not so fast, stud," Rica said, bracing her arm on Carter's chest. Carter's eyes had already taken on that intense focus that signaled she was aroused, and as much as Rica loved to know that she could put that look in her lover's eyes in under a minute, she didn't want to get distracted. Well, she did, but not just yet.

"After a greeting like that, you're going to put the brakes on?" Carter tugged Rica closer and caught Rica's earlobe between her teeth. She nipped and grumbled, "Tease."

"Mmm, like you mind." Rica kept her arms around Carter's neck, but leaned back in her embrace, preventing Carter from enticing her into more kisses. Kissing Carter was an addiction she had no desire to control, and once she started, she wasn't likely to stop. "I didn't expect to see you so soon. That was just a little hello kiss."

Carter contented herself with running her hands up and down Rica's slender back. Rica had left her long, wavy midnight hair down, and it flowed around her pale, oval face like a frame on a classic painting. Rica's ebony, almond-shaped eyes glowed with happiness and excitement, and that was all Carter needed to see for her world to feel complete. She kissed Rica's forehead. "Tell me your news."

Rica tilted her head, studying Carter with a playful expression. "What makes you think there's news?"

"It's written all over your face." Carter skimmed her thumb over the faint dent in Rica's chin. "Give."

"I've just landed a new client—Gillian Fitzgerald."

"The expressionist?" Carter whistled. "She's hot right now, isn't she?"

"The *New York Times* is calling her one of the most exciting avant-garde painters of the last half-century. And she's agreed to let me open her new works here, before we move them to Manhattan."

"You'll need to spend some time in the city, then," Carter said casually. She didn't like the idea of Rica moving back into the kind of circles where she would be vulnerable to her father's or his associates' influence. Don Alfonse Pareto had been suspiciously absent from Rica's life in the last six months, but Carter didn't believe the reprieve was permanent. Rica was the don's only child, and Pareto had made it well known that he expected to turn his *business* enterprises over to his daughter, or his daughter's husband, when he retired. Just because Rica had informed her father that she had no interest in his business at the same time she'd told him she was a lesbian *and* in love with Carter, didn't mean the don was on board with Rica's program. But Pareto was Rica's father, and she loved him, so Carter said nothing.

"I know what you're thinking," Rica said quietly.

"Do you?" Carter nuzzled Rica's neck. "Then you'll leave that sign on the front door and sneak out the back with me for an hour or two."

Rica laughed and stroked Carter's cheek. "Darling, you wouldn't last an hour." At Carter's look of mock hurt, Rica kissed her lingeringly. "You know I don't mind. I love to make you lose control."

"Rica," Carter warned. "Don't tease if you're not going to finish."

"I'm going to finish. Just not right now." Rica grasped Carter's hands and stepped back, keeping her fingers threaded through Carter's. "You're worried about my father. He can't force me to do anything I don't want to do. My spending time at the gallery in Manhattan won't make any difference. Try not to worry."

Carter nodded. "All right."

"What happened when you talked to Reese?"

"I'll be spending my nights in a patrol car again," Carter said with a grin.

"Are you going to be all right with that?" Rica asked gently.

"Perfectly fine." Carter kissed Rica on the nose. "Piece of cake."

Rica searched Carter's eyes for some sign of disappointment. Carter had been a decorated officer in the Massachusetts State Police, but because of her association with Rica she'd been interrogated by the FBI, her professional integrity had been called into question, and some of her colleagues no longer trusted her. Carter insisted her decision to walk away from her career as an undercover detective had nothing to do with their relationship, but Rica wondered if Carter had been completely honest with herself. Rica had seen that Carter was bored with practicing law after just a few months even though she insisted otherwise, and her boredom wasn't just because small-town law lacked challenges. Carter would have been dissatisfied in a big-city law office too. Carter was a cop, not a lawyer, but starting over again in a small provincial department had to be hard for her.

"Stop looking for something that isn't there," Carter said. "I'm okay with this. I'm grateful Conlon is willing to take me on."

"Why wouldn't she want you? Because of my father?" Rica asked angrily.

"Hell no. Baby, that's not what I meant." Carter drew Rica over to the love seat that was crammed, along with Rica's desk and file cabinets, into the small back room Rica used as her business office at the gallery. Sitting, she tugged Rica down on her lap and wrapped her arms around her waist. She kissed the base of her throat. "You and your father have nothing to do with the trouble I got myself into. Conlon knows I played fast and loose with the feds and some of the guys on my team. She's a straight-up, by-the-book commander. She won't look the other way for anything."

Rica threaded her fingers through Carter's thick chestnut hair. She loved her strength. She loved her passion and her devotion. She hated to think of the sacrifices Carter had made for her, but she would not dishonor those sacrifices by seeming ungrateful. "I love you."

With a sigh, Carter rested her cheek between Rica's breasts. "For a long time, I didn't know who I was or what mattered. Now I do. I know who I am because of you, Rica."

"You're mine," Rica whispered, holding her close.

❖

"Adam seven," Gladys's voice intoned over the cruiser's radio, "you copy?"

"Adam seven, go ahead," Allie answered.

"Reese wants you code thirteen."

"Affirmative, Adam seven code thirteen." Allie glanced at Bri, who met her eyes and shrugged. Reese wanted them back at the station. Allie hooked the mic back on the dashboard. "Well, hell. There goes my chance to make a date for tonight."

"You got all afternoon, and it won't take you but a minute and a smile."

Allie laughed. "You're good for my ego, Parker. I'm not really worried about it. There's always someone at the Vixen looking for company."

"Uh-huh." Bri made a U-turn in Michael Shay's parking lot and headed back down Bradford toward the center of town. "Are you okay about Ash?" Out of the corner of her eye, she saw Allie's hands clench into fists. She probably shouldn't have said anything, but usually when Allie was this hot for a date, it was because she was hurting or there was something she wanted to forget, or both. "I mean, you didn't know she was coming or anything, did y—"

"How would I know she was coming?" Allie shot back. "It's not like we've been talking. I haven't heard from her in months. We both moved on, remember? And I'm not one of those dykes who likes to play best friends with all of her exes."

"You're friends with Deo," Bri pointed out quietly.

"Deo and I slept together a couple of times. She's a sweetheart and I really like her. Besides," Allie said moodily, "I was never in lo…"

Bri glanced over at her. "What, Al? What were you going to say?"

Allie bit her lip and shook her head. After a minute, she said quietly, "Nothing. I wasn't going to say anything at all."

CHAPTER THREE

You can go on in. Sheriff's waiting," Gladys said when Bri and Allie walked into the office.

Bri shot Allie a quick glance, tapped on Reese's door, and pushed it open. Reese looked up from her desk and motioned them in.

"There's been a change in the duty roster," Reese said. "Parker, I'm switching you to nights for the next couple of weeks. You'll ride with Officer Wayne."

"Yes ma'am."

Reese noted the look of displeasure cross Bri's face, but unlike a year ago when she would have argued, Bri merely stared straight ahead. She was young still, not yet twenty-three, but she had a natural instinct for the job. Plus, five years of dedicated martial arts training had taught her restraint, if not true patience. That would come. Allie Tremont was a different story. She was a skilled officer, smart and dedicated, but she lacked Bri's steadiness, as if some part of her was still searching for a solid foundation. Reese knew of Allie's fast-and-loose reputation—the town was too small not to know just about everybody's business. But Allie never missed a shift or showed up for work impaired in any way, unless Reese counted lack of sleep. But being exhausted was not a disciplinary offense. If it were, she'd have to put herself on report along with just about every other officer in her department.

"Tremont," Reese said.

Allie straightened, her eyes wary. "Sheriff?"

"I need you as liaison with Ash Walker. She's going to be looking into—"

"Let Bri do it," Allie exclaimed. "I'll ride with Wayne."

Bri sucked in a breath and muttered, "Al. Shut up."

"That was an order, not a request for advice, Officer." Reese had expected one or both of her young officers to complain about being split up. Bri and Allie had gone through the academy together. They were used to working with each other and they were friends. Riding separately for a few weeks would give them a chance to develop skills in the areas where they depended on the other now. Bri was a loner. There was nothing wrong with that, but if she was going to command one day, she needed to learn how to read people. How to evaluate those she would lead. Right now Bri let Allie handle a lot of the interpersonal parts of the job. Riding with Carter would force her out of her comfort zone.

Allie, for her part, was too comfortable with Bri taking charge. Working as the department's rep with Ash would give her a chance to develop her own style and approach to problem-solving. However, Allie wasn't complaining about the partnership being split up, she was complaining about working with Walker.

"Is there some reason you don't want to work with Walker?" Reese asked. "Some problem with her I should know about?"

"No ma'am. Nothing of that nature," Allie said stiffly.

"Then unless there's a professional problem—which I expect you to bring to my attention," Reese said, reaching for the next pile of paperwork, "I want you to contact Walker immediately to review her schedule and get her anything she needs. I also expect you to coordinate her site visits on a daily basis and accompany her to any claim where we have open files. Maybe we can clear some of the backlog. Parker, you're off duty until midnight tonight. You're dismissed."

"Ma'am," both Allie and Bri said simultaneously.

Reese did not look up as they left.

"You've got to be kidding me," Allie snarled as soon as Reese's door closed behind them.

"Not here, Allie," Bri said urgently when Gladys and one of the other officers glanced their way curiously. She grabbed Allie's arm and dragged her down the hall leading to the locker rooms. "You know better than to complain about an order in front of the others."

Allie stopped in the hall and rounded on Bri. "It's bullshit and you know it! Jesus, Bri, half the town is still underwater and we've got all we can do to investigate complaints. Sticking me with a babysitting—"

"*Fuck*, Al." Bri grabbed Allie by the shoulders, frog-marched her the rest of the way to the locker room, and pushed her through the door with a hand in the middle of her back. "Do you want to get suspended? You think Reese is going to put up with you mouthing off about your assignment in hearing range of the squad?"

"And what's this about putting you with Carter? Why not put Wayne with one of the guys on the night shift—Smith has been around longer than you have!"

Silently, Bri agreed with her, but she wasn't going to say so. She liked riding with Allie. She liked working the day shift too, even though she had to do her fair amount of night duty when her name came around in rotation. When she worked nights she got to see a lot less of Carre, and that always made her edgy and put her off her game. Sleeping next to Carre replenished some vital part of her spirit. But Reese was her boss, and more importantly, Bri trusted her. "Reese must have her reasons. That's why she's the sheriff."

"Fuck that." Allie abruptly turned her back on Bri. "I'm not doing it."

"Just take a few minutes to cool off," Bri said after a long pause. This wasn't the Allie she knew. That Allie always had a who-gives-a-damn smile and a smart comeback when things didn't go her way. From the way Allie's shoulders were shaking slightly, Bri thought she might be crying. Crap. Taking a tentative step closer, she rested her hands on Allie's shoulders. "Hey, Al. What's going on?"

Wordlessly, Allie shook her head. She reached up to cover Bri's hands with hers and leaned back against Bri's chest. The move put her practically in Bri's arms, and for a couple of seconds, Bri panicked. But she wasn't getting the old Allie sex vibe, and although she was glad for it, she was also nervous. She didn't have a clue what to do for the new Allie.

"If you want me to talk to Reese for you, I will," Bri said finally.

Allie laughed, a short, choked laugh, and dropped her head against Bri's shoulder. "Wow. You must really be worried."

"Hey," Bri said, trying to lighten the mood. "I know you're still really pissed at Ash. I don't blame you for not wanting to work with her."

"Yeah, I'm pissed at her. But I've been pissed at you before too. This is different." Allie let go of Bri's hands and turned to face her. "She hurt me, Bri. She really hurt me."

"I'm sorry, Al." Bri hated feeling so helpless, and she hated Allie hurting.

"Me too," Allie said flatly, the expression in her eyes unforgiving. "Me too."

❖

"Hey, baby!" Caroline Clark smiled brightly when Bri walked into their apartment in the middle of the afternoon. She put her paintbrush down on the easel and wiped her hands on a clean cloth. "If I'd known you were coming home, I would've made lunch or something."

"I didn't know myself." Bri hung her gun belt over the back of a kitchen chair, put her weapon in the top drawer next to the sink, and unbuckled her belt. Caroline had pulled her shoulder-length flaxen hair back in a ponytail, and with her smooth skin and big baby blues, she still looked sixteen instead of twenty-two. "I'm not hungry for lunch."

"Um, baby?" Caroline's eyebrows rose as Bri unzipped her pants, stepped out of them, and draped them over the chair. By the time Bri started on the buttons on her uniform shirt Caroline had reached her and joined in. Nothing turned her on faster than Bri being hot for her. "You can tell me later why you're here. How much time do we have?"

Laughing, Bri wrapped her arms around Caroline's waist and nibbled at her neck. "Until about eleven thirty tonight. Reese just switched me to nights."

"Oh damn." Caroline stripped off Bri's shirt, tugged up the bottom of the tight tank she wore beneath it, and ran her hands over Bri's chest. "I hate not sleeping with you."

"I know. I'm sorry." Bri popped the button on Caroline's jeans and pushed them down. Then she reached under Caroline's T-shirt, released the clasp on her bra, and skimmed them both over Caroline's head. Leaving Caroline just in her panties, Bri walked her backward toward the bedroom. "Maybe I can make it up to you a little bit right now."

When the backs of Caroline's knees hit the bed, she flopped down and pulled Bri on top of her. Caroline spread her legs so Bri's naked thigh came to rest high up between her legs, and hooked one ankle around Bri's calf. She tilted her pelvis and rubbed herself over Bri's thigh. "You can make it up to me *a lot* right now, baby."

"That was my plan, babe." Bri shot her a cocky grin.

Caroline worked her hands under Bri's tank and played with her nipples, laughing when Bri squeezed her eyes shut and groaned. She loved teasing her tough-girl lover. Bri tried so hard to be brave and strong, and she was. She really was. From the very first day they'd met in high school, Bri had stood up for them, against their peers and their parents and those who wanted to hurt them for daring to love each other. And then she joined the sheriff's department and put her heart and soul and body on the line every day, still trying to do the right thing. A few people knew the softer side of her, but only Caroline really knew how tender she was, how sometimes in the night she'd cry out in her sleep, trembling, until Caroline pulled her close. Bri needed *her* and wasn't ashamed to admit it, and that's all that mattered between them. Caroline arched up and kissed Bri. "I love you."

Bri met Caroline's gaze, the deep blue of her eyes turning stormy with excitement. Hands shaking, she yanked off her top and fumbled with her briefs. Caroline reached down to help her.

"Fuck, you make me so hot, babe," Bri muttered as she got up on her knees to get the last of her clothing off.

"I know." Caroline sighed with satisfaction and quickly shed her panties. She grasped Bri's hand and pulled it between her legs. She was wet. "That's what happened the minute *you* walked in the door."

Bri groaned and slipped inside her. Leaning on one elbow, she kissed her slow and deep. While she gently slid in and out of Caroline's warm, tight depths, she licked the inside of Caroline's lips and teased her tongue. "I want you to come. I love it when you come."

"Don't think...you're getting off with just a quickie." Caroline gripped the thick dark hair at the back of Bri's neck, arching against her as her hips lifted and fell with each thrust of Bri's hand. She shivered, her legs tightening. "Oh, damn. Dammit. I'm going to come right away."

"Feel me inside you," Bri said with fierce concentration, avidly watching Caroline's face. She angled her palm to hit Caroline's clitoris and Caroline's inner muscles spasmed. "Oh yeah. Here it comes."

"Uh-huh," Caroline gasped, "right now."

Bri rolled half on top of Caroline, straddling Caroline's thigh and burying her face in Caroline's neck. Pulling the soft flesh between her lips, she sucked as Caroline pulsed around her fingers. With two hard thrusts of her hips, she came.

"You cheated," Caroline protested a few minutes later, stroking the back of Bri's head.

"Can't help it," Bri mumbled, her head pillowed on Caroline's shoulder, her fingers still deep inside her. "Love you."

"So how come you're home early?" Caroline kissed Bri's forehead, felt around for the sheet, and covered them. "You're not in trouble, are you?"

"Nah." Bri couldn't move and didn't even try to open her eyes. The late-afternoon sun coming through the skylight over their heads warmed her shoulders. She felt so peaceful, so safe. "Carter Wayne just joined the department, and I've got to ride with her on the late shift for a couple of weeks."

"Okay. That explains why you're home. Any special reason you're so horny?"

Bri sighed and lightly stroked between Caroline's legs. She remembered the pain in Allie's eyes earlier, and never ever wanted to do anything to put that look in Caroline's. "It's you, babe. It's just you."

Caroline took advantage of Bri's relaxed state and pushed her over onto her back. Then she made her way down between her legs. Right before she put her mouth on her, she said, "I'll always be here, baby. Always."

❖

Ash took stock of the three-room suite she'd been lucky to score at the Crown. The bedroom was set off on the short end of an L, with a small gas fireplace occupying the corner. The long arm of the suite contained a sitting area with a desk and a spacious bath on the far side of that, and at the end closest to the door from the courtyard, an efficiency kitchen. Compared to the many Motel 6 equivalents she'd stayed in over the last month, this place was a palace. After having traveled most of the night, she was looking forward to a shower and change of clothes before she started to work again.

A knock sounded at the door, and assuming the attendant had returned with the extra towels she'd requested, she called *come in*.

Opening her suitcase on the bed, she added over her shoulder, "Go ahead and leave them on the counter in the kitchen. Thanks."

When she heard the door close, she pushed down her jeans, pulled off her polo shirt, and headed for the bathroom in her briefs. She stumbled to a stop when she realized she wasn't alone. Covering her nakedness seemed ridiculous when the woman standing just inside her door had seen all of her in far more compromising positions. Watching Allie's eyes widen and skim down her body, she almost covered her breasts when she felt her nipples harden.

"Sorry," Allie said sharply. "I thought you said come in."

"I did." Galvanized by the frigid look in Allie's eyes, Ash backed toward the bedroom. "I thought you were someone else."

"So I gathered." Allie looked away, desperately wanting to flee, but not wanting to reveal her discomfort to Ash. She did not want Ash Walker to have the slightest inkling that she still had any power to affect her at all. She definitely didn't want to betray the way her heart had tripped over itself when she'd first seen Ash step into the room naked. Even exhausted and ten pounds too thin, she was gorgeous, just as gorgeous as she had been the last time Allie had touched her. Long limbed and sleekly muscled, firm oval breasts tipped by small light brown nipples, concave abdomen with a shallow, round navel that she used to love to dip her tongue into. God, she didn't want to think about that. Not now. Not ever ever again. Resurrecting her anger, she said tightly, "Since you're expecting company, I won't keep you."

"Just wait, Allie," Ash said. "No one's coming. It was just a misunderstanding."

"Yeah, that happens a lot with you."

"Just…wait. Jesus." Ash bolted back to the bedroom, grabbed a pair of jeans and a T-shirt, and hastily dressed. The entire time, she listened for the sound of the door opening and closing. She couldn't believe how much Allie hated her. She half expected Allie to be gone, but when she returned to the living area, Allie was still there, just inside the door. The rush of relief was so strong and so unexpected, she swayed with a surge of dizziness.

"You all right?" Allie asked almost begrudgingly.

Embarrassed, Ash waved away Allie's concern. "Yeah. Fine."

"When's the last time you ate?"

Ash blinked. "What?"

"You fucking look like you're going to fall over, Walker." Allie stomped to the counter and jerked an apple out of the welcome basket the innkeepers had left. Pivoting sharply, she flung it across the room. "Eat that."

"Christ, Allie," Ash exclaimed, catching the apple just before it hit her in the face. "Would you…" She took a breath and forced herself to speak softly. "Thanks."

Allie turned her back and looked out the door toward the plant-filled flagstone courtyard.

"What are you doing here?" Ash knew better than to think Allie had come to see her for any personal reason.

"Apparently Reese thinks you need an escort."

"What!" Ash swallowed the chunk of apple she was chewing so quickly she almost choked on it. Coughing, she cleared her throat. "Reese told me she wanted a list of places I plan to check out. And that she'd have someone provide records for me. You didn't need to come over here in person."

"Believe me, it wasn't my idea." Allie looked back over her shoulder. "Reese ordered me to get together with you. I'm supposed to be your liaison, as in work with you on behalf of the department."

"That's crazy."

"For once, we agree."

Ash tossed the apple in the trash can and jammed her hands into the pockets of her jeans. "Look, let me get settled and I'll stop by the station and talk to Reese again. I'll leave you a list of the records I need you to pull. You won't even have to see me."

For just a second, Allie thought she heard a whisper of sadness in Ash's voice and she felt a quick pain around her heart. Just as quickly, she squashed the feeling. Ashley Walker was nothing to her now, and she wasn't going to waste one single emotion on her. Ash could work herself into the ground for all she cared. Because she didn't care.

"Leave your list this afternoon," Allie said, her hand on the doorknob. "I'd like nothing better than to never see you again, but I have orders, and until Reese changes her mind and tells me differently, I'm at least going to meet with you every day to go over your schedule. What time do you want to start tomorrow?"

"Allie," Ash said softly. "I'll talk to Reese today. I'll tell her—"

"Don't do me any favors," Allie said harshly. "You'll only make it worse."

Ash pushed her hand through her hair. "Okay. Okay. I'll see you at eight tomorrow, then."

"Fine." Allie pulled open the door.

"Allie," Ash called. "I'm sorry about this."

Allie turned back, her face a careful mask. "It's too late to be sorry. It's too late for anything at all."

Chapter Four

He did not fear being discovered.

Most of the houses on Bradford west of Atlantic showed signs of storm damage—blown-out windows, missing sections of roof, debris-filled yards, and downed trees. Many of the residents had not returned. Scattered sections of Commercial Street remained flooded and closed to anything except official vehicles. Power had yet to be restored to some residential enclaves, and streetlights were out all over town. No one paid any attention to a lone man dressed in generic work clothes moving purposefully down the street. Or into a yard. Or through an open garage or unhinged back door.

He sat on the edge of her bed, ran his hand over the depression in her pillow where her face had pressed while she slept. He leaned over and took a deep breath. Her scent was primal female, light and airy with the teasing undercurrent of lush fertility. He slid his hand between the sheets and imagined her body splayed open, hungry for a touch. His touch.

For a moment, he contemplated pulling back the covers and lying naked where her flesh had been, absorbing the warmth she'd left behind. Too risky. Too soon. The hunt was far too enjoyable to rush. Sighing, he rose, adjusted the heaviness in his pants, and moved to the closet. Her clothes shared space with those of the pretender. He barely resisted the urge to yank the carefully pressed shirts and trousers from the hangers and fling them to the floor. But he wasn't ready to announce himself yet. He fingered the silky sleeve of a red shirt, lifted it to his mouth, ran it over his lips. The silk became her hair twining through his fingers, and closing his eyes, he saw his hand twisting in her lustrous locks—yanking her head back, exposing her vulnerable throat to his mouth, his lips, his teeth. He'd bite her, mark her, make sure the world understood she was his.

But not yet. Not while the anticipation excited him, not while the fantasies of what was to come still satisfied him. Shuddering, he pulled the shirt from the hanger, wadded it up, and pushed it inside his clothes. He smoothed out the silk over his bare abdomen, carefully sliding one sleeve down the front of his pants where he could feel it like slick fingers stroking him every time he moved.

Not yet. But soon.

Tory stuck her head into the examining room where her associate, Nita Burgoyne, was finishing with their last patient. Even after a twelve-hour day, Nita looked fresh and elegant in a sage shirt, slightly deeper green skirt, and low heels. Her coffee-colored skin glowed and her dark eyes sparkled with happiness. Tory smiled inwardly at how good love looked on her. "I'm going to head home, Nita. I've got the beeper if anything comes up."

Nita finished wrapping an Ace bandage around Joey Torres's injured hand. "Go ahead. Joey and I are going to wait until Deo comes to pick us up." She gave the handsome dark-haired youth a stern glance. "Because Joey isn't ready to drive yet, right, Joey?"

"Yes ma'am," he said with an utterly charming grin. "Not until you say."

"How is Deo?" Tory asked. Deo Camara, Nita's lover and Joey's cousin, had been injured while trying to salvage a pier and boathouse from one of the many fires that had started the night of the hurricane.

"*She* says she's fine," Nita said. "Of course, getting her to admit that anything hurts is a major undertaking."

Tory laughed. "Now there's a familiar story. Good night, you two. Nita, I'll see you in the morning."

After gathering some files she wanted to finish at home and grabbing her cane, Tory made her way through the empty clinic, turning out lights as she went. She rarely used her cane anymore, relying on just her light ankle splint to support her damaged leg, and sometimes not even that. But she'd been on her feet constantly for the last ten days, and her leg was swollen and partially numb. She wasn't so proud that she'd risk falling on her ass rather than use her cane for a few days.

She left the lights on in the hall and the reception area for Nita and Joey, and pulled open the front door. Deo was just striding up the walk from the gravel parking lot in front of the single-story health clinic Tory had opened almost ten years before. Deo could have been Joey's twin—same dark good looks, same devilish grin, same muscular body. Until Nita, she'd broken hearts all over town. But not any longer.

"Hi, Deo. Nita is in the back with Joey. You can go on through. We're done with patients for the day."

"Thanks, Tory." Deo hurried to hold the door as Tory maneuvered through with her briefcase and armful of files. "I'm glad I caught you. I'll be by to take care of your deck and the damage to your doors sometime this week."

Tory waved a hand. "Don't worry about it. I'm sure you've got much bigger projects to see to. How's the recovery going?"

Deo grimaced. "I hate to say that a storm like this is great for business, but we've got more work than we know what to do with. Right now, we're just trying to put Band-Aids on places to prevent further damage. Roofs, windows, that kind of thing."

"Well, like I said, our house is livable, so I don't mind waiting."

"Thanks, I appreciate it." Deo sketched a salute in the air. "See you soon, then."

"'Night."

Tory piled her things on the front seat of her Jeep and drove out of the parking lot with a sigh. Almost six thirty. With any luck, Reese really would be able to get home by seven. Then they could have a quick dinner and make love. Tory smiled, thinking about having a few uninterrupted hours with Reese.

A brilliant sunset colored the sky above the harbor with swaths of pink and orange, bleeding into purple closer to the water. Despite the devastation to the town, the natural beauty of the sky and sea, the majesty of the sweeping dunes, remained eternal. The storm had arrived so suddenly and had wrought such fierce destruction so quickly, everyone was left in shock. Tory had seen tragedy upon tragedy in her years as a physician, had suffered the loss of her own dreams more than once, and still this event had shaken her. Had made her realize how quickly life can change, how all she cherished could be lost in a matter of hours. She'd been thinking about that a lot lately.

She pulled into the driveway beside their house in the far east end of Provincetown. They'd been lucky. A tree had come down in the front yard, narrowly missing the house, although it had smashed the front steps. Some shingles had blown off, but the roof had held and the upper floors were dry. The major damage was on the harbor side of the house—the panes in the sliding glass doors on the rear deck had finally cracked under the onslaught of flying debris, and something heavy, or a number of heavy somethings, had smashed the door frame and demolished part of the railing. Still, their house was habitable. A great many people couldn't say the same thing.

She slowly climbed the stairs to the side door and, once inside, dumped her briefcase and files on the counter that separated the kitchen from the living-dining room and propped her cane against one of the bar stools. As she walked toward the damaged double glass doors leading out to the rear deck, hoping to catch a last glimpse of the sunset, she thought idly about what she'd make for supper. Something quick and easy. She didn't want to waste a minute of her alone time with Reese.

Frowning, she noticed the deck doors were open an inch or two. She couldn't think why, unless Reese had been home during the day. That seemed unlikely, and even then, they hadn't been using the doors for the last few days because they were worried that the glass panes might fall out. Maybe the wind…

Somewhere overhead, a thud. Not a random tree branch falling, not a timber shifting. A door closing.

Tory spun around, her gaze sweeping the first floor. Nothing seemed out of place. The house was completely silent. Then she saw the trail of sand on the hardwood floor just inside the deck doors that shouldn't be open. She yanked her cell phone off her waistband as she grabbed the handle on the slider and pulled. The door caught in the warped frame, screeching like an animal in pain. Ignoring a surge of panic, she shoved harder, but the force just deformed the bent track further and she couldn't get the slider to open far enough for her to squeeze through. Through the thundering of her heart, she heard footsteps pounding above her. Pushing Reese's number on speed dial, she raced across the room toward the outside door.

❖

Reese tossed her hat onto the dashboard and settled behind the wheel with a satisfied sigh. She'd actually managed to reduce the stack of paperwork on her desk by several inches. Even more importantly, she'd convinced the town council to allocate emergency funds so she could approve overtime for her officers and schedule the work that had to be done. And after several strategic phone calls to collect on a few favors, she'd gotten the official go-ahead to hire Carter Wayne. Not bad for a day's work, even if she did have a headache. As soon as she was home with Tory, that would be history.

Her phone rang as she turned left onto Bradford, and she muttered a curse under her breath. It wouldn't be the first time she'd barely been out of the station house before she had to turn around and go back. When she glanced at the readout, she relaxed and pressed On.

"Hi, love," Reese said. "You need me to—"

"Reese! Someone's in the house!"

"Get out of there, Tory," Reese snapped, jamming her foot down on the accelerator as she hit the lights and siren.

"I...oh God..."

"Tory? Tory!" Reese's vision went completely blank. The road disappeared. The sky turned black—blacker than a starless night. The black of an endless void. Pain slashed through her chest and she cried out. She couldn't breathe. Couldn't breathe.

"No," she shouted, sucking in a huge breath. The road ahead shot into focus as the cruiser rocketed over the narrow, two-lane road. She jerked the mic off the dashboard and shouted for backup. Then she dropped it, leaving it to dangle by its curling black cord, as she unholstered her weapon. Twisting the wheel viciously with one hand, she careened into her driveway and slammed to a halt.

It couldn't have taken more than a minute for her to get home, but sometimes a minute could change a lifetime. Tory lay face down on the ground a few feet from the stairs. Time stopped for Reese. The world ground to a halt. Life as she knew it hovered on a precipice.

"Tory!" Reese tumbled from the car, racing forward, her weapon raised, her eyes scanning the area by instinct. Nothing moved. She anticipated the flare of incendiary devices and the smell of burning flesh, braced herself for the hail of bullets, waited stoically for the agonizing pain. Nothing came. She dropped to her knees on the crushed-shell driveway, her weapon falling uselessly to the ground. "Tory. God, Tory."

For the first time in her life, Reese was paralyzed. In the midst of battle, with death all around her, she'd acted. Instinct, a lifetime of training, had won out over fear and suffering and horror. She'd protected, she'd defended, she'd saved lives at the risk of her own. Now she couldn't move. She heard a car screech into the driveway behind her, dimly registered radio static and voices shouting. She couldn't move.

Tory moaned, rolled onto her side, and reached for her. "Reese."

The earth shifted back onto its axis. Reese's mind cleared as if someone had changed the channel on a television set. Sights, sounds, smells became suddenly razor sharp. She touched Tory's cheek. She was warm. Alive.

"Lie still, love. You've got blood on your forehead." Never taking her eyes from Tory's face, Reese shouted, "We need an ambulance."

"No, we don't," Tory said, her throat dry and her voice scratchy. "It's my leg. I fell down the stairs. God *damn* it."

Tory tried to sit up and Reese gently pressed down on her shoulder. "No. Stay there until the EMTs can check you out."

"Reese," Tory said urgently. "There was someone in the house. Upstairs."

"Did he touch you?" Reese's guts twisted when she asked the question.

"No. No, I think he ran away, but I'm not sure."

Reese looked up and met Allie Tremont's wide eyes. Bobby Strope, a part-time officer who worked the swing shift, stood behind her, red-faced and breathing hard. "Tremont. Take Strope and clear the house."

"Yes ma'am," Allie said crisply. She motioned to Strope and headed up the walk to the side door, her weapon out in front of her. She looked rock steady.

The EMT vehicle angled off the side of the road at the head of the driveway and two techs raced toward them, each carrying a red equipment box.

"I'm all right," Tory told them as they knelt on either side of her.

She recognized the sandy-haired man. "Dave, I'm okay. I just…it was stupid. I fell."

"We'll just take a look at you, Doc," Dave said affably while expertly wrapping a blood pressure cuff around her upper left arm. "You meet my new mate, Flynn Edwards?"

A blonde with cornsilk gold hair and eyes as blue as the July sky grinned down at her as she grasped Tory's wrist and took her pulse. "Dr. King. Good to meet you."

"BP's one-forty over eighty-two," Dave said.

"Pulse is eighty-eight. Nice and strong," Flynn reported. She flipped open her tackle box and pulled out a clean pair of gloves. After extracting a four-by-four gauze pad, she soaked it with saline and dabbed Tory's forehead. "This is just a scratch. Probably from one of the shells when you fell."

"I'll put some antibiotic ointment on it later." Tory gripped Reese's arm and pulled herself upright. "Listen, you two. I'm okay. Let me sign your release so you can get back to doing serious work."

Dave eased back on his heels. "Would you mind if I took a look at your leg, Doc?"

"If you take the splint off, it will swell," Reese said sharply. She shifted positions, slid her arms behind Tory's shoulders and under her knees, and pushed upright, cradling Tory against her chest. "She needs to be in bed before we take it off. I'll see to it as soon as the house is clear."

Dave and Flynn exchanged a look.

"I'm fine, really," Tory said gently, stroking Reese's cheek. "Sweetheart, I'm fine."

Flynn put her head down and began busily storing her equipment. Dave cleared his throat and said, "I'll get the paperwork."

"All clear, Sheriff," Allie called as she exited the house, holstering her weapon. Her lips parted in surprise when she took in Reese standing with Tory in her arms, and then her expression went carefully blank. "I sent Strope out to check the perimeter. You'll need to document whether anything is missing…after you get Dr. King squared away, that is. If it's okay with you, I'll dust for prints too."

"Thank you, Officer," Reese said, settled and calm now that Tory's heart beat close to hers. "Once you're done here, canvass the surrounding houses. Check with any owners who are home to see if they've had any problems with vandals. Look for any signs of forced entry in any houses that are empty."

"Yes ma'am."

"Fill me in when you're done, Tremont."

Allie saluted. "Yes ma'am."

Reese smiled briefly. "Well done, Tremont."

❖

"She didn't sign the release form," Dave muttered.

"Give it to me," Allie said, holding out her hand as she watched Reese climb the stairs as effortlessly as if she weren't carrying a hundred and thirty pounds of woman in her arms. No wonder everyone thought she was hot. She *was* hot.

"Impressive," a husky female voice said beside her.

"Understatement," Allie murmured. She glanced at Flynn and laughed. "How are you doing?"

"Busy, but getting settled." Flynn flipped a shock of blond hair off her forehead with long, slender fingers. "You?"

"About to get a lot busier."

"Yeah." Flynn glanced toward the house. "What do you think? Vandalism?"

Allie shrugged. "Maybe. Looting has been a problem, what with so many places standing empty. There's also a lot of new faces in town. Disaster always draws a crowd."

"Yeah, I saw that after nine-eleven."

"You were there?"

Flynn colored and glanced away. "I volunteered with a…uh, group of people. Got there just a couple days after. It was…it was bad."

"I believe it. How long were you there?"

"Two months."

Allie was impressed. "That's pretty amazing."

"Not so much. No big deal." Clearly embarrassed, Flynn looked over her shoulder where Dave waited by the truck. "Listen, I've got to get back to work."

"Me too," Allie said.

"So how about we get together for drinks some night. Tonight, maybe," Flynn said quickly.

Allie hesitated, and for no good reason at all, flashed on Ash standing naked in a room on Bradford. "I've got a couple more hours of work here at least. But yeah, later. Later would be good."

"I'll call you," Flynn said, backing away, her eyes sparkling. "Tonight?"

"Tonight." Allie called out her cell number. "Can you remember that?"

Flynn patted her chest. "Already etched on my heart."

Laughing, Allie shook her head and watched Flynn climb into the truck. It felt good to laugh. It felt a lot better than crying.

CHAPTER FIVE

"My cane is right over there," Tory said, pointing toward the counter. "You can put me down, sweetheart. I can walk with that."

"No," Reese said gruffly. She couldn't put her down. She was afraid, afraid in some animal part of her being to relinquish her protective hold on her mate while there was still the slightest possibility of danger. Struggling not to let her fear bleed over to her lover, she started toward the stairs. "We should see to your leg. I'll take you to the bedroom."

"Stop. Wait a minute." When Reese kept walking, Tory grasped a fistful of Reese's starched uniform shirt and tugged on it to get her attention. "Reese. Look at me."

Reluctantly, Reese paused, one foot on the lower stair, Tory resting in the cradle formed by the curve of her body. She didn't want to meet Tory's eyes because she couldn't hide what was in her own. She didn't want Tory to see her fear or her fury. "You're hurt, baby. Let me take care of you."

"You are. You do." Tory smoothed her hand over the wrinkles in Reese's shirt, caressing her chest through the thin barrier. She understood Reese's need to safeguard her, and she would never try to change that. Reese's sense of duty, her loyalty to her family and her friends, her need to defend those she loved was fundamental to her life. Tory loved her for it. But she'd seen the haunted look in Reese's eyes just a few minutes before, heard the pain in her voice. As strong as Reese was, she'd been hurt in more than body in that desert horror, and she wasn't completely healed. "Put me down on the couch. We'll wait together for Allie to report in." She kissed Reese's neck above the crisp line of her collar. "I love you."

Reese shuddered and buried her face in Tory's hair. She took great gulping breaths, purging the bitter taste of loss from the back of her throat with the sweet fragrance of Tory's shampoo. "I saw you there on the ground and…for a second, I thought…" Reese's legs suddenly felt weak and she abruptly sat down on the stairs, pulling Tory tighter to her chest, bracing Tory's injured leg on her thigh to cushion the damaged ankle.

Tory threaded her arms around Reese's neck and twisted in her lap so her breasts were pressed to Reese's chest. She kissed her, and when she heard Reese moan, she caressed the back of Reese's neck and murmured against her mouth, "I'm all right. I'm right here with you. Right where I'll always be."

"I love you so much," Reese whispered.

"I know, darling. I know." Tory feathered her fingers through Reese's hair and kissed her gently. "I love the way you love me. Don't ever change."

❖

On his way up from the beach to the darkened house where he'd been staying after forcing the rear door a few days before, he caught a glimmer of light flashing through the scrub pines bordering the property. Slowing, he eased his way cautiously through the brush until he could see the rear deck. A figure moved slowly from window to window, shining a flashlight into the house. He slid his hand to the waistband of his pants and gripped his H&K. The moon came out from behind a cloud, bathing the deck in silver. He saw a woman, young, and with a body that even the drab uniform couldn't camouflage.

Pity. Such a waste. He extended the gun and cradled his right hand in the palm of his left, sighting on her head. In the distance, the crackle of police radios and the flashing light bars on top of the cruisers cast a red glow through the trees, lighting the sky as if the night were on fire. The sound of the shot would carry, but he would be just another shadow by the time anyone arrived.

She reached for the back door handle and he drew in a long, steady breath in preparation for squeezing the trigger. He didn't have to kill her. He hadn't left behind anything of consequence. He just wanted to. He was tired of being hunted. Tired of being driven from safety. Tired of watching from the shadows.

"Hey, Allie," a male voice called just as an arc of white light cut a swath over the trees where he crouched. A man made his way along the flagstone path from the street toward the back of the house. "Anything?"

"Not sure," the woman replied. "There's a trash bag in the middle of the kitchen floor. It looks like it's almost full—food trash, looks like. Doesn't that seem weird to you? I mean, if you were evacuating, would you leave that stuff inside the house when you didn't know when you'd be back?"

"Huh."

"And I think the door's unlocked," the woman said.

The officers drew their weapons.

Calculating the possibility of taking them both out, he judged the odds of clean kills to be low. He could not risk one or both of them returning fire. He heard a grinding sound and realized it was his teeth, and he forced his jaws to relax. He saw the woman's face in the reflected light of her partner's flashlight. She was beautiful and young. So many to choose from.

Next time. Next time he might have her. She would do, while he waited.

❖

Reese reclined in the corner of the couch with Tory nestled in her arms, Tory's legs stretched out and her injured foot propped on several pillows. She stroked Tory's hair and listened to her slow, even breathing. Her service weapon rested on the arm of the sofa millimeters from her right hand. She trusted Allie, but she wanted to clear the house herself and until she did, she wasn't leaving Tory's side. Some things were too important to leave to anyone else.

As each minute passed, her focus sharpened. She didn't doubt that someone had been in the house. Tory was as levelheaded and objective in a crisis as anyone she'd ever met. After she had a chance to look around, she might have a better idea of exactly what happened. She considered the possibilities. Random vandalism was certainly an option, although any local resident would know she lived here, which ought to make the house less of a target. However, criminals did not tend to be the most intelligent members of the population, and everyone in town knew that Tory was a doctor and Reese the sheriff. Whoever had broken in might have thought there were drugs or guns and ammunition in the house. There were also a higher than usual number of strangers in town, having been drawn by the disaster as seemed to be the case whenever misfortune struck. The final possibility was that the house and its contents were not the target, but that some member of the household was.

She was the sheriff, which wasn't always a popular position, although she couldn't think of anyone in their small village who she'd arrested for anything more serious than car theft. Except for the man who had molested Bri Parker. She'd broken his arm, and had contemplated worse. He must have felt how close she'd come to pulling the trigger of the gun she'd held to his head. She'd bested him hand-to-hand and humiliated him. For some men that was enough to exact payback. She made a note to check his whereabouts. He'd received the maximum sentence for the attempted rape and assault on a police officer, but he might have gotten early parole.

Tory saw dozens of patients every day, and although Reese doubted that anyone would be angry enough over a diagnosis or some other perceived slight to want to hurt her, the possibility of a stalker was very real. In her capacity as a physician, Tory was intimately involved in people's lives, often making the difference between life and death. Some unstable individual could easily fixate on her. Just the idea of anyone getting close to Tory, harming her, froze the breath in her chest.

"What are you thinking about?" Tory murmured.

"Nothing," Reese whispered, kissing the top of her head. "Go back to sleep."

"I wasn't sleeping. I was just lying here thinking how much I love lying here in your arms."

Reese's stomach tightened and heat shot through her. Adrenaline and desire tangled and pulsed. She sucked in a breath, her hips lifting almost imperceptibly. She forced herself to breathe evenly. "How does your leg feel?"

"Your body just got tight as a drum. So don't tell me you weren't thinking about anything important. What's worrying you?"

"I'm concerned about your leg," Reese said, which was true. "You wouldn't have fallen down the stairs tonight if you hadn't already put too much strain on it. You need to take it easy, baby. You're working too much."

"I'm not working any more than anyone else, and I can't leave Nita to handle it all on her own." Tory shifted until she could look up into Reese's face. "The medical problems never go away, and now we're seeing a lot more minor trauma, and some of it that's *not* so minor, because of all of the recovery efforts. We're swamped, sweetheart."

"I know. But you still need to leave at a reasonable hour." Reese tapped Tory's chin. "That doesn't mean ten o'clock at night."

"I left early tonight. I had big plans for you, you know." Tory sighed. "Dinner and then sex. Lots of sex."

"In a little while I'll take care of dinner. The other..." Reese grinned. "I'll take care of that in a couple of days."

Tory's eyebrows shot up and she laughed incredulously. "The hell you will. I have no intention of waiting a couple of days." Then just as quickly, her face grew serious. "What about the baby? Do you think we should have Jean and Kate keep her at their place for a few days? What if I'd been here alone with her?"

"Let's see what the investigation turns up tonight." Reese smoothed her thumb over the worry lines on Tory's forehead. "This will probably all turn out to be nothing."

"Probably." Tory struggled to sit up and Reese swiftly moved the pillow to the coffee table. Tory eased her leg onto the pillow and said, "So what do you really think happened?"

"I don't know yet. I need to look around the house. In the meantime, I want you to think about anyone you've seen at the clinic in the last three months who's been acting strangely."

"Strangely how?"

"Paying too much attention to you, maybe calling on the phone with bogus complaints or asking for special appointments. Anything that seems excessive or inappropriate."

"You think someone is stalking me," Tory said quietly.

Reese shook her head. "I don't think anything at all just yet.

But that's on my list. I have a few other things to look into as soon as Allie—"

"I know you need to talk to Allie tonight," Tory said. "But after she reports, I don't want you to go back to work. Not tonight." When Reese said nothing, Tory took her hand. "You need to be here with me. And I need you here."

Reese brought Tory's hand to her lips and kissed it. "I'll be right beside you, all night long."

❖

"Hey," Bri said to Allie as she walked into the locker room at the station house shortly before ten thirty. "Smith said something happened out at Reese's. What's going on? How come no one called me?"

Standing in front of her open locker, Allie shot a look over her shoulder. She'd already changed into her jeans and, except for her scanty black lace bra, was bare from the waist up. She saw Bri's gaze drop and laughed. "Eyes up, Parker."

Bri blushed. "Sorry. Reflex."

"Yeah yeah." Allie slipped into a tight, scoop-necked black top and tucked it into her jeans, then pulled on her black cowboy boots. "Tory walked in on someone in the house. She's fine. And I didn't call you because I took the call and you weren't on duty. I handled it."

"Jesus, Allie. It's Reese and Tory!"

Allie patted Bri's chest. "I know, baby. But I was going to call you when you came on shift and fill you in. There wasn't anything for you to do."

"You think I should go out there?" Bri paced in a small tight circle, her hands jammed into the pockets of her low-slung black jeans.

"No. Strope and I checked the whole neighborhood. It looks like someone might've been squatting in the house right next door. We did a quick check inside when I found the back door unlocked, and there was fresh trash in the kitchen. And someone had probably been sleeping in the living room." Allie pulled a black leather bag out of her locker and slid her holstered weapon into it. "Nothing to identify who it might've been. We stayed while Reese checked through their house again, and she didn't come up with anything."

"It doesn't feel right," Bri muttered. "Just doing nothing."

Allie straddled the narrow wooden bench between the lockers and propped her bag against her leg. Bri sat down facing her, their knees touching.

"I don't like it either," Allie said softly. "The whole thing just feels creepy." She rested her hand on Bri's thigh. "But there really wasn't anything for you to do, and I didn't think Reese and Tory needed all of us showing up at their house."

"I'll do some extra drive-bys tonight," Bri said.

"Good. I figured you would." Allie grinned. "You've got an awesome hickey on your neck, by the way. I guess you probably know that."

Bri tried to frown while rubbing the sore spot, but her smile came off self-satisfied. "Well, I had the afternoon off."

"Yeah, well," Allie said, squelching a surge of envy, and maybe a little jealousy. "Maybe I'll get lucky tonight. I'm on my way to the Pied to meet Flynn."

"That was fast!"

"We ran into each other at Reese and Tory's." She stood and lightly swatted Bri's shoulder. "Don't be giving me that look. We're just having a drink. And then, if…" She shrugged. "We're both legal. And I haven't had any since Deo, and that was weeks and weeks ago."

"Well, it's not like it's a terminal illness or anything."

"Oh yeah, like you go what…more than a day without it?"

Bri swung her leg over the bench and straightened up. "That's different. I'm married."

"You're supposed to get *less* when you get married."

"Says who?"

"Says everyone. That's why I prefer variety."

"Just be careful, okay?"

Allie frowned at her. "What do you mean, be careful? You know I don't go in for drugs or anything like—"

"That's not what I'm saying." Bri placed her fingertips gently on Allie's chest, at the top of her left breast. "I'm talking about this, Al. About getting hurt in here."

"Don't," Allie said softly. "Don't get all sweet and gentle on me. It makes me want to kiss you."

Bri snorted and shook her head. "Jesus, you make me crazy."

"I can't help the way I am, especially when you pull that fierce butch stuff. It just does something to me." Allie smiled tremulously. "It's just a date. Nothing to worry about. Promise."

"Okay. Look, I'm sorry." Bri shrugged. "I just… Well, you know, with Ash in town and—"

"Walker has nothing to do with anything," Allie said curtly. "Nothing at all." She ruffled Bri's hair and strode toward the door. "I gotta go. Flynn is really hot, and I don't want to keep her waiting."

"Yeah, right. I hear you." Bri turned and watched the door swing closed behind Allie. She might have believed her, except she'd seen the hurt skate across Allie's face at the mention of Ash's name.

He watched her turn the sign in the window of the shop door to *Closed*. When she came out and turned right to walk down Commercial Street, he fell in behind her.

CHAPTER SIX

"D o you need more ice on that?" Reese repositioned the pillow under Tory's ankle.

"No, it feels much better now." Tory took in Reese in her faded regulation-green boxers and T-shirt. The shrapnel wound on her leg and the burn scars on her arm and shoulder were still red and angry. She'd gained back a little of the weight she'd lost while deployed, but she still appeared wraithlike in the dim light cast by the lamp on the far side of the room. Reese had been nothing but gentle and tender and attentive all evening, but she vibrated with a violent energy Tory knew she was struggling to hide. Tory patted the bed beside her. "Stretch out next to me."

Reese frowned. "I thought I would make you some tea. Or maybe a glass of wine?"

Tory smiled. "Wine. In a few minutes." She pushed the sheets down. "Come here, first."

"I'm just going to keep you awake," Reese muttered as she slipped under the covers. "You need to rest and I'm not tire—"

"I'm going to sleep like a baby tonight, I promise." Tory traced Reese's lower lip with her index finger, then leaned over and kissed her. In the middle of the kiss, she worked her hand underneath the bottom of Reese's T-shirt and caressed her abdomen. The skin felt stapled to the ridges of muscle underneath, stretched tight and humming with tension. She flicked her tongue over Reese's lip and murmured against her mouth, "But first, I have unfinished business."

"Tory," Reese groaned, partly in frustration and partly with anticipation she couldn't conceal. Tory knew her body better than she did herself. Tory knew what she needed, when she needed it, how she needed it—Tory knew what to do so her tension would ebb, her mind clear, and her dreams become comfort rather than torment. But not tonight. Tory had been taking care of her for months, although they both pretended otherwise. But not tonight. "You need to be careful of your leg."

When Reese started to roll away, Tory slid her hand higher, between Reese's breasts, and held her down. "You'd be surprised what I can do without moving very much at all."

"No, I wouldn't be." Reese pulled Tory closer and kissed her again. "I know exactly how talented you are, but that still doesn't mean I want you to wear yourself—"

"Sweetheart," Tory said lightly, "shut up."

Reese couldn't answer because Tory was kissing her again, kissing her and massaging her chest, brushing her palm over her nipples, scraping her nails down the center of her abdomen and then stroking to smooth the thin trails of fire left behind. When Tory's tongue plunged deeper into her mouth, Reese automatically lifted her hips, her thighs turning to iron.

"Be very good now," Tory whispered as she drew back and leaned on one elbow, "and do exactly as I say."

"Be careful." Reese fixed on Tory's gaze. In the yellow glow of the lamplight, Tory's green eyes danced with flecks of gold, and although Reese was reminded of sparks escaping flames, she didn't hear the roar of artillery or feel the scathing pain as fire consumed the earth. She saw strength and desire and safety. Here, in the one place only Tory could take her, she did not have to fight.

Tory skimmed her hand down the center of Reese's body and underneath the waistband of her boxers. Reese arched and sucked in her breath. Smiling, Tory watched Reese's face as she slowly and unerringly found her clitoris and began to stroke. "That's right, darling. Let me have you."

"Tory," Reese murmured, drifting on Tory's smile. "You always have me."

"Mmm. But not like this." Tory nipped Reese's chin. "Helpless. At my mercy." She squeezed and Reese hissed, her stomach muscles rippling under Tory's forearm. "So hard and so hot." She picked up speed and Reese's breath followed suit, coming faster and harsher with each passing second. The muscles along the edge of Reese's jaw bunched, and she groaned. An urgent warning. Instantly, Tory released her grip, cupping Reese in her palm as she claimed her mouth with another deep kiss.

Reese twisted on the bed, desperate for Tory to stroke her. Tory's tongue danced over hers, teasing and tormenting. She throbbed under Tory's hand, teetering on the edge. She grasped a handful of Tory's hair and tugged Tory's mouth away from hers. "Do it, baby. Please. Keep going."

Tory's vision wavered and arousal swept through her so brutally she couldn't get enough air to talk. She loved this moment, when Reese needed her and only her for everything. Reese was hers, completely, just as she was Reese's. "No. Not so soon." She circled the slick, smooth prominence with just her fingertip, thrilling to the sight of Reese's fierce blue eyes losing focus as pleasure stole through her. "Just me. Just feel me." She kissed her, caressed her. "Mmm. Yes, like that."

"You're going to make me come," Reese gasped.

Tory stopped.

"Oh Christ," Reese moaned, her entire body stiff and quivering. She clamped her hand around Tory's wrist inside her boxers and tried to press Tory's fingers where she needed them. "I can't."

"You can." Tory kissed Reese's damp temple, then her eyelids, then her mouth, infinitely tender. "Trust me. I know what you need."

"Okay. Okay," Reese said breathlessly. She forced herself to relax her grip on Tory's arm. "Did I…hurt you?"

"Oh, sweetheart, no. Never." Tory's head pounded with the effort not to move, not to climb on top of her, not to push inside her. She pressed her forehead to Reese's shoulder, shaking with need. "I want you so much."

Reese wrapped her arm around Tory's shoulders and tried to turn her onto her back.

"No," Tory said quickly. "No no no. You are not taking charge, Sheriff."

"Let me please you."

"You do." Tory dipped into Reese's wetness and massaged her clitoris. "*This* pleases me."

Reese rocketed toward orgasm. Her hips bucked under Tory's fingers. "Close to coming. *Close.*"

"Mmm. I feel it." Tory sped up—circled, pressed, stroked and squeezed. She listened for the hitch in Reese's breathing, waited for the sudden stiffness beneath her fingers, and then she stopped. Reese broke out in a sweat and moaned against Tory's breasts. She started, she listened, she stopped. Again and again.

"Beautiful," Tory breathed as Reese trembled in her arms. Reese was so close now her clitoris never softened, even when Tory stopped touching her. She took her hand away completely and caressed Reese's abdomen. "I love you."

"Please, I need you."

"I need you." Tory kissed her gently, a brush of lips, a soft caress of tongue and teeth. "I need you more than I will ever be able to show you. But I'll try." She slipped under Reese's boxers again.

"This time," Reese groaned when Tory resumed stroking. "Need to come this time. Please don't stop this time, baby."

Tory kissed her forehead and picked up speed. "All of it, darling. Give me everything."

Reese's body bowed, her breath halted in her chest, and Tory took her surely and certainly to the edge, and beyond.

❖

Bri cruised past Reese and Tory's darkened house, slowing to check that no one loitered around the driveway or in the neighboring yards. "Everything looks quiet around here."

"The guy is probably miles away by now," Carter said to her new partner. Bri had been quiet since they'd met at the station house. After a short briefing, Bri had palmed the keys to the cruiser on their way out, and Carter didn't even consider asking to drive. Right now, her first night on the job, all of her experience meant nothing. Not in the delicate hierarchy of her new posting. She didn't mind needing to earn her stripes, and she didn't mind not driving. She preferred to ride shotgun because she could watch the streets more carefully. Given a choice, she'd rather walk the streets than ride them, but right now, she went where she was told.

"Yeah. It doesn't make sense he was local," Bri muttered, slowly heading west on Commercial. In the East End, the galleries and restaurants were all closed for the night. As they drew closer to

MacMillan Wharf, activity picked up. More people on the street, making the rounds of the bars and clubs along Commercial and tucked away in narrow alleys. "You'd have to be crazy to break into the sheriff's house!"

"Can't rule out that possibility," Carter said quietly. "Crazy, I mean."

"Yeah. I hear that."

"So what's the routine?" Carter asked.

Bri shot her a glance and then looked back to the street. She was used to riding with Allie. They had a rhythm. They didn't have to talk about what they'd do, how they'd handle a situation when they took the call, how the shift would spin out. Thinking about it now, she realized that she'd kind of fallen into the role of shift leader, not because Allie wasn't capable, but because Allie really didn't care who was in charge. And that suited Bri fine. She couldn't take any of that for granted with Carter, but it seemed as if Carter was handing her the ball. "We'll cruise for a while if no calls come in, and then when the bars start to close, take a walk through town. Check for trouble."

"Drunk and disorderlies?"

"We can always count on a few fistfights, some lewd and lascivious that's so in-your-face we can't ignore it. Once in a while a drunk gets rolled and we'll need to get the EMTs out."

"Much trouble with DUIs?"

Bri nodded. "Yeah. We'll need to head out to Six when the ones who aren't staying in town start heading back up Cape."

"And there's what, one other car out?"

"Smith and one of the seasonal guys—Girelli. They'll mostly stick to the highway and out around the beaches. Since the storm, there hasn't been much action out that way, but we've had problems with boats bringing drugs in."

"For a sleepy little town, there's a lot going on here," Carter remarked.

Bri laughed and then quieted abruptly as the radio crackled.

"Charlie five, copy?" the officer manning the desk back at the station asked.

Carter grabbed the mic. "Charlie five, go ahead."

"Auto burglary—parking lot at Bradford and Standish. Female motorist needs assistance."

"Charlie five, affirmative. Suspect in the vicinity?"

"Negative. Requested motorist wait with vehicle—break…"

"Go ahead."

"Gray Lexus, Massachusetts license Victor Bravo three-seven-one."

A lead weight dropped into Carter's stomach. "That's Rica's car."

Bri leaned forward, flipped on the sirens and light bar in one fluid motion, and floored the gas pedal.

Ash wasn't sure why she'd come out to the Pied. She hadn't had more than a few hours' sleep a night in almost two weeks and had logged over ten thousand miles driving up and down the eastern seaboard from one devastated area to another. But sleep wasn't what she wanted. Her head buzzed with stress and her skin tingled with restless energy, so she'd changed into a navy shirt and jeans and sought out the one place where she might find a diversion. She'd never been much of a drinker, but she seemed to be leaning on alcohol a lot lately to soothe her nerves and dull the constant low-level ache of loneliness that threatened to mushroom into the unrelenting pain of despair. When she thought about it, which she tried not to, the last eight months had been pretty much a blur. She worked as much as she could, until she was physically exhausted and mentally too weary to think about the direction her life had taken. When work wasn't enough to keep her from questioning the decision she'd made, she tried to block out her unhappiness with transient trysts. Frantic couplings in no-name motels with women whose faces all ran together. There hadn't even been much of that lately because she couldn't muster enough interest to pretend she cared about the women she was with, and she couldn't tolerate the self-loathing in the morning. Even a one-night stand deserved to be seen.

"Is this seat taken?"

Ash looked up from her beer at the slight, curvaceous blonde in the very short skirt and low, tight top who stood with one hip canted and a smoldering look on her face that said she knew exactly how sexy she was. She had to be a dozen years younger than Ash, if not more, and the irony was not lost on her. The same twelve years separated her and Allie. Shaking her head, Ash said, "The seat's free, but you don't want to sit here."

Surprise flashed across the blonde's delicate features and she tapped one manicured nail on the tabletop. "What makes you think so?"

"I'm halfway drunk and I can't offer anything except a quick fuck and good-bye in the morning."

Laughing, the blonde pulled out a chair and sat down. She was braless and when she leaned toward Ash her pert round breasts swayed invitingly. "So you think you've got it all figured out? What makes you think I want any kind of fuck?"

"My apologies." Ash lifted her beer bottle and when the woman reached out to take it away, she let her. "I'm afraid my conversational skills are impaired at the moment as well."

"What about a dance? Can you manage that?"

Ash frowned and focused on the music. "If it doesn't get any faster."

"If it does, we'll pretend we don't notice. My name is Lisa."

"Ash. Ash Walker."

Lisa stood and held out her hand. "Then come along, Ash Walker, and dance with me."

❖

Allie waved to the women on the door at the Pied and some of the locals she knew as she made her way through the late-night crowd toward the bar. She hadn't been out in weeks. The last woman she'd dated had gone and fallen in love with someone else. As every weekend rolled around, she'd kept telling herself she'd go out, relax, find a woman to play with for a few days or a few weeks, but she hadn't. She'd always found something else she needed to do that kept her from spending a night with a stranger. And before those few weeks with Deo Camara, who was the first woman since Ash she'd thought she might be able to get serious about, she hadn't been to bed with anyone for a few months. So to say the last six months had been a dry spell was an understatement. She was twenty-three years old and she liked sex, and even more than that, she liked to wake up to the feel of a woman in her arms. She was lonely and she was horny, and she was tired of being both.

Flynn was easy to pick out, leaning against the bar. She wasn't wearing her navy blue EMT jumpsuit now. Taller than Allie by a head, with her thick blond hair slicked back from her strong, bold face, she looked lean and sexy in tight black pants, a white open-collared shirt, and black motorcycle boots.

"Wow. You look hot," Allie said as she sidled up next to Flynn.

Grinning, Flynn ducked her head and kissed Allie's cheek. Her gaze drifted down Allie's body, taking in the rich fall of ebony hair, the full breasts straining against the stretchy top, and the hip-hugger jeans accentuating a tight round butt. "And you look gorgeous."

"Thank you." Allie smiled and waved at the bartender. "Sammy! Draft?"

"Got ya covered, baby," the husky dyke called back. "One minute."

"So how was the rest of your night?" Flynn asked.

"Quiet." Allie paid for her beer and took a sip. "You?"

"A couple of minor callouts. Nothing serious."

Allie liked the way Flynn leaned with one elbow on the bar, her eyes fixed on Allie's face, as if they were alone together and not in the middle of a packed bar. "Where are you from?"

Flynn looked momentarily taken aback, as if the question had thrown her somehow. Then she quickly said, "Chicago."

"This place must seem like a big change," Allie said lightly, having noticed Flynn's hesitation. Okay, so she didn't want to talk about her past. Fair enough.

"Yeah." A look of relief tinged with sadness passed over Flynn's handsome features. "I've only been here a few weeks, but it already feels like home."

"I know what you mean." Allie ran her fingers down Flynn's arm and squeezed her hand. "I hope that means you'll be staying."

"Don't worry," Flynn replied, the mischievous light returning to her eyes. "Now that I've gotten your attention, you won't get rid of me so easily."

Allie laughed, enjoying the flirtation. "Believe me, you've had my attention all along."

Flynn eased a little closer and settled one hand on Allie's hip. She ducked her head and whispered in Allie's ear, "Well then, I want to be sure to keep it."

"You're doing pretty good so far." The pressure of Flynn's hand on her hip, the tease of warm breath in her ear, stirred a tingle of excitement low in Allie's belly. She tilted her head just a little to bare her neck to Flynn's mouth. Flynn's lips were so close she could almost feel the kiss about to drop onto her skin. Enjoying the pleasant anticipation, she let her gaze drift over Flynn's shoulder out to the dance floor, and thought she glimpsed a familiar face. She blinked, not quite believing, as Ash's face came into sharp focus.

Flynn kissed her neck and murmured, "How about now? Still good?"

Allie wanted to look away but she couldn't. Ash stared into Allie's eyes, her mouth twisting sardonically. Then Ash buried her face in the neck of the slinky blonde who was plastered against her body, her hands sliding down to cup the woman's ass.

"Even better," Allie said, her voice sounding flat to her own ears. She tugged on Flynn's hand. "Let's get out of here."

Flynn lifted her head, clearly surprised, but she smiled and let Allie pull her hurriedly through the crowd and out into the street.

❖

"There she is!" Carter pointed to Rica standing next to her Lexus, parked halfway down the outer row of cars. The huge parking lot was separated from the street by a thicket of trees. Despite the late hour, the lot was still half full, but the attendant's booth was at the far end, around a bend. The section where Rica had parked was isolated, and the street lamps, mounted on poles every thirty feet or so, left substantial areas in darkness.

"Man, this place is a setup for robberies and assaults," Carter said, bolting from the cruiser before Bri had even pulled to a stop. She reached Rica in three long strides and slipped an arm around Rica's waist. Hustling her back to the cruiser, she pulled open the rear door. "Wait inside, babe."

"Carter," Rica began, but Carter just shook her head, guided her into the vehicle, and closed the door.

Bri came around the front of the cruiser and together they approached Rica's car. Carter scanned the lot but saw no sign of anyone else. The driver's side window of the Lexus was smashed, glass littering the ground.

"The perp was most likely gone by the time she got here," Carter said, her mouth dry and her stomach twisting. "Christ, if she'd walked up on him—"

"It was probably a smash and grab," Bri said, shining her Maglite into the front seat. "Radio's still there. We'll need to find out if she left something in the car."

"Maybe, but Rica is usually careful." Carter took a breath, clearing her head. "We should walk around, see if any of the other cars have been broken into."

"You take the back half, I'll canvass up here," Bri said. "Check back with me in five."

"Got it."

They separated, slowly wending their way up and down the rows of cars.

He'd checked his watch when she'd discovered her car and made a call on her cell phone. Less than three minutes passed before the police had arrived. He could accomplish a lot in three minutes. There was plenty of light for him to make a body shot. Even a head shot, although he didn't think they were wearing vests. Not in this town, not for routine patrols. And of course, she was completely unprotected. Vulnerable to anything he wanted. Just like all of them. He slid his fingers over the smooth length of the knife in his pocket. Of course, if he got close to her, he could get much more personal. Much more.

CHAPTER SEVEN

When the music switched to a faster tempo, Ash started to pull back, but Lisa tightened her arms around Ash's neck and murmured, "No, I like your hands on my ass."

"Sorry," Ash murmured, realizing she'd been blatantly feeling Lisa up on the dance floor. And the reason she'd done it had nothing to do with Lisa. She'd been dancing with Lisa but watching Allie. Watching Allie flirt and play with a good-looking butch her own age. Just exactly what Ash had told her she should do. Except when Allie had tilted her head back so the woman could kiss her neck, Ash had tried to block the hard pain by fondling the woman in her arms. Not a response she was proud of. She jerked her hands back up to the center of Lisa's back and repeated, "Sorry."

"Baby, I just told you I liked it." Lisa undulated seductively. "You can put your hands anywhere you want."

Ash tried to lose herself in the kind of mindless arousal that didn't really work for her even when she *wasn't* thinking of Allie. Now she couldn't think of anything else. Lisa was a few inches shorter than Allie and fuller breasted, and although her body was tantalizing, she didn't fit in Ash's arms the way Allie had. Allie. Allie apparently didn't have any problems fitting into someone else's embrace. Ash could still see the way Allie offered her neck, that smooth ivory column that was so responsive to a kiss or the scrape of teeth, to the stranger. The stranger who'd left the bar with Allie. The stranger who was probably kissing that neck right now, sliding her hands under the tight skimpy top that had displayed Allie's ripe young breasts so teasingly. Caressing her, making her whimper softly, plaintively, the way she did when she was getting excited…

"Fuck," Ash whispered, not intending to speak out loud.

"I was thinking the same thing." Lisa leaned back in Ash's arms and rolled her pelvis against Ash's. Her eyes were liquid, her lids heavy, as her gaze drifted over Ash's face and came to rest on her mouth. "Are you as ready as I am?"

Ash gripped her ass again and, under cover of the darkened dance floor, pumped her crotch once, hard, into Lisa's. "What do you think?"

"Oh yeah." Lisa flicked her tongue over her full lower lip. "I think you're ready. I think you'd love to put your mouth on my—"

"Come on," Ash said gruffly. "Where are you staying?"

"With two other girls at the Boatslip." Lisa grabbed her purse from the chair at their table while Ash downed the rest of her beer.

"Are they going to be home?" Ash held Lisa's drink out to her, and when Lisa shook her head, she finished that too. She could tell from the hungry look in Lisa's eyes it was going to be a long night.

"They won't be back for quite a while, and I've got the single bedroom." She smiled and tugged on Ash's fly. "But I don't mind a crowd if you don't."

Ash grinned grimly. "Maybe some other night."

Right now, all she wanted was to get rid of the movie playing inexorably in her head, one starring Allie. First she saw herself making Allie scream with pleasure, only to be replaced by an image of the muscular blonde, her mouth at Allie's breast, her hand between Allie's legs. A sharp pain shot through Ash's head and she gritted her teeth. Swiftly, she grabbed Lisa's arm, jerked her close and kissed her, willing the heat of Lisa's mouth and the lush pliancy of her body to burn the unwanted pictures from her brain.

❖

"We'll follow you home," Carter said to Rica after she and Bri had checked the parking lot and found nothing else amiss. She wasn't sure how to interpret the absence of any other break-ins. In crimes of opportunity, the perpetrators wanted to get as much merchandise as they could, so more than one vehicle was usually targeted. But only

Rica's Lexus appeared to have been vandalized, and Carter wondered uneasily if her car had been singled out intentionally.

"You don't need to do that," Rica said quietly. "I'm fine. It's only a mile."

Carter shook her head. "No. I want to be sure there's no further problem."

What she didn't say was she wanted to check the house. There was no reason at all to think that Rica was in danger, but Rica was not an ordinary woman. She was the daughter of one of the most powerful organized crime figures in the country, and even though Rica steadfastly repudiated her heritage, she could not deny it. She was her father's daughter, and as such she was a potential target for men who might want to influence or retaliate against him. Pareto had pulled back Rica's bodyguards at Rica's insistence, and although Carter was glad, right now she wished one of them were around.

Bri joined them by the side of the cruiser. "Was there anything lying in plain view on the front seat or the floor?"

Rica shook her head. "No. Nothing. I never leave anything of value visible."

"I checked under the dash," Bri said, "and I didn't see any sign that the wiring had been tampered with. No one hotwired it in an attempt to steal it. The sound system connections are all intact. Looks like the broken window is the only damage." Bri glanced at Carter and hooked one thumb over her gun belt before focusing on Rica again. "Have you had a run-in with anyone lately? An irritated customer, maybe?"

"No, no one," Rica said quickly. "Why?"

Carter cleared her throat and Bri said immediately, "Just running the list of possibilities."

"Oh, bullshit," Rica said irritably. "Don't you two pull that cop stuff on me. You think someone was trying to send me a message? A warning of some kind?"

"It's possible," Bri said. "And it's just as possible this was a completely random act. Plenty of kids get drunk and show off for their friends. Someone may have just tossed a rock at the window to prove how bad they are."

Carter took Rica's hand. "Right now there's no reason to think it's anything more than what Bri just said. But be careful, okay? If you notice anything at any time that seems the least bit off, call me."

"I will, baby," Rica murmured. "Right now, I just want to go home."

As they followed Rica's Lexus down Bradford, Carter automatically checked for a tail. A single car followed at a distance but turned off before they reached their street. Rica would probably say Carter's years undercover had made her paranoid, but being paranoid was what had kept her alive.

"You don't think her car being hit was an accident?" Bri asked.

"I don't know."

"I don't like the feel of it."

"No," Carter said. "Neither do I."

He waited, watching, until the police cruiser followed the Lexus out of the parking lot. It was late, well after midnight, but he wasn't tired. He felt invigorated. So many choices. He could follow her home. She'd be alone for the rest of the night. He could watch her undressing through the windows, from the safety of the dunes. He could slip in through an unlocked window or an unattended patio door. He might be able to see her through the misty glass of the shower doors or watch her sleep with moonlight slanting across her face. Or he might visit one of the others. Which one would be first? Whistling, he made his way down the narrow twisting streets to Commercial Street and imagined all the possibilities. Finally he was in charge.

Allie moaned quietly, clutching Flynn's shoulders as Flynn leaned over her, pressing her back into the soft sofa cushions. Allie had guessed from Flynn's slightly cocky manner and to-die-for-body that she would be good at this, and she hadn't been wrong. Flynn really, really knew her way around a woman. Right now, Flynn was doing an awesome job of kissing her. Flynn's second-story, one-bedroom apartment faced the harbor in the far West End. The sofa, where they were currently entangled, sat in front of double sliding glass doors, which were open to the cool early-September breeze. The air outside could have been frigid for all the effect it had on her, because Flynn was stoking her fires like no one had done in far too long. God, Flynn's tongue felt good playing inside her mouth, making her tingle and tighten in so many places at once she couldn't think of anything else. She couldn't think. She couldn't remember. She couldn't ache for what she didn't have. This was good. This was so good. This was good enough.

Allie grabbed the back of Flynn's shirt and yanked it out of her jeans, then dipped a hand under the waistband. Her whole body tensed when she encountered nothing but bare skin, and she dug her fingers into the hard muscle. Flynn groaned and worked a thigh between Allie's legs. Allie whimpered with the sudden pressure.

"You're so hot," Flynn muttered, massaging Allie's breast through her top. "You're making me crazy."

"Good." Allie arched beneath her and gripped her ass even harder. Flynn pushed her hand under Allie's clothes and palmed her breast. Flynn's fingers were dry and warm, and Allie's breasts ached wonderfully as Flynn worked her way back and forth between them, fondling and massaging. "Yeah, really good."

"Want you so bad," Flynn groaned.

"Then kiss me." Allie dragged Flynn back down and opened her mouth to pull her in. Flynn shifted fully on top of her, punctuating each thrust of her tongue with a hard hip pump. Allie opened her legs wider. Dry humping had never gotten her off, but the way she felt right now, so desperate to let go of the last fragments of awareness, so frantic for just a few minutes of pleasure, of not hurting, she thought she might come. God, she would explode if Ash would just squeeze her nipple a little harder, the way she liked it. The way she always did when she wanted to make her come. She murmured breathlessly, "Please..." *Ash, please... Ash.*

Allie jerked back into the moment and felt every ounce of blood drain from her head. She pulled out of the kiss, turning her face away. Gasping, she said, "Wait, please."

Flynn went rigid. After a few seconds of silence, she eased some of her weight off Allie's body, bracing herself on her arms with their lower bodies still touching. "Allie?"

"Oh my God, Flynn. I'm so sorry. I...I just..." Allie took a shuddering breath. What the hell was happening? She'd been about ten seconds away from an awesome orgasm. This had never happened before. Not that long ago she'd made love with Deo, more than once, and she'd been fine. All systems go. She hadn't had the slightest problem coming, and she hadn't thought of Ash once. Not really. All right, maybe sometimes, but never when she'd been with Deo. Well, never when Deo had been making love to her at least. Flynn was an amazing lover. Flynn had been making her feel terrific. Flynn had been about to make her come. "I don't know what happened."

Liar. You do know what happened. God damn it. She doesn't want you. Stop thinking of her!

"It's okay." Flynn, breathing hard, rolled off until they were half sitting up, side by side on the sofa. She stroked a few strands of hair off Allie's cheek. Her eyes glittered in the moonlight, and her smile seemed a little rueful. "We might've been moving a little fast. I kinda lost it there."

Allie threaded her fingers through Flynn's and held their joined hands in her lap. "Believe me, I was right there with you." She laughed and shook her head. "Actually, I was probably a little ahead of you."

"I thought you were going to come," Flynn murmured quietly.

Allie's face flamed hot. "You're pretty amazing. I was really worked up."

"Yeah, me too."

"Oh God, I'm sorry. You must think I'm an enormous tease." Allie thought of how many times Bri had accused her of being a tease. She *was* a tease, sometimes. Sometimes teasing girls was just a form of foreplay. But nothing about what had just happened was intentional. "I'm sorry."

Flynn straightened and turned so their eyes met. "Allie! Don't be crazy. I meant it when I said maybe we were fast-forwarding a little too much. It's our first date, and…" She shrugged. "I'd been thinking about you ever since we ran into each other earlier, so I was pretty revved up when you walked into the bar. And then you just looked so hot and you felt so good, and I stopped thinking about anything except… Well, you know. But I don't usually have sex with a woman the first time we hook up."

I do, Allie wanted to say, because it was true. Most of the last year at least, when she'd gone out at all, the only thing she'd wanted from a woman had been hard, hot sex and as much of it as she could get. But she didn't say it because she didn't want Flynn to think that's what tonight had been all about. Maybe it had been mostly about sex, right up until a few minutes ago. But it wasn't about that anymore. Flynn was nice. Too nice to just be a convenient mouth and pair of hands.

"I think this might be the most insane thing to ever come out of my mouth," Allie said, "but would you mind if we just took things a little slower for a while?"

"So does that mean I get another date?"

A date. Allie thought about that. Flynn was gorgeous. Flynn was smart and funny. Flynn had amazing hands and an incredible mouth and a killer body. Well, duh. Allie kissed her, and Flynn's tongue skating over hers was like a power surge electrifying every atom in her body. She pulled back before she short-circuited completely. "Yes. Definitely, yes."

Flynn grinned and pulled her to her feet. "Come on, I'll walk you to your car."

"That's probably a good idea." Allie wrapped her arm around Flynn's waist. "Because believe me, restraint is not my strong suit."

"You won't hear me complaining."

Allie laughed, strangely relieved to be going home, even though she still wasn't sure why she was saying no. Maybe it was because as she and Flynn walked hand in hand down the dark quiet streets, she kept wondering where Ash was, and with whom.

❖

"Oh baby," the blonde panted as Ash worked her nipple roughly between her teeth, "you're going to make me come. You're going to make me come."

Again. The woman didn't quit, and Ash didn't want her to, driving her with her mouth and her hands and her tongue and her teeth from one peak to the next. She wanted to make her come, needed to make her come, desperate for her cries of ecstasy to block out the sounds of another woman's climax from her consciousness. Still, despite the pain of nails raking down her back and teeth sinking into the muscles at the base of her neck, she couldn't obliterate the pictures, couldn't erase the memories. She groaned and pushed her hand deeper, thrust harder and faster.

"That's it. That's it! Here I go again. Oh God!"

Ash squeezed her eyes shut, unable to endure the chasm that

threatened to swallow her up when she stared into a stranger's eyes. During a moment when she should have felt most connected, she felt nothing. Empty. Adrift. Lost. Her muscles quivered with unrelieved tension, her head ached, her heart pounded so hard her chest hurt.

When the woman…Linda…Laurie…Lisa…tugged weakly at her jeans and murmured, "Take these off so I can do you too, baby," Ash thumbed the woman's still pulsating clit to distract her. Lisa writhed under her and went back to chewing on her neck. After a few more pumps, Lisa forgot all about pleasuring Ash, which was exactly what Ash wanted.

"Fuck me, baby. Fuck me, fuck me, fuck me!"

Ash did, until the woman finally stopped coming and just drifted off into an exhausted sleep. Trembling, Ash sat on the side of the bed until her legs would hold her. Then she found her shirt on the floor, missing a couple of buttons, and pulled it on. She still had her boots and jeans on, and after checking to make sure she had her wallet, she let herself out. As she stumbled home, exhausted and a little high, she became aware of the uncomfortable pressure in her groin and the painful press of her swollen clitoris against the rough denim. She didn't know how long she'd been with the blonde—hours, she thought. She hadn't come once. Hadn't wanted to. She knew if she went home and tried to come, she wouldn't be able to. If she was lucky, a shot or two of whiskey would let her sleep. And if she couldn't sleep, it was only a few hours until morning.

Morning. And she'd see Allie again. For the first time since she'd left the bar, she felt something besides numb. And no matter how hard she tried, she couldn't kill the sweet surge of anticipation.

CHAPTER EIGHT

A little after five a.m., Reese slipped out of bed, grabbed her clothes, and carried them downstairs to shower and dress in the guest bathroom so she wouldn't wake Tory. Then she settled on a stool at the breakfast counter and called the station house.

"It's Reese. Is Officer Wayne there?"

"They just came in a few minutes ago, Sheriff," Smith said. "Hey, Carter. Phone for you."

"Hello?" Carter said.

"Carter, it's Reese. I need you to run a check on an inmate—William Everly. He should be doing time at Cedar Junction. If he's out, get me his last known address and a number for his parole officer."

"On it."

"And, Carter, keep it quiet for now."

"Yes ma'am."

"I'll be in for shift change. Anything I need to know now?"

"Nothing I can put my finger on, but..."

When Carter hesitated, Reese said, "Trust your gut, Carter."

Carter sighed. "Rica's car was broken into in the lot on Bradford last night."

"Is she okay?"

"Yes. There was no one there by the time she found it."

"You don't figure it was random."

"I don't know," Carter said. "That's what's bugging me."

"I'll put some extra cars in your neighborhood and make sure street patrol checks Rica's gallery frequently."

"Thanks. I'll get on this other thing right away."

"Good. I'll check with you when I get in." Reese disconnected and swiveled around at the sound of footsteps behind her.

Tory, barefoot except for her ankle brace and wearing only a thigh-length pale green sleep shirt, slid between Reese's legs and wrapped her arms around Reese's waist. She kissed the corner of her mouth and said, "Good morning, darling. You're up awfully early."

"And you should still be asleep. How's your leg?"

"I've got some numbness on the side of my foot. More annoying than any kind of functional problem." Tory sighed. "It's from the swelling, which is pretty bad. I'll need to elevate it as much as I can."

Reese raised an eyebrow. "You don't usually admit it when anything's bothering you this much."

"You'd see it. You'd know." Tory rested her cheek against Reese's shoulder. "And I can hardly expect you to come clean with me if I don't do the same."

"Can you stay home today?"

Tory shook her head silently.

Reese closed her eyes and breathed in Tory's scent, a combination of coconut and fresh salt air. "Half a day?"

"Maybe. I'll try." Tory leaned back, searching Reese's face. She looked tired. "What about you? You didn't get much sleep last night."

"Yeah, but I had a hell of a bedtime sedative."

Tory laughed. "Mmm, that was nice." She kissed Reese again. "In fact, now that I think of it, we've got time for a repeat."

"I'm already dressed for work!"

"That's what buttons are for, darling," Tory said, swiftly opening Reese's uniform shirt. "They open and close so you can take your shirt off and put it back on again."

Reese slid her hands up the back of Tory's thighs and underneath the lower edge of her sleep shirt, encountering bare skin all the way up to her ass. She groaned and pulled Tory tighter into her crotch. "Love, I really need to go to work."

Tory slid her hand inside Reese's shirt and toyed with her nipple through her undershirt. "I know what time your day starts. They don't need you right away."

"I've got Carter running a check for me on the guy who assaulted Bri. I need to meet her before shift change."

"You think it was him last night?" Tory slipped her hand out of Reese's shirt.

"I don't even know if he's been released yet. Just covering the bases. If he *is* out, I want to know about it. I don't want Bri and Caroline becoming targets."

"Or you. He has every reason to go after you, but, of course, you'll worry about everyone *except* you," Tory said with an edge. Reese had been home from Iraq for less than half a year. While she'd been deployed, she'd nearly died. Tory tried not to think about that. She tried very hard to erase the utter desolation she'd felt during the days when she hadn't known if Reese was ever coming home. She'd mostly learned to live with the inherent danger of Reese's job, but the fear still rode close to the surface. Especially when she was reminded that Reese never put her own safety before that of others.

"Hey, hey! Love, we're getting way ahead of ourselves." Reese ran her hands up and down Tory's back, soothing caresses meant to calm rather than excite. She kept it up until she felt Tory relax. "One step at a time, okay?"

Tory nodded and pressed her face to Reese's neck. "There's something I need to tell you. I was going to do it last night, but then..." She sighed. "I know how much work there is to be done in the next few weeks with the recovery in town, and now with this...who knows when we'll ever have time to ourselves."

Reese's heart jumped into overdrive. "Is something wrong? What's the matter?"

"Nothing. Darling, nothing's the matter." Tory caressed the back of Reese's neck and smiled. "I want to have another baby."

"Another..." Reese's head pounded and her vision dimmed, the way it had in the middle of the firefight in the desert, the way it had last night when Tory had called her on the phone and said there was someone in the house...

"Reese," Tory said gently. "Reese, how do you feel right now?"

Shuddering and trying to hide it, Reese forced a smile. "Just surprised."

"No. Something else." Tory took Reese's hand. "Come sit down and tell me what just happened."

Reese shook her head. "It's nothing. I'm all right."

Tory stroked Reese's cheek. "Do not do this. I'm a doctor, Reese, but anyone could have seen you turn pale and your pupils dilate. Right now, you're shaking. Tell me how you feel."

"I'm okay now," Reese said. "For just a second, maybe two, there was a roaring in my head and I couldn't focus, couldn't hear. Goes away really fast if I just hang on for a few seconds."

"How often?" Tory asked, ignoring the churning in her stomach, keeping her voice level and quiet. "How often has it happened?"

Reese shrugged. "I don't really know. Just a couple of times in the last few weeks. Before that, nothing felt right, so I can't even remember if it was happening then." She gripped Tory's hand. "Look, I'm okay. It was just a second. Let's talk about you and us and another baby."

"Has it happened on the job?"

"No," Reese said quickly.

"I want you to come in for a physical. Today."

Reese grimaced. "Tory, I don't have time—"

"Do it today, Reese, or I'll rescind your medical release to return to active duty."

"Jesus, Tory." Reese rubbed her forehead. "You wouldn't—"

"I would. I'd do anything to protect you." Tory turned abruptly, but Reese still held her hand and she couldn't escape. She didn't want Reese to see her fear. Or her anger.

"I wasn't intentionally keeping anything from you. I just didn't think it was important."

"No, when it's about you, you never do."

"That's not fair, Tor," Reese said quietly. She stood and gently gripped Tory's shoulders. "I'm trying."

Tory spun back around and slid her arms behind Reese's neck. "I know, darling. I know you are. I'm sorry. Sometimes, I just get scared."

"I'm sorry too. For ever making you frightened."

"Shh." Tory kissed the base of Reese's throat, then her neck, then the corner of her mouth. "It's not your fault. I love you. You can't possibly know how much."

"I do, love. I do know." Reese kissed Tory, a deep lingering kiss. "I'll come by the clinic as soon as I can get away today, okay?"

"Thank you," Tory murmured against Reese's mouth, the kiss filling her with warmth and calm.

"About the other thing—"

Tory pressed her fingers to Reese's lips. "We'll talk about it later."

Reese frowned. "No, Tor, this is important. If you—"

"Later." Tory leaned against Reese. "I think I need to get off my leg. Will you help me up the stairs?"

"I'll do more than that. Put your arms around my neck."

"I think carrying me up the stairs once this week is enough."

Reese laughed. "I don't get enough exercise behind the desk. Hold on to me."

And because she needed her, because she needed to feel surrounded by Reese's solid strength and unwavering love, Tory let herself be carried. Talk of another child would need to wait. Right now, all she cared about was finding the cause of Reese's symptoms.

Carter cruised through her neighborhood a little after seven thirty, noting that many of the early-morning joggers were absent. She didn't recognize half of the cars and vans parked on her own street. Most of the unfamiliar vehicles were probably those of workmen who had come from up Cape or inland to start repairs on damaged homes. Determining who belonged and who didn't was impossible. Still, she took her time, working street by street, looking for anything or anyone out of place. At eight o'clock, she pulled into the driveway in front of Rica's hilltop home, *their* home now. Surrounded on three sides by pine and beech trees, the house commanded a sweeping view across protected wetlands and dunes to Herring Cove. Rica's Lexus was in the garage, and when Carter walked through to the spacious eat-in kitchen, she heard Rica talking on the phone outside on the deck.

"I need you to tell me the truth, Papa," Rica said, leaning against the railing. Her hair was loose, still damp from the shower, and she wore only the short black silk robe that Carter loved to slowly take off her. "No one?"

Carter halted, not wanting to eavesdrop. Rica had spent her whole life struggling to reconcile her love for her father with her repulsion for his "business." She and her father rarely spoke of it directly, but their relationship had been even more strained since Rica became involved with Carter. Alfonse Pareto tolerated Carter, a cop, so close to the seat of his empire for only two reasons—he believed that Carter loved Rica and would protect her, and he knew that Rica would cut off all ties to her family if he attempted to keep them apart. Carter did not want to make Rica's life any more difficult. She started to back out of the room just as Rica turned and saw her.

Rica waved Carter out onto the deck while listening to her father interrogate her as to why she wanted to know if he had assigned any of his men to shadow her. She wasn't used to seeing Carter in a uniform. The night before, Rica had been working late at the gallery and Carter had dropped by in her regulation khaki pants, tab-collar shirt, and dark tie before her shift. Rica had been sorely tempted to drag her into the back room and divest her of said uniform. Now she could, since she didn't have to worry about making Carter late for work.

"I know you said you wouldn't, Papa." Rica slipped her arm around Carter's waist and pulled her close. "But sometimes you change your mind and forget to tell me."

At Carter's raised eyebrows, Rica shook her head, rolled her eyes, and gave her a kiss. When Carter tugged her a little closer and nipped at her lower lip, Rica stifled a moan.

"I need to go, Papa. I have another call."

"When will you be home for a visit, *cara*?"

"I don't know. Soon."

"I miss you," Pareto said. *"Ti amo."*

"I love you too, Papa." Rica fumbled for the Off button, wrapped her free arm around Carter's neck, and blindly set the phone down on the top of the railing. "Mmm, I missed you in bed last night."

"Sorry," Carter muttered, kissing her way up Rica's neck to her ear. "I won't have the night shift forever."

"I think I might like you coming home in the morning when I'm all rested and you're a little rumpled and tired. It'll make it easy for me to have my way with you."

"Like you don't always." Carter laughed and pulled Rica over to one of the cushioned lounge chairs. She tugged her down and wrapped her in her arms. "How's your father?"

"The same." Rica unbuckled Carter's belt, pulled her shirt up, and caressed her abdomen. "How tired are you?"

"Not tired at all." Carter opened Rica's robe and cupped Rica's breast.

Rica murmured her approval and pressed closer, nibbling Carter's ear. "I think I'd like it if you made love to me out here. I've been thinking about it since I woke up. I'm already wet."

Carter groaned. "Are you?"

"Why don't you see for yourself?" Rica flicked her tongue along the edge of Carter's jaw, then kissed her. Carter smoothed her palm down Rica's abdomen and caressed between her legs. Rica's hips flexed and she whimpered softly against Carter's mouth.

"Jesus," Carter muttered. "Baby, you're so ready."

"Then don't make me wait," Rica said, breathing quickly, her dark eyes turning glassy as Carter stroked and stroked. "I think if you just go inside me, I'll…"

Carter pushed deeper and filled her.

"…come," Rica gasped, closing her eyes and burying her face against Carter's neck. She quivered, her fingers trembling against Carter's face as she came in long, undulating waves of exquisite pleasure.

"I love you, baby," Carter whispered.

"I love you." Rica sighed, melting bonelessly into the lean, hard planes of Carter's body. "And I *really* love this uniform."

Carter chuckled and ran her fingers through Rica's silky hair. The midnight waves sparkled in the early morning sunlight. "You're so beautiful, Rica. So beautiful."

"I never thought I could be this happy."

"Neither did I." Carter closed her eyes and luxuriated in the unbelievable pleasure of having everything in her life she'd ever wanted. This woman, this one woman, was everything that mattered.

"In a few minutes I'll be able to move again," Rica murmured lazily. "So be patient. The other thing I've been thinking about since I woke up was you coming in my mouth."

Carter jerked, the muscles in her stomach dancing. "Rica, baby. You're killing me."

Rica smiled and ran her fingertips over Carter's lips. "Good."

"So are you going to tell me why you called your father first thing this morning?"

"I wondered when you'd ask me that."

"Did something happen?" Carter knew Rica would try to shield her from anything that might have to do with her father's business. "I don't need you to protect me."

"No? But it's all right for you to protect me?"

Carter sighed. "I didn't mean it that way."

"How did you mean it?"

"I'm not investigating your family—it's not like it was when I was undercover before. Plus, Reese knows about your father. My job is not in danger because of your father's business dealings, so you don't have to keep things from me. That's all I meant."

Rica tucked her head under Carter's chin and slid her hand under Carter's shirt again. "I'm sorry. I know. It's just, they hurt you the last time. I couldn't stand it if—"

"Nothing is going to happen to me." Carter caressed Rica's face. "If you called your father, you're worried about something. What is it?"

"I got to thinking about the car last night. I know it was probably just some kids or something, but—on my way to the parking lot, I had this weird feeling. I forgot all about it until I got home."

Carter tensed, then forced herself to relax. She didn't want her worry to influence Rica. "What kind of weird feeling?"

"Like someone was…I don't know…watching me, maybe."

"Did you see anyone?"

"No, which is why I'm sure it's just my imagination, but I thought maybe Papa had sent another one of his men to keep an eye on me. You know how he is."

"What did he say?"

"He said he didn't."

"You believe him?" Carter didn't trust Rica's father, for many reasons. The don was not above lying to his daughter if he thought it was for her own good.

"I do. If I really thought he had men watching me, I wouldn't have let you ravish me out here—even if only the seagulls could possibly see onto this deck."

"What about the shop? Has anyone been in who seemed out of place? Someone who might have been inappropriate, pushed you to go out with them?"

Rica laughed. "No. No! I would have told you." She sat up and braced her hands on Carter's shoulders. "I'm sorry I even brought it up. You're going to worry, and there's no reason to. I just had this... feeling."

"Sometimes it's those kinds of feelings that keep us alive."

"I'm not an undercover police officer, darling. I'm not in danger."

Carter didn't agree with her, but she wasn't going to frighten her by enumerating all the reasons why someone might want to hurt her. "Just promise me you'll be careful, and tell me if you have any more of these feelings. Promise me that."

"I promise." Rica tipped her head and kissed Carter. "Now that I've regained my strength, it's time to take you upstairs and put you to bed." She kissed her again. "And I know just how to do it."

Carter let Rica take her upstairs, but she put her weapon in the dresser next to the bed before she finally surrendered to Rica's plans for her.

❖

"You wanted to see me, Sheriff," Bri said.

"Come on in and close the door." Reese leaned against the front of her desk, her arms folded over her chest.

Bri carefully closed the door and stepped forward, unconsciously standing at attention.

"Relax, Bri," Reese said softly.

"Is there a problem, Sheriff?" Bri didn't know how to act. Reese was usually pretty cool and distant at work, the way a commander should be. But Reese was looking at her now with a kind of tenderness in her eyes that made her heart flutter a little bit and her stomach get queasy. Reese looked like something was hurting *her*. Something bad had to be wrong. "Is my dad—"

"No, Nelson is fine." Reese clasped Bri's shoulder. "William Everly is out. He was released on parole a little over a month ago. He hasn't checked in with his parole officer for the last three weeks."

Bri shivered, trying to process what Reese had just said. She hadn't heard anything after his name. "I'm sorry. I...what did..." Bri felt Reese's hand tighten on her shoulder, felt the warmth of her touch, and something deep inside her shifted, steadied, and she took a breath. "Okay. He's out and he's gone off the grid. You think he's here?"

"I don't know. But we're going to find out. He's got family and friends and we'll be checking with all of them."

"Give me the list. I'll check—"

"No," Reese said. "You won't be looking for him, Bri. I'll do it with Tremont or Wayne. Not you. If he turns up, you stay away from him, understood?"

Bri stiffened. "You don't think I can handle him?"

"I *know* you can handle him. But I don't want you to *have* to handle him. That's an order, Bri."

"Why? Just tell me why?" Bri searched Reese's face, needing to know that Reese trusted her. Believed in her.

"Because he hurt you and no amount of jail time will ever make up for that," Reese said quietly. "And I don't want you to have to choose between justice and your badge."

"I think I understand," Bri said, her voice cracking. "But just so you know, I'd choose the badge."

Reese pulled her close and cradled the back of her head. "I believe you. I should probably tell you that if he went after you, I might kill him myself."

Bri closed her eyes, letting herself be held by one of the only people in her life she trusted completely. "Okay, I won't go looking for him. I don't want you getting in trouble."

Reese laughed quietly and stroked her hair before letting her go. "Thanks."

CHAPTER NINE

Allie watched Bri come out of Reese's office and head down the hall to the locker room. Bri looked shaky, her eyes not quite focused. After a minute, Allie set aside the reports she was scanning and followed her into the locker room. Bri sat on the long narrow bench between two rows of lockers, her hands between her knees, staring at the floor. Allie sat down beside her, leaving an inch of space between them.

"You okay?" Allie asked.

"Yeah. Sure." Bri grinned weakly. "Never better."

"You in trouble with the boss?"

Bri shook her head.

"You want me to go?"

Bri hesitated. "No. Stay. Reese will probably brief you this morning anyhow." She grimaced. "Hell, everyone will hear about it sooner or later."

"Hear about what?" Allie rubbed Bri's leg just above her knee. Bri's muscles tensed and jumped. She was really wired. "Bri? Honey? What's going on?"

Bri tried to figure out how to tell her what she'd never talked about to anyone except Caroline, and Reese and Tory. She'd been a lot younger when it had happened, and not as strong. William Everly had only been a few years older, but he'd been twice her size. She didn't think about it much anymore, and it rattled her that just the mention of his name could throw her. She thought she was stronger than that. She *had* to be stronger than that. She was a cop now. And Caroline needed her to be strong.

"When Caroline and I were in high school, a guy stalked Caroline.

Stalked us both, sort of. He figured she should be with him instead of me." Bri laughed bitterly. "Most people did."

"Not Caroline," Allie whispered. "Smart girl."

Bri laughed, a little of the tension draining away. "Crazy girl, maybe."

Allie nudged her shoulder. "What happened?"

"He came after her one night, but he got me instead. He put me in the hospital."

Allie fought down a wave of fury and steeled herself to the pain that instantly settled around her heart. She hurt for Bri, but her pain was far less then Bri's. Bri needed to talk, and wouldn't if she knew Allie was hurting. So Allie said with as much cool as she could fake, "How bad was it?"

"Could've been worse." Bri gave Allie a fleeting smile, a shadow of her usual cocky grin. "He broke my jaw. Few ribs. Pretty much beat the crap out of me."

"Motherfucker." Allie hesitated, wondering if she should ask the obvious question. With another girl, she might not have, but this was Bri. If she didn't ask, Bri would figure Allie didn't think she could handle it. Crazy turned-around thinking, but that was Bri. Allie had recognized the first day they were together in the academy that Bri's tough-guy attitude was all about needing to prove to other people that she was strong. That she could handle herself. The only way Bri would ever let anyone take care of her was if she believed *they* believed in her. Somehow, Caroline figured that out about Bri years ago, and that was the big reason why Caroline was the right girl for Bri. But Bri was Allie's friend, and Allie loved her, so she didn't shy away from the hard stuff. "Did he rape you?"

Bri jerked, then straightened her shoulders. "No. He tried. I fought, but he was bigger. God, he was strong. But when he got on top of me, I broke his nose. And then I guess he just got pissed and beat me some more. But not that."

"Did they get him?"

"Reese did."

"Good," Allie said through gritted teeth. "I hope she kicked the shit out of him."

"He resisted a little and she took care of him." Bri sighed. "Anyhow, he's out and he's in the wind. He's local, so he might turn up back here. Reese will fill you in."

"How are you feeling?"

"Okay, I guess. I just didn't expect it. I don't know why not. Nobody goes away for very long for that kind of thing. Because he resisted, and probably because I was a cop's kid, he got the maximum. Better than I could have hoped."

"Do you think he'll bother you again?"

"I don't know. A lot of times these guys do. You know that. They get fixated on a girl, or they blame her for going to jail." Bri turned on the bench, her blue eyes dark and cloudy. "I'm worried about Carre. She's the one he wanted, and she's not going back to school until the spring semester. She's going to be home alone while I'm working."

"Look, we'll find this guy. And until we do, all of us will keep an eye on her." Allie put her arm around Bri's shoulders and kissed her cheek. "Don't worry, okay?"

"Yeah. Okay."

"And as far as people knowing about what happened? You stood up. You hurt him. You're a hero, baby." Allie ruffled Bri's hair. "Now go home and let your girl take care of you."

Bri laughed. "You think sex cures everything."

"Don't you?"

"Yeah, most of the time." Bri stood, opened her locker, and unbuttoned her uniform shirt. "So how did things go with Flynn last night?"

"Oh God, she is so fucking hot."

Bri rolled her eyes. "Yeah, you said that before."

"Seriously, she just kissed me and I almost came in my pants."

"For real?"

"Believe it," Allie said, her face flushing. "And I never do that." Almost never. She squashed the memory of the last time she had—when she'd been making out with Ash and Ash had played with her nipples so long and so hard she'd climaxed. Not going there. Not. Not. Not.

"Okay—major stud points," Bri said, impressed. "So I take it your dry spell is over?"

Allie looked away. "Not exactly."

Bri rolled up her shirt, tossed it into the laundry hamper, and pulled on her T-shirt. As she unbuckled her belt, she cut Allie a look. She'd heard something in Allie's voice she'd never heard before. Regret. Longing. More than a little sadness. "What's going on?"

"Nothing, really," Allie said with forced brightness. "Hey, just because I don't put out for every girl who looks my way doesn't mean there's something wrong."

"Yeah yeah. This is me you're talking to. I saw her cruising you the first time she saw you. And you were already sizing her up before you even went out. *Now* you tell me she's so hot you're losing your stuff just kissing. So—if you didn't get it on with her, why not?"

"She's nice, Bri," Allie said softly. "She's somebody I might like to have as a friend, you know? Sometimes sex messes things up."

Bri pulled on her jeans and her boots, closed her locker door, and leaned back against it. "What the fuck, Al? You've never minded fucking friends, and you've never had any trouble being friends with women you've have sex with—look at Deo."

"Yeah. Look at Walker," Allie said bitterly.

"Oh."

"Oh what?"

"Are you still hung up on her?"

"No!" Allie glared. "It's got nothing to do with her. She's ancient history. I just didn't feel like fucking Flynn last night!"

"Okay." Bri held her hands up in surrender. "Okay. So take things slow with Flynn if that makes you feel better." She tapped her boot against Allie's foot. "But Jesus, don't wait too long. I can't stand it when you're horny. You get bitchy."

"Fuck you, Parker."

Bri grinned. "See? Proves my point."

"Oh, go home already." Allie rose. "About that other thing. If anything breaks, I'll let you know."

"Thanks."

Allie walked Bri to the side door, waved good-bye, and headed back into the bullpen.

"Well, fuck me," she muttered to herself. Ash Walker was sitting at her desk.

❖

Ash stood up quickly as Allie, doing a pretty decent impression of a thundercloud, stomped toward her. Allie obviously wasn't looking forward to seeing her, not that she expected anything different.

"I just stopped by to go through those files," Ash said.

Allie pointed to a stack on the corner of her desk. "Those are all open—mostly alleged vandalism, break-ins, or arsons. We still have to sort out what's storm damage and what isn't. The ones with the red stickers have not yet been cleared to enter by the fire marshal. Those you can't investigate yet."

"I am certified for fire investigation, Allie," Ash said quietly.

"Oh, I know your qualifications. You were evaluating a fire claim the first time you blew in."

"If you've got a spare desk somewhere, I'll go through these files and cross-reference them with my list." Ash was too tired and too queasy for a fight. She'd only been partially right the night before. When she got home, she'd stripped and immediately climbed into the shower to wash away the sex sweat and try to clear some of the alcohol from her brain. With the hot water beating down on her neck and shoulders, she'd closed her eyes and tried to blank her mind. No luck. All she'd been able to see was Allie—not Allie in a bar with a stranger's hands all over her, but Allie lying under her, teasing her with light kisses and taunting her with whispered dares. *I dare you not to come while you're fucking me. I dare you not to come when I go down on you. I dare you not to come when I fuck you. I dare you, baby. I dare you.*

The pressure in her pelvis got so bad she'd tried to get off, picturing Allie's teasing smile, hearing Allie dare her not to come in her mouth while she sucked her. She wanted to come, but she couldn't. She got close a couple times, so close she kept trying, but she couldn't hold on to the feel of Allie's lips long enough to push herself over. She worked at it until the water ran cold and her legs wouldn't hold her up anymore, and then she stumbled into the kitchen, found the bottle of Johnny Walker, and took a slug. Thirty minutes later she was still awake, tossing and turning and working up another kind of sweat. Fatigue and frustration and futility. She drank a bit more and finally her body just quit on her, and she slept. When she woke a few hours later, she felt like crap. Another shower, a cold one this time, cleared her head some but didn't do much for her stomach.

Allie cocked her hip and folded her arms beneath her breasts. "You look like total shit, Walker. And you've got fucking *teeth* marks all over your neck. Did you even get to sleep or did you come here straight from spending the whole night fucking that blonde with the big tits?"

"Don't, Allie," Ash whispered.

"You know what? You're right. It doesn't matter at all," Allie said coldly. "Give me your list. I'll do the cross checks. You're not fit to work. Go home and get some sleep."

Ash stiffened. "I'm fine."

"I'll come by and pick you up at noon." Allie held out her hand. "Give me your goddamned list."

Ash would have argued, but Reese stood in the doorway of her office watching them. If she put up a fight, Allie would get caught in the middle and she didn't want that. She opened her briefcase, found the folder with the local cases, and handed it to Allie. The papers shook in her trembling hand. "I'd like to start in the West End where the damage is the worst. It will help me set up an assessment scale for the area."

"Fine. I'll see you at noon."

"Okay." Ash turned, nodded to Reese, and quickly left.

Allie watched her go, thinking now she knew where Ash had been the night before. She'd gotten it on with the blonde she was pawing on the dance floor at the Pied. From the looks of her neck, they'd been going at it hard. While *she* hadn't even been able to let a sweet, hot, sexy woman make love to her, Ash had spent the night fucking her brains out. Nice.

And stupid for you to care, she muttered. *Really stupid, Allie.*

❖

"Nita," Tory said when Nita came out of one of the examining rooms. "Can I talk to you for a second?"

Nita finished making a note in the chart and left it in the file holder next to the door. "Sure."

Tory led the way back to her office and closed the door behind them. She gestured to one of the chairs in front of her desk and took the other one. Facing Nita, she said, "Reese is on her way over. I'd like you to examine her for me."

"Of course. What's the problem?"

"That's just the thing. I'm not sure there's anything wrong." Tory told Nita about Reese's episode the night before. "She looked disoriented. Her eyes were unfocused. She said she had trouble seeing. It was all very quick. Anyone else might not even have noticed." Tory sighed. "The thing that bothers me is that it's happened more than once."

"What exactly were the extent of her combat injuries?" Nita asked quietly.

"She was in a firefight. Their convoy was hit in the middle of the night with rocket fire. Several of the trucks exploded. She doesn't remember all of the details, but she had a forehead laceration from being struck with a rifle butt. Shrapnel in her leg. Her clavicle was broken. Burns to her..." Tory stopped, her throat closing.

"I'm sorry. That was thoughtless of me."

Tory shook her head. "No. It's necessary. I keep thinking I'm past it. She's home. She's fine. But when I think of what happened, how close she came to not coming home..." Tory smiled unsteadily. "I'm just thankful she's not going to be deployed ever again. Because honestly, I don't think I could stand it."

Nita squeezed Tory's hand. "You could stand whatever you had to stand. But I'm glad she's home for good too."

"What else..." Tory forced her mind into doctor mode. "She was captured, beaten. She can't remember if she was unconscious or for how long, but I'm certain that she had some head trauma."

"And how has she been since she's been home?"

"About how you would expect. From all the reports I've seen, more than two-thirds of returning troops have signs of PTSD, even the ones who weren't injured in combat. She's had trouble sleeping, nightmares, hypervigilance—some hyperreactivity."

"Depression?"

"No. Reese is a Marine. She's incredibly strong, psychologically. She's trained for what she went through. It's the things that she can't control that have been the biggest problem."

"Aggression?" Nita asked gently.

"No," Tory said, her gaze steady on Nita's. "Never."

"Okay," Nita said briskly. "Let me know as soon as she gets here. Do you want to observe?"

Tory laughed. "Of course I do. But I think it will be better if I don't. Reese might be more comfortable. She might tell you something that she doesn't want me to know. And I never think it's a good idea for us to treat family."

"Are you okay?"

"I don't mind telling you, I'm scared." Tory hesitated. "There's something else too. I told her this morning, right before she had this episode, that I wanted to have another baby."

Nita's eyebrows rose, then she smiled broadly. "Really! That's terrific."

"My timing was probably terrible, but..." Tory grinned ruefully. "I'm almost forty-one years old. I don't have any more time. I'd like Regina to have a sibling by the time she's two."

"What did Reese say?"

"Nothing. When I told her I had something I wanted to talk to her about she jumped to the conclusion that something was wrong, and then she had the reaction."

"Immediately? So you think it was triggered by stress? Fear?"

"Maybe. An adrenaline surge could have produced those symptoms." Tory stood and started to pace. "God, I hadn't thought about that. Nita! What if it's endocrine? An adrenal tumor or..."

"Whoa. Whoa. Remember, you're not Dr. King right now. You're Tory, Reese's partner. And my advice to you is to wait and not play what-if. Okay? Is that a deal?"

"Yes. Yes. Deal." Tory slumped into the chair. "Lord, I'm a mess."

Nita smiled fondly. "You love her. That's messy sometimes, but wonderful."

The phone rang on Tory's desk, and she leaned over to answer it. "Yes?"

"Reese is here to see you," Randy said. "I already told her you're double booked the entire day."

"It's okay, Randy, send her back. And would you bring Reese's chart to Nita."

"Certainly," Randy said immediately, his voice sobering. "Right away."

Nita rose and brushed Tory's shoulder with her fingertips. "Don't worry. I'll take care of her."

"Thanks." Tory schooled her features to hide her anxiety. She didn't want Reese to know how frightened she was. Rationally she knew her worst fears were probably unfounded, but that didn't help calm her frayed nerves. Reese was everything to her. Everything.

CHAPTER TEN

A llie parked the patrol car halfway up on the sidewalk in front of the Crown, got out, and followed the winding flagstone path, flanked with the last valiant flowers of the season, through the side gate to Ash's suite. The blinds were drawn and the room was silent. She tapped on the door.

"Walker," she said, "it's me." She waited a minute and knocked again. She didn't try the knob. She didn't want a repeat of yesterday's unexpected view of Ash naked. Especially not after knowing what Ash had been doing all night. The last thing she wanted to feel was even a reflex attraction to her. She was about to walk away when the door opened. Ash didn't look much better than she had earlier. Her white shirt was rumpled and her eyes red rimmed. Allie's stomach twisted with an unexpected surge of concern and, whipping her gaze to a point past Ash's shoulder, she said, "You ready?"

"Yes," Ash said hoarsely and followed as Allie abruptly about-faced and stalked away. When Ash reached the patrol car, Allie was already behind the wheel. Ash slid into the front seat across from her. She hadn't been able to sleep, but she had managed to get down a little breakfast, and after a couple of cups of coffee, her head was clear. "Let's start on the harbor side of Commercial in the far West End. I've got a lot of claims down there."

"Fine." Allie stared straight through the windshield, one hand on the wheel, the other resting on her right thigh. She recognized the familiar spicy Dolce & Gabbana cologne Ash was wearing, because she'd given it to her. She remembered laughing while Ash opened the package, telling Ash she had gotten that particular scent because it smelled like something she wanted to eat. Ash had unbuttoned her shirt and dabbed a little just below her belly button.

Hungry now? Ash said.

Allie had met the challenge in Ash's eyes and immediately dropped to her knees, unzipped Ash's fly, and gone down on her, savoring the aromas of fine cologne and even finer woman. Ash had come hard and fast, and considering that they were standing next to Ash's car in the parking lot on Bradford, that was probably a good thing.

Allie gunned the motor and pulled out into the street so fast that Ash slammed back in her seat. Ignoring Ash's grunt of surprise, Allie snatched her radio off the dash and reported her destination.

Ash gripped the armrest and gazed out the window. About half of the businesses on Commercial were open, although many had sheets of plywood covering shattered front windows. Rubble was piled along the edge of the sidewalks, waiting for removal. Here and there portions of roofs were missing and big yellow warning signs were stapled to the doors, forbidding entry by order of the fire marshal.

"You took a heavy hit," Ash murmured.

Allie said nothing. She wasn't in the mood for casual conversation. What she wanted, more than anything else, was to be able to look at Ash and not remember anything. So far, that wasn't working so well, and that just pissed her off.

"You happy with the job?" Ash asked.

"I like my job, I love the town, I'm dating a hot woman. That's my story. Can we stick to business now?" Allie said.

Ash sucked in a breath. What did she expect? She'd been the one to break off the relationship because when she'd felt herself falling in love, she'd panicked. She'd been convinced that Allie was too young for a long-term relationship, and even if Allie had been ready for a commitment, she was too young *for Ash*. More than a decade Ash's junior, and a big decade. The difference between forty-two and fifty-five was light-years away from the difference between twenty-two and thirty-five. Ash knew from painful experience how hard it was to build and keep a relationship. She'd failed herself a couple of times and seen her sister's marriage fall apart after eight years and three kids. Hell, not a single one of her friends from college had managed to make a go of their marriages. She'd looked at Allie and couldn't imagine her being satisfied with Ash when there were so many women waiting in her future. Allie was like a supernova, shining so bright that everything in her path burned with her. She was smart and vital and embraced life with a carefree sensuality that Ash envied. She would gladly have incinerated in Allie's blaze. She feared not immolation, but that she would survive, forever scarred, forever wanting. So she'd walked away, and damned herself to exactly the future she had tried to avoid.

"You can let me out here," Ash said when Allie slowed the cruiser in front of a barricade blocking off a flooded portion of the street.

"I told you, Reese wants me to go with you to clear our open files."

Ash opened the door when Allie halted the cruiser. She stepped out, leaned a forearm on the roof, and peered back in. "If I see anything suspicious, I'll tell you. Otherwise, you can clear your cases as I go through them. I'll give you a list at the end of every day. I know you're all pulling double shifts. You don't need to do this."

Allie jammed the car into Park and hopped out with the engine still running. She glared at Ash across the roof. "What part of *orders* don't you understand? Reese assigned me to work *with* you. So I'm coming *with* you. Now move the barricade so I can get the cruiser through."

"Allie, there's probably three feet of water down there in some places. You'll stall out."

"Fine." Allie reached in, cut the ignition, and pocketed the keys. She slammed the door. "Let's walk."

Ash winced, the shock shooting up her arm and into her head. "Okay. Jesus. Take it easy."

"Maybe if you weren't hungover, you wouldn't be so sensitive."

"Look, can we declare a truce here?" Ash asked quietly. "I know you're pissed off at—"

"You don't know anything about me," Allie said succinctly. "You never bothered to look at me, Ash. You just saw what you wanted to see. Nice tits and a pretty face."

Ash jolted with shock. "Allie. Baby," she whispered, "that's not true. I nev—"

"Don't you dare call me that," Allie said furiously. "I'm not your baby. I never was. That was just your first mistake."

"Okay," Ash said, feeling the earth tilt under her feet. She pressed her palms flat against the top of the car to fight the wave of dizziness.

The core of pain she always carried in her chest expanded until every breath felt like a knife piercing her heart. "I apologize. I won't do it again."

"Let's go." Allie strode around the front of the car and sloshed through six inches of water to the sidewalk. She'd seen the pain arc across Ash's features and settle in her eyes. She'd wanted to hurt her, and she had. She just wished she felt a little bit better about it. Payback wasn't nearly as satisfying as she'd imagined.

❖

"Hi, love," Reese said as she walked into Tory's office.

Tory closed the door, put her arms around Reese's neck, and kissed her. "How is your day going?"

Reese took a moment to kiss her back. "Everly is out on parole, and he's missing. I told Bri this morning."

"Oh, darling. Damn it. How is she?"

"It rocked her a little, but she's okay." Reese grinned fondly. "She's tough."

"Do you think we have a problem?"

"It's premature to say that." Reese squeezed Tory's hand. "We'll need to run him down, if we can. If we find him, that will solve the problem, because he'll go away again on the parole violation."

"What about fingerprints? Didn't Allie check our door and upstairs? His prints would be on file, right?"

"Oh, they're on file all right. But trying to isolate a foreign print in a family residence is really difficult. And chances are whoever was in the house was wearing gloves. We'll run random samples, but…" She sighed. "Honestly, Tor, we're not likely to find anything, and trying to sort through hundreds of prints is just too expensive."

Tory laughed ruefully. "Darling, you don't need to explain cost-effectiveness to me. That's all medicine is about these days." She rubbed Reese's arm. "You will be careful if you go looking for him, though, won't you?"

Reese kissed her forehead. "It's been my experience that men who attack women are cowards. He's not going to put up a fight if I find him."

"Just the same—"

"Just the same," Reese said, "I intend to be very careful."

"Thank you." Tory gestured toward the hall. "Are you ready? I asked Nita to look at you."

"Yes. Whatever you need me to do."

Suddenly all Tory needed was right there within arm's reach. She wrapped her arms around Reese's waist and laid her cheek against Reese's chest. "This. This is what I need."

Reese stroked her hair. "Done."

"Kate called," Tory murmured. "They should be back around four."

"Do you want me to swing by and get Reggie and the dog on my way home?" Reese asked.

"Call me. Whichever one of us is free can do it." With a sigh, Tory let her go. "Come on. Let's get you checked out."

❖

"Darling," Rica called from the bedroom when Carter stepped out of the shower, "didn't you pick up the dry-cleaning the other day?"

Carter briskly toweled her hair and walked naked into the bedroom. "Uh-huh. Last Tuesday. That was everything we brought in before the storm. Why?"

"Oh, nothing." Rica frowned and sorted through her clothes again. "I can't find my red silk shirt."

"It's in there. I saw it the other day."

"That's what I thought too. But it's not here."

Carter strode to the closet and scanned Rica's section. She had a good memory for details. Most cops did. On the job, she had maybe a second to take in the position of potential assailants or make a judgment call as to whether a man crouched in the shadows with a gun was a cop or a perp. She noticed things. And she remembered. "It was here a couple of days ago. Have you noticed anything else missing or out of place?"

"I don't think so. But—"

"Not just clothes. Anything." Carter yanked a pair of jeans off a hanger and stepped into them. As she zipped her fly, she crossed to the bedside table, extracted her holstered weapon, and clipped it to the waistband. "Jewelry? Personal items of any kind?"

"You think someone stole my shirt? You think someone was in here?"

"Someone was in Reese and Tory's place last night. Then your car was broken into." Carter shook her head. "I don't like coincidences."

"I'll have to look through my jewelry box."

"Do it. I'm going to check the rest of the house."

"Carter. Darling. Put on a shirt."

Carter looked down, then grinned sheepishly. "Oh."

"And be careful."

"I'll be right back. Then maybe I'll take my shirt off again."

Rica smiled. "Maybe you will."

❖

Reese sat on the examining table waiting for Nita. She kept her pants on but had stripped from the waist up. After checking out the paper gown, she tossed it aside and put her uniform shirt back on, leaving it unbuttoned. She didn't wait long.

"Hi, Reese," Nita said as she entered and closed the door behind her. "How are you doing?"

"Tory's worried about me."

Nita dropped Reese's chart onto the small pull-down desk attached to the wall, then leaned against the counter that held the sink and cabinets. "What about you? Are you worried?"

"I haven't been."

"How do you feel?"

Reese sighed. "That's a really tough question."

Nita nodded. "I get that. I really do. There's no right answer, or even *one* answer. Let me ask some questions and we'll see if we can get to a few of them. Does anything bother you physically?"

"No," Reese said immediately. "No pain."

"Fatigue? Weakness? Generally just not feeling up to par?"

"I haven't noticed any change since I…got back." Reese frowned. "You know, I can't really remember what I felt like before I went."

"Sometimes the experiences that change our lives reset our entire worldview. Even of ourselves."

"I'm not much of a philosopher, Nita," Reese said ruefully. "I used to be a Marine. Now I'm a cop. I've got three things in my life that matter to me. Tory, our daughter, and my job. Nothing will ever change that."

Nita smiled. "How are you sleeping?"

"A little erratically. I have nightmares sometimes. I'm sure Tory told you."

"What about when you're awake? Are you having flashbacks?"

"Brief ones. Not as often as I did." Reese grimaced. "A couple of times I've had sort of mini-flashbacks." She described the episode she'd had when Tory had called to say someone was in the house.

"Can you remember any physical symptoms associated with that? Severe headache, a strange smell? Numbness or tingling in your hands or feet? Weakness in your arms or legs?"

"No," Reese said with certainty. "Nothing like that."

"Have you had any chest pain, the sensation that your heart was racing out of control?"

"No."

"Night sweats?"

Reese hesitated. "Sometimes, yeah."

Gently, Nita asked, "Have you ever had these symptoms while you were making love?"

"No."

"Okay." Nita pulled the blood pressure cuff out of its metal holder on the wall. "I'm going to examine you and then draw some blood for a battery of tests. Would you take your shirt off, please."

"Will you do me a favor?" Reese asked as she shrugged off her shirt.

Nita nodded, taking in the scars on Reese's shoulder, arm, and abdomen. "Of course."

"If you find something wrong with me, will you tell me before you tell Tory?"

"Will you promise not to keep anything from her?"

"Yes. But I don't want her to find out alone. I don't want her to be frightened without me there."

"Let's not get ahead of ourselves, okay?" Nita pulled her stethoscope out of the pocket of her white coat. "You've made a rapid and impressive recovery from a series of severe traumatic events. You've returned to a very high-stress job in record time. You're functioning exceptionally well. The symptoms you're experiencing may be variants of posttraumatic stress. They're not typical because you are a very unusual woman."

"They could be something else, right? A brain tumor or something?"

"It's possible, but with such isolated symptoms, not as likely." Nita paused after wrapping the cuff around Reese's arm. "Are you concerned about that?"

"Only for her."

"Tory can handle anything, Reese. Trust her."

"I do."

"Good," Nita said casually, watching the pressure on the gauge. She let the cuff down all the way, then inflated it again. "I understand you might be having another child." She felt Reese tense and took her blood pressure again. Both her pulse and blood pressure had jumped dramatically. "How are you feeling right now?"

"Nervous."

"About what?"

"You weren't here when Reggie was born. Tory almost died."

"I remember her telling me. She had preeclampsia. That can come on fast and get out of control quickly. They'll be looking for that next time."

"But there's no guarantee they can prevent it," Reese said, her voice gravelly.

"No, there isn't." Nita reached for the ophthalmoscope. "You and Tory will have to have some frank discussions with your obstetrician. I'm sure that will help."

Reese didn't say anything. She would give Tory anything she wanted, if she could. She would do anything to ensure Tory's happiness and well-being. But she couldn't face the possibility of losing her, not even for something that Tory wanted as much as she wanted another child. And she didn't know how to tell her that.

CHAPTER ELEVEN

When Reese returned, Carter was waiting in her office. Reese closed the frosted glass door, hung her hat on the spindly wooden rack next to it, and walked around behind her desk.

"Sorry to bother you in the middle of the day," Carter said, dressed in jeans and a loose gray sweatshirt with her weapon on her hip. She was supposed to be off duty but something was clearly up.

"What's going on?" Reese waved a hand for Carter to sit, but Carter just shook her head and paced a step, then caught herself. She looked about ready to ignite.

"Someone's been in our house."

"Run it for me." Reese settled into her chair, folded her hands in her lap, and listened as Carter resumed pacing and told her about a missing shirt. "That's it. Just the shirt?"

"As near as we can tell. Look, I know it's not much—"

"Carter, if you say someone took it, then someone took it. The question is, why?"

"I've got a lot more questions than that." Carter couldn't stay still. She was angry and agitated and confused, and worried. She didn't know what was going on, and if she didn't understand it, she couldn't do anything to prevent a problem. "Somebody's messing around with Rica. The car last night. The shirt. Someone is targeting her. God damn it. God *damn* it."

"Someone was in my house too."

"I know. And that doesn't make any sense. Messing with cops? That's just plain stupid."

"We don't know the events are related. Could be a thrill seeker. Could be kids acting on a dare."

Carter snorted. "You don't believe that."

"I'm not discounting it, but I'm not looking for an easy answer either. Not when so much is at stake." Reese told Carter about William Everly, his history with Bri, and the fact that he might also factor into the mix.

"I can see where Everly might go after Bri or Bri's girl, or you or your family. But Rica and I weren't here then. He doesn't know us."

"Doesn't Caroline Clark spend time with Rica? At the gallery?"

"Sure. Caroline's a local artist and Rica knows her. She thinks Caroline is really talented and they've gotten to be friends. I think Caroline even helps out sometimes—" Carter grimaced. "Well, hell. We already know the guy is a stalker. If he's been watching Caroline, then he probably knows Rica. You think he'd go after Caroline's friends before her—if it *is* him?"

"Maybe. If Everly spent the last few years thinking about payback, maybe he doesn't want it to be over so soon. Maybe he wants to circle around his real target for a while. A guy like that is going to need some way to blow off steam while he waits. So he'll play with secondary targets first. If he hurts someone his primary target cares for—a friend or a lover—then he'll also be removing a potential competitor."

"I don't mind telling you, I don't like this one bit," Carter said. "I don't even want Rica to go to work, but I don't want her home alone either. As if I could get her to stay home."

"No one is going to get close to our families." Reese stood. "How about you and I go pay *this* guy's family a visit."

"You think we'll get lucky?" Carter wished it could be so easy, but her experience said otherwise.

"If he's not there, we'll sit on the place until he shows," Reese said flatly. "They always come home. Sooner or later, they always come home."

❖

Allie kept silent as Ash evaluated the first two claims, watching her climb over piles of rubble to take photographs of the damaged buildings, measure sections of missing roofs, and sort through the detritus of the hurricane. The third building on their list was a fire-ravaged classic Cape Cod structure with its Wedgwood blue shutters hanging askew, most of the rear portion collapsed, and a yellow warning sign from the fire marshal on the door. A blackened oval plaque next to the front porch denoted it as one of the historic structures that had been floated over from Long Point on rafts. Allie's curiosity finally overcame her still-smoldering anger and she asked, "What are you looking for exactly?"

Ash stopped halfway up the walkway to the entry, surprised that Allie had actually said something that wasn't a biting criticism. The sun had long ago burned off the early morning fog, and she was sweating in the bright afternoon sun. Her shirt clung to the center of her back and chest, and she imagined she could smell the alcohol steaming out of her system. Maybe it wasn't her imagination. She swiped an arm across her forehead. Being with Allie for the last two hours had been a study in masochistic gratification. She hadn't been this close to Allie, for this long, in almost a year, and she took every opportunity to steal glances at her when Allie wasn't looking. Allie was beautiful in anything she wore, but her full breasts and curvaceous backside looked great in a tailored uniform. Ash got more excited just *looking* at her than she had with most of the women she'd actually been in bed with. She felt as if she were awakening after a long hibernation, living and breathing again, all of her senses vibrating. She couldn't stop herself, didn't want to stop herself, from indulging in the illicit pleasure. But the exhilaration came at the price of knowing someone else would be the recipient of Allie's smile, someone else would be holding her, someone else would be running her hands over that body. Probably in a few hours. The pictures playing in her head of Allie and the blonde together were methodically cutting her to pieces.

"What time is it?" Ash asked.

"What?" Allie checked her watch. "Almost three. Why?"

"No reason." Ash wanted a drink at three o'clock in the afternoon. She didn't want it because she craved the alcohol. She wanted it because she craved the sweet oblivion. Being around Allie reminded her of exactly what she'd been running from. Maybe it was time to stop running and let the pain kill or cure her. She shivered and fought down a swell of nausea. "What did you ask me just now?"

Allie studied her, trying not to care that Ash looked like she was on the verge of collapsing. Rivulets of sweat streaked her temples and her crimson hair clung to the back of her neck in wet strands. Even though Ash looked like a refugee from a rehab center, the way her shirt clung to the muscular curves of her chest and the etched surface of her abdomen gave Allie a charge. Jesus, talk about being a hopeless case.

"What are you looking for in these places?" Allie repeated.

"Oh," Ash said, happy to divert her attention from Allie. When she worked, her pain and self-loathing were bearable. Sometimes, she even forgot about the emptiness of her life for a few hours. "I usually investigate commercial claims because the incidence of fraud is highest in those. After a huge natural disaster like this hurricane, there are far too many claims for the regular adjusters to assess. So the investigators, like me, get pulled in to do a lot of the routine cases." She shrugged. "It's most cost-effective to have me focus on resort areas like this, where every building has a commercial function. More chance of fraudulent claims or criminal mischief."

"So tell me about the red flags." Allie enjoyed puzzles. That was one of the things that drew her to law enforcement. She liked crime solving, and this was an opportunity to learn from an expert. Ash wasn't a cop, but she was an experienced investigator. Experienced enough that Reese had worked hand in hand with her the year before.

"Okay," Ash said, cutting across the small front yard, its once immaculate lawn littered with downed limbs and debris, to the side of the building where most of the fire damage had occurred. "A fire claim is always suspicious because it's one of the best ways to totally destroy a building. Plus the claims are usually high. Fires are also common during natural disasters because of the disruption of gas lines, the abundance of flammable material, you know what I mean…"

Ash stopped to photograph the exterior of the building. A huge hole had been punched in the side of the building and when Allie peered inside, she could see that the second floor had partially collapsed. Blue sky showed through huge gaps in the roof above that. Mounds of fallen beams—partially burned and piled like pick-up sticks—were covered with ceiling plaster and filled the lower floor to knee height.

"Major mess in there," Allie said.

"From what I understand, this part of town was largely cut off and even if it hadn't been, there were so many fires, it's doubtful all of them could have been contained," Ash said.

Allie nodded. "A fire on one of the piers threatened to destroy the biggest boat building in town. Most of the volunteers were there. They couldn't get to a lot of the individual structure fires until well after the buildings were fully involved."

"Nobody's fault, but it happens a lot in situations like this." Ash climbed through a fire-scorched opening and straddled a pile of charred flooring material while she photographed the interior. When she heard Allie clambering toward her, she said, "This structure hasn't been cleared yet. You should wait outside."

"You're in here," Allie pointed out testily.

"I know where to step." Ash pivoted and forgot about the job. Allie was backlit by sunlight, her hair a dark halo around her pale, achingly beautiful face. "I don't want you to get hurt."

"I think we've established it's a little late for that."

"I've apologized and you've moved on, so—"

"You're right. That was bitchy." Allie ignored the impulse to shout that she *hadn't* moved on. That she wanted to, but she couldn't. Ash didn't need to know that. And now that she had found Flynn, the perfect person to help her finally manage a clean break, she wasn't about to tell Ash. *Flynn.* Thinking about Flynn helped. She took a breath and struggled for the only neutral ground they had. "So tell me how you decide if this fire is arson or not."

"Okay." Ash appreciated Allie's attempt to smooth things over. They were going to spend a lot time together the next few weeks. It would be good not to keep drawing blood. "For someone to deliberately torch a building, they need three things—some kind of fuel, a heat source, and oxygen to sustain the blaze. We call that the fire triangle. So when we evaluate a fire site, first we look for the typical accidental sources of a blaze—faulty wiring, malfunctioning space heaters, a source of open flames like a fireplace or a kitchen stove—but we're also looking for signs that any of the three points of the fire triangle were intentionally manipulated."

"Like someone pouring gasoline on the floor or punching holes in the ceiling and walls to augment air flow. Right?"

"Exactly." Ash checked her file. "This place had a first-floor rear coffee shop. So we want to look there first as the most likely site for an accidental blaze to start."

Allie stepped in Ash's footprints as Ash carefully picked her way through the debris toward the back of the building. Almost two weeks after the fire, the atmosphere was still thick with the acrid odor of charred wood and synthetics. Their footsteps stirred up fresh soot that rose in clouds around them. Allie coughed, her eyes tearing.

"You okay?" Ash asked.

"Yeah. Sensitive nose."

"If you weren't so stubborn, you could wait outside. I'll call you if I find anything."

"Just shut up, Walker, and keep talking. If I have to traipse around in this shit, I want to get something out of it."

Ash laughed, having forgotten how tough Allie was beneath her seductive siren exterior. Her own laughter sounded foreign to her. She couldn't remember the last time anyone had made her laugh. "Okay. Lesson one. Most arsonists, especially amateurs, believe that the fire itself will destroy all evidence of the crime."

"Almost never true, right?"

"Only with the very best. Usually some trace of an accelerant or the heat source is left behind. Or they use multiple points of ignition—a dead giveaway." Ash stopped in the middle of what had once been the small coffee shop and began to take more pictures. Three of the four walls had collapsed, and sunlight cut sharp swaths through the murky air. "Our problem is that the firefighters themselves are often the best observers of a fire's suspicious origins. They arrive before signs of the arson are destroyed in the fire. The color of the smoke often indicates what type of accelerant was used. The pattern of closed doors and open windows may indicate intentional venting to speed up the burn. Firefighters are trained to look for suspicious signs, but we don't have the benefit of firsthand accounts with most of these cases. So we're going to have to try to reconstruct and hope that any arsonists we might be dealing with are not pros."

"Or hope that the storm put the fires out while there was still some evidence left," Allie said. She watched Ash work in silence for a while, appreciating her focus and efficiency, before asking, "Can I take notes for you or anything?"

"That would be great." Ash handed Allie a folder with a pen clipped to it. "I'll just talk us through this scene, and you can check off the boxes and make notes. It's all pretty self-explanatory."

"Okay."

Slowly, they worked their way through the structure. Occasionally

Allie would ask a question and Ash would elaborate on some point of the investigation. Allie hadn't had this much fun doing fieldwork since she'd been at the academy. She'd always loved treasure hunts and playing Clue. She liked the idea of pitting her mind against that of a perp—that was one of the fun things about being a cop. She didn't notice the time pass until Ash started using her flashlight because it had gotten so dark inside.

"We're going to have to quit," Ash said, starting back the way they had come. "It's not safe with the visibility so bad. Stay close to me on the way out."

"So what do you think about this place?" Allie asked, dogging Ash's steps.

Ash slowed, pointing to one wall that was still standing. The window in its center was still intact. "What do you see over there?"

Allie squinted through the gloom and trained her Maglite on the wall, which was covered with floral-patterned wallpaper above beaded dark wood wainscoting. The wallpaper was streaked with black and curling in places. "It looks like the interior wall started burning, but the fire went out for some reason. Not enough air flow, maybe," she mused, surveying the intact ceiling above.

"What do you see up there?"

Frowning, Allie studied the beaten tin ceiling. The halogen beam from her Mag reflected off a shiny surface, and she focused on a two-inch stainless steel fixture. "A sprinkler."

"Uh-huh. Except where are the water marks on the wall? Where is the water damage on the wall and floor?"

"So it didn't work." Allie shrugged. "Lots of sprinkler systems don't work very well. Maybe it wasn't hot enough in here to set it off?"

"Maybe. Or maybe the water was turned off at the source. We'll have to find out."

We'll have to find out.

Allie didn't want to leave. She wanted to keep searching the site. She was hot and sticky and downright filthy, but she was also charged. Teaming with Ash the last couple of hours had been easy. More than easy. Fun and exciting. This was the kind of work she loved. This was one of the things that had attracted her to Ash Walker, besides how downright scorching hot she was. They shared a mutual respect for their jobs. Ash was an intense, savvy investigator. She was also one of the best. Allie had loved discussing cases with her, and Ash had always been a good sounding board for her. They had connected on a really important level.

Just as Allie decided this assignment might not be so bad, she caught Ash in her flashlight beam as Ash plucked her sweat-soaked shirt away from her chest. She was braless and the hard points of her nipples stood out beneath the thin white cotton. Allie couldn't look away from Ash's breasts, picturing Ash braced above her, one hard, lean thigh pumping between her legs, Ash's bullet-hard nipples just above her lips. A wave of heat coursed through her, and she ground her teeth together. *Damn it.* She didn't want the unwelcome memories to spoil what had almost been a pleasant interlude. When she finally dragged her gaze up, she found Ash staring at her, her eyes glittering dangerously in the half-light.

"You're right, it's getting dark. Let's get out of here." Pivoting abruptly, Allie jumped over a gap in the floor she hadn't noticed before. When she landed, beams shifted beneath her feet. Her balance wavering, she saw Ash flailing as a mound of debris seemed to pitch upward and then just disappear. She lunged for Ash, grabbing for her shirt. "Ash. Ash!"

Her hand closed on empty air.

CHAPTER TWELVE

Reese pulled into the driveway of a tidy, pale pink one-story bungalow bordering the north side of the Winslow Street Cemetery. A well-kept ten-year-old Toyota hatchback was parked in the gravel drive in front of an open, single-car detached garage. A dusty black Ford pickup, along with stacks of aluminum lawn furniture and a push mower, took up most of the space inside the garage. The buildings appeared to have weathered the hurricane fairly well. A broken window box lying on the grass in front of the low front porch was the only sign of casualties.

Reese preceded Carter across the lawn to the porch and rapped on the pitted metal storm door. The inner door was open and she could hear the drone of a television. After a minute, she knocked again, louder, and saw a shadow pass across the shaft of blue light from the television, and then a woman appeared at the door. In her sixties, she had straight gray hair cut in a short, layered, no-frills style and wore shapeless black slacks with a fuzzy sweater a shade darker than the pink of the house.

When she saw Reese her lips thinned, but she opened the door a sliver and said pleasantly, "Hello, Sheriff. Hot enough for you?"

Her gaze flickered past Reese to Carter, sharp and appraising.

"Feels like August again," Reese agreed. "Mrs. Everly, this is Officer Wayne. May we come in and talk to you for a few minutes?"

"I don't see why not." Her tone was mild but her expression said she wasn't happy about it. She pushed the door open another inch, and when Reese caught the edge, she turned and walked away, leaving them to follow her through the small living room into an eat-in kitchen. "Get you two something to drink?"

"Thank you, but there's no need for you to bother," Reese replied.

She'd seen no sign of William Everly on her quick walk through the house. No beer cans, no men's magazines, no sign of any men's clothing lying around. One plate and one glass in the dish drainer next to the sink. Two doors leading off the living room were closed. Those were presumably the bedrooms. She doubted Everly could be staying in the small house without leaving some sign of himself in plain sight. But she didn't rule it out. Assumptions got you killed.

"What can I do for you, Sheriff?" Mrs. Everly said, folding her arms under her ample breasts.

"We're looking for William, Mrs. Everly."

"Billy?" Her face and voice registered surprise. "Why, you know where he is, Sheriff Conlon. You're the one who put him there."

"You didn't know he was out on parole?" Carter asked, her voice low and tight. Not exactly intimidating, but she was a stranger to Mrs. Everly, whereas Reese was not. Being questioned by someone she didn't know might shake the woman up just enough to make her slip up, if she were hiding something.

"Parole! You mean he's out?" Everly's mother shook her head. "He didn't tell me. Are you sure? We talk on the phone every month, and I try to get down there to see him as often as I can."

"When did you last speak to him?" Carter asked.

"Let me see...about the first of August, I'd say."

"And he didn't mention he was no longer in prison?" Carter let her incredulity show.

"No," Mrs. Everly said, smiling politely. "I'm sure I would have remembered that."

Reese changed tack. "Do you know where he might go if he didn't come home? Friends or a girlfriend, maybe?"

Mrs. Everly narrowed her eyes. "You don't know where he is?"

"He hasn't checked in with his parole officer in several weeks."

"I only knew his friends in high school and that was some time ago, as you know. He had a girlfriend, more than a few," she said with a faint trace of disapproval. "But I don't think any of them have been waiting around for him."

"Would you remember any of their names?"

"The girls? Oh my, no. As to the fellas, Billy was popular. On the football team and all that. He had a lot of friends."

"If you talk to him, it's very important that he contact his parole officer immediately," Reese said. "The longer he goes without checking in, the more problems he's making for himself."

"I'll do that, Sheriff. I'm sure he doesn't mean to be causing any trouble."

"No," Reese said. "Of course not."

Carter wanted to push her more, but when Reese turned and signaled they were leaving, she followed. If she let her temper get the best of her, Reese was going to shut her out of the investigation. She couldn't let that happen. She couldn't sit back and leave it to someone else to figure out what was going on, not when Rica was involved. Not even Reese, whom she respected more than anyone she'd ever worked with.

"I'll never stop being amazed at the powers of denial," Carter said when she slid into the front seat of the cruiser and slammed the door. "*Of course* he doesn't mean to cause any trouble. At least she didn't start in on what a good boy he's always been." She thumped the dashboard with her fist. "God damn it."

"We don't know Everly has anything to do with what's happening here in town."

Carter tilted her head back and closed her eyes. She'd just promised herself she wouldn't lose her temper, and she already was. "I know. Sorry. I'm just strung a little tight about this. Rica…" She shook her head. "Thanks for letting me ride along."

"We'll have a patrol car swing by here, couple of times a shift. His mother may not be expecting him, but odds are, he'll turn up here." Reese started the engine and backed out of the driveway. "I want to take a walk around your house."

"Sure. Now?"

"Is Rica home?"

"No, she went to the gallery."

"Then this ought to be a good time."

Reese's radio crackled to life and the dispatcher said, "All available units. Code eight—officer needs assistance. Fifty-six Commercial."

"This is Conlon," Reese said as she hit the sirens and made a tight, fast U-turn in the middle of the street. "What do we have?"

"It's Tremont. Building collapse. Paramedics are on the way."

❖

"Ash!" Allie had been knocked to her knees when half the floor collapsed. Now she edged toward the gaping pit where Ash had just been standing. The bitter taste of bile flooded her mouth and she swallowed around her terror. "Ash?"

She heard a muffled groan and her heart soared with relief and gratitude. "It's all right. Help is on the way. It's all right, Ash."

"Allie, get out of here."

Ash sounded strained, as if each word was a struggle.

"Are you hurt?" Allie eased her weight forward onto what looked like an intact section of plywood subflooring. The floor tiles had all cracked into fragments from the heat or been burned away. As she put her hand down, she felt the floor shift beneath her with an ominous grating sound. "Oh shit."

Ash's voice was stronger now. "Get the fuck out!"

"Just shut up, will you," Allie barked back. "I'm not leaving you down there. Are you hurt?"

"I don't think so. But I can't move without risking more collapse. You're not safe up there."

"I'm coming to get you."

Allie heard sirens approaching from all directions. It was totally dark inside now and everything looked different as she shone her Maglite in front of her. Nothing was where it had been five minutes ago. Sweat trickled into her eyes and her lungs screamed with every breath. Her hands were bleeding, but they didn't hurt.

"Allie. Please. Listen to me, baby, I—"

"What did I tell you about calling me that?" Allie couldn't ever remember Ash being scared, but she sounded scared now, and that scared Allie more than the thought of falling into the blackness. She moved another few inches. Something sharp tore through her pants and she muffled a cry at the sudden pain.

"Allie? You okay?"

"Yes." Allie heard the thunk of timber falling and her stomach turned over. "What just happened? Ash?"

"Nothing. Go outside, Allie. Just back up slowly the way we came in."

"I'm not leaving you there. Can't you ever just trust me?"

"I—"

"Tremont?" Reese called loudly. "Tremont, what's your twenty?"

"Here." Allie raised her Mag and looked over her shoulder, blinking as a half dozen lights focused on her. "Part of the floor collapsed. Ash Walker is down there."

"This is the fire marshal." A big dark shadow appeared beside Reese. "Stay right where you are, Officer. We're coming to get you out."

"No, not until—"

"You'll evacuate as ordered, Officer," Reese said. "We don't need another casualty. You can't help Ash if you're under a pile of rubble yourself."

As firefighters in turnout gear and halogen headlamps slowly drew near, Allie turned back to the black hole that had swallowed Ash. She couldn't leave her there. She couldn't. She focused her light in front of her again and started to crawl forward when a firm hand grasped her shoulder.

"You'll just endanger her, Allie," the fire marshal said. "We'll get her out."

Another firefighter appeared next to her and Allie had no choice. She let herself be guided out into the crisp, clean night air.

"It's my fault," Allie said, her voice breaking.

"What happened?" Reese asked.

"We were almost finished and then I misstepped and everything just collapsed."

"What's her status?"

"She's conscious. She says she's all right, but—" Allie heard her voice shaking and consciously steadied it. She didn't want Reese to think she couldn't handle an emergency. "I haven't had any visual contact since the collapse."

Flynn appeared by Allie's side out of the throng of officers, volunteer firefighters, and EMTs. "Allie," she said urgently, "are you hurt?"

"No, I'm okay."

"You don't look it." Flynn's expression was tight and tense, but her voice was calm and professional. "Your hands are bleeding, your pants are ripped, and there's blood running down your leg. Let me get you back to the rig and check you out."

"No," Allie said, although she felt shaky all of a sudden. "I need to—"

"Go with her," Reese said. "You're all in, Tremont. You'll be shocky in another few minutes."

Allie stiffened her shoulders. "Sheriff, I—"

"I'll update you as soon as they get her out. But I don't want to see your face back here until you've been cleared by medical."

"Yes ma'am." Allie was cold and dizzy, and when Flynn put her arm around her waist to guide her through the crowd, she leaned into her, grateful for her strength and her warmth.

❖

Tory rapped on the examining room door and stuck her head in. "Dr. Burgoyne? Got a minute?"

Nita patted the knee of the elderly woman she'd been examining. "I'll be right back, June." Outside in the hall, she asked, "Problem?"

"Reese just called. The EMTs are bringing Allie Tremont over. She and Ashley Walker, an insurance investigator, were caught in a building collapse. Allie is going to need some stitches. I don't know Ash's status. If she's seriously injured, we'll have the EMTs transport her to the airport and medevac her out of here."

"Do you want me to take care of Allie or pick up your patients?"

"If you don't mind, I'd like to see to Allie myself. She's one of Reese's people, and Reese always takes it hard when she has an officer injured. I'm just going to be hovering otherwise."

Nita laughed softly. "I understand. If one of Deo's crew were injured, I'd feel the same way."

"Thanks. If they end up bringing Ash here, I may need you to evaluate her if I'm tied up."

"No problem. Just have Randy call me." Nita sighed. "I hate to hear about this kind of thing. Deo and her crew are in and out of those unstable buildings all day long. I know they're all professionals, but the chance of an accident is so much higher than on a regular job."

"I know." Tory squeezed Nita's hand, oddly comforted that she wasn't the only one worrying in silence about her partner. "Trust her. Deo's good at what she does."

Nina cocked her head and smiled. "Is that what you tell yourself about Reese?"

"Every day," Tory said. "Every single day."

❖

"Hey, Allie," Tory said as two EMTs wheeled Allie on a gurney into the treatment room. Allie had an IV running in her left hand and a blood pressure cuff around her right biceps. She was pale but alert. "How are you doing?"

"Her BP dropped to sixty palp so we started an IV," the good-looking blond EMT Tory had seen the night before reported, efficiently releasing the buckles on the straps that secured Allie to the gurney.

"I know we met last night," Tory said. "I'm sorry. Flynn, is it?"

"That's right. No reason you should remember, Dr. King."

"Quite the contrary. Thank you for all your help." Tory turned her attention back to Allie. "Let's get her over here so I can have a look."

Flynn slid her hands under Allie's shoulders and said to her partner, "Chuck, get her hips."

"I can move," Allie said irritably. "I'm fine. I wasn't the one that had a building fall on me."

"Let them do their jobs, Allie," Tory said calmly, leaning across the treatment table to help in the transfer. "So tell me what happened."

"Nothing happened to *me*. Part of the floor collapsed and Ash... Ash went down. They didn't have her out yet when we left." Allie glared at the EMTs. "I didn't need to be brought in right away."

"Uh-huh." Tory ignored the all-too-familiar complaints and quickly scanned the EMT records. Allie's pulse was rapid, her blood pressure erratic. "Nothing fell on you? Hit you?"

"No. I fell when the floor buckled, but it was nothing."

Flynn rested her hand on Allie's shoulder. "Stop fussing and let Dr. King check you out."

Tory peeled back the leg of Allie's uniform pants where someone had applied a field dressing to her left thigh. After donning gloves, Tory removed the bandage. "You've got a fifteen-centimeter laceration here. It's fairly deep. I'll need to irrigate it out and suture it. Are you allergic to any drugs?"

"No."

"Do you remember when your last tetanus shot was?"

"No," Allie said distractedly, looking up at Flynn. "Do you think you can radio someone in the field and find out what's happening with Ash?"

"Sure." Flynn stroked Allie's hair for a second and then stepped away to the far corner of the room.

"Reese will make sure she's taken care of," Tory murmured. "How about letting me get you taken care of?"

"Fine. Whatever. Do anything you want." Exhausted, guilty, and just plain scared, Allie closed her eyes. "I can't freaking believe this. The sheriff puts me in charge and I totally fuck it up."

"Somehow, I find that hard to believe."

Allie didn't think she would ever forget the sight of Ash falling, just disappearing. Even though she'd lost Ash long ago, the thought of truly losing her forever was the most terrifying feeling she'd ever experienced.

"It's going to hurt a little bit," Tory murmured as she began injecting the wound edges with lidocaine. "Okay?"

"Don't worry about it," Allie whispered. The pain in her leg was nothing compared to the pain in her heart.

❖

"Stand by on the line," the firefighter shouted up to the team on the surface, who waited to winch up the rescue sked, a molded plastic litter that could be used to immobilize and drag a victim out of the tightest of confined spaces.

"Have them drop a rope ladder," Ash repeated for the tenth time. "I can climb out now that you've got the sides braced."

The young dark-haired man in a bright yellow turnout coat ignored her and tightened the safety straps around her waist and thighs that secured her in the narrow stretcher. After an hour of carefully removing loose debris and shoring up the remaining support structures, he'd slowly worked his way down into the V-shaped depression where she'd been lodged when a portion of the floor had fallen into the basement. Fortunately, she'd tobogganed down on top of the debris and none of it had fallen on her. The steep angles of the cavity and the instability of the structure had made it impossible for her to climb out before. She was still worried that the vibration set up by her ascent might trigger further collapse, and the young firefighter would be beneath her handling the guide ropes. She didn't want him at risk. "I'm not injured. I can climb."

"This is safer until we can get a medic to look you over."

Ash grimaced. "I'm banged up a little, but nothing serious. We'll stand less chance of destabilizing this area if we don't use the winch."

"Can't do it, ma'am. Protocol."

"Listen, hotshot, imagine how you'd feel if you dropped through a floor and your buddies had to bring you out in a basket."

He grinned, his grime-streaked face devilishly handsome in the bright light of the halogen lamps shining down on them. "Definitely a dick-shrinking thought."

"Damn right. So have a little pity. It's your call to make, so unstrap me and tell them we're climbing."

He tugged on the guideline attached to the bright orange sked. "On the line," he called up. Then he gave her a charming boyish smile. "Don't worry, ma'am. The shrinkage is only temporary."

She gripped his hand. "What's your name?"

"Mike Torres."

"Thanks, Mike. And be careful down here."

"I'll be right behind you."

After five painstaking minutes, she was at the surface and being rapidly transferred into the back of the waiting fire rescue van. She peered up at the small African American woman guiding the front of the stretcher into the brightly lit rear compartment. "What happened to Allie Tremont? The officer who was with me? Is she all right?"

"I think she went to the clinic in the first truck," the woman said as she efficiently slapped on EKG leads and ripped open the plastic sheath around a bag of IV solution.

"What do you mean, she went to the clinic?" Ash grabbed the woman's arm and tried to sit up, fumbling frantically to release the safety strap. "She's hurt? Where did they take her? How badly is she hurt?"

"Hey! Whoa. Take it easy," the tech said. "Let's worry about you first."

"I've been telling everybody for the last hour, I'm okay." She'd landed on her left side, and her hip and shoulder pounded unmercifully. Still, she could move everything. She'd been hurt on the job before, and she'd be in for a couple of weeks of discomfort, but this was nothing major. "I want to talk to someone in charge. I want to know what happened to her."

"Look. We're on our way to the clinic right now. As soon as I get you lined up, I'll see if I can get some information. But you have to cooperate."

Ash slumped down, suddenly exhausted. "Okay. Okay, fine. But call someone, please." The jostling of the vehicle set her back and hips on fire, and she closed her eyes to fight down the pain. Time became fluid, and the voice of the technician reporting her vital signs drifted into an incoherent rumble in the recesses of her mind.

When the vehicle came to an abrupt halt, she groaned and opened her eyes. The double doors sprang open and she was being lifted out into a parking lot.

"Where's Allie?" she demanded again.

"She's inside," a new voice said.

Ash focused on the woman walking beside the stretcher. Blond, young, chiseled face and tight body. She knew her. She'd seen her the night before. Allie's girlfriend. "Is she all right?"

"The doc's about finished with her. She's fine." Flynn looked down, grinning. "I thought I was going to have to tie her down to keep her from going back after you. She'll be happy to see you."

"Tell her I'm okay. She doesn't have to hang around here."

"I'll tell her, but you know your partner." Flynn guided the stretcher up the few stairs to the main entrance and pulled the door open. "I doubt she'll leave until she's satisfied that you're all right."

Partner. Ash gritted her teeth. Allie wasn't her partner, not in any sense of the word, and the very last thing she wanted was Allie and her new squeeze waiting around. "Do me a favor and get her to go home. There's nothing she can do here. Nothing at all."

CHAPTER THIRTEEN

R eese pulled into the clinic parking lot right behind the EMT rig, left her cruiser, and followed Ash and the EMS personnel inside to the treatment area. At the far end of the hall, Tory directed the medics guiding Ash's stretcher into an open treatment room.

"How's everyone doing?" Reese asked.

"I've only got a minute because I need to see to Ash," Tory said, "but Allie's okay."

"Nothing serious?"

"Lacerations and abrasions," Tory said. "She's shook up and she's going to be sore for a while. She's handling it well, but I'd still recommend putting her on desk duty for a day or two. Any problems getting Ash extricated?"

"It all went smoothly. She's pretty banged up too, but from what I could tell, she got lucky. They both did."

"How are you?" Tory asked.

"Me?"

Tory smiled at Reese's genuine confusion and stroked her arm. "Things must've been pretty harrowing there for a while."

Reese glanced around to make sure they were still alone. "I didn't have any recurrence of those symptoms. That's what you're worried about, isn't it?"

"Let's say concerned."

"Don't be. I'm okay. You've got enough to do taking care of my people."

"You'll always come first," Tory murmured.

Reese glanced at her watch. "By my count, you've been standing for close to ten hours again. How is your leg?"

"Better than I'd hoped."

"That's a cagey answer, Doctor. I know you can't leave now, but as soon as you can, all right?" When Tory nodded, Reese kissed her quickly. "Can I see Allie?"

"Yes. She's across the hall in three. I'll update you on Ash when I know something."

"Thanks. I'll call Kate and tell her I'll be by to pick Reggie up in an hour or so."

"Good. I hope I'll be home about then too. I'll see you later, darling."

Tory left to see Ash, and Reese crossed to the other treatment room. Just as she was about to knock on the door, Bri barreled in from the reception area. She looked like she'd just jumped out of the shower—her dark hair was wet and windblown, and she wore threadbare jeans, a faded blue polo shirt, and her motorcycle boots. From the wild look in her eyes, she'd probably rushed over to the clinic after hearing about the cave-in on her police scanner. Reese held up a hand.

"Take it easy. Everybody's okay."

"Allie?" Bri asked, panting from her run in from the parking lot.

Reese nodded. "Cuts and bruises. Nothing worse. I was just about to check on her."

Bri let out a long sigh of relief. "Man, that's good news. Can I go in with you?"

"Yes." Reese checked behind her. They were still alone. "I told Carter about Everly. We checked his mother's house today. No sign of him."

"Thanks for the heads up." Bri added casually, "I'm okay with you telling whoever needs to know."

"Did you talk to Caroline?"

"Not yet. She was just leaving when I got home. I'll tell her tonight."

"Don't wait any longer. There may be nothing to worry about, but make sure she's careful."

"Don't worry. As soon as I leave here, I'll do it. She's been with Rica at the gallery all day, so I figured she was safe."

"Good enough." Reese reached for the doorknob on treatment room three. "Let's go see how your partner's doing."

❖

"You talked to her?" Allie asked Flynn as she pushed herself up on the side of the stretcher and started buttoning her shirt. Tory had removed the IV and cleared her to go home, but she couldn't leave until she knew Ash was all right. "She looked okay?"

"She was stable when I talked to her." Flynn rubbed Allie's back soothingly. "Awake and asking about you."

Allie stiffened, resisting the little trill of pleasure that came from just knowing Ash had asked about her. "What did the EMTs say? Is she hurt seriously?"

"I only got a quick report from Sharon, the medic who brought her in, but it sounds like she's in good shape. She looked it to me."

"Good," Allie said briskly. "That's good."

Flynn clasped Allie's hand. "It will probably be a while before Dr. King is done with the x-rays. Maybe you ought to go home."

"I feel pretty normal right now." Allie squeezed Flynn's hand. "Thanks for looking after me and making sure I got here okay. I guess I was more shook up than I realized."

"You had a right to be shook up—you were both really lucky." Flynn kissed Allie's cheek. "When I heard what happened, I was pretty scared."

Allie forced a laugh, feeling oddly guilty about Flynn's concern. After all, the entire debacle had been her fault, and since it happened, she hadn't been able to think about anything except Ash. Through the whole thing, Flynn had been a rock—supporting her, comforting her, looking after her. "You were great, Flynn. I'm really glad you were there and I really appreciate—"

"I wanted to be there. I want to be *here*. Don't thank me," Flynn murmured, dipping her head to kiss Allie on the lips.

Allie jerked away when she heard the door open. Reese and Bri stood in the doorway. Reese's face was completely expressionless. Bri smirked ever so slightly.

"Officer Tremont," Reese said, continuing into the room. "I

understand Tory has cleared you to leave. I suggest you head home and get some rest. I'm taking you off rotation tomorrow. You'll be on the desk when you come back the next day. I'll need your report before that, including anything that you or Ash might have found suspicious in the structure. Can you take care of that while at home?"

"Yes, Sheriff," Allie said formally, processing the news about desk duty. Was she being reprimanded because she'd screwed up? Probably. She could've gotten Ash killed just because she'd let her personal feelings compromise her judgment, even if for only a few seconds. Maybe Ash was right all along. Maybe she wasn't mature enough for anything—a relationship *or* her job. "I'll type up the report tonight and e-mail it to you. You'll have it on your desk by start of first shift tomorrow."

"Tomorrow by noon will be fine, Tremont," Reese said. "Take it easy tonight."

"Thank you, but I want to finish what I started."

Reese glanced at Bri. "Can you take her home?"

Bri shook her head. "Sorry, Sheriff, but I came on my bike. I don't think she should—"

"I'll see that she gets home all right," Flynn said. She'd released Allie's hand but still stood close by her side.

"Good enough," Reese said. "I'll check in with you later, Tremont."

"Okay, Sheriff." Allie waited until the door closed behind Reese and Bri, then said to Flynn, "Don't you have to get back to work?"

"I'll take some personal time. It's no problem. I'll keep my radio on and leave if I have to."

"You sure?"

Flynn slipped her arm around Allie's waist. "Yeah, positive. I want to stay with you a while."

"Can you wait just a minute while I find out if I can see Ash?"

"Sure. I'll wait out in the hall for you. I have to call the station house anyhow."

"Thanks, Flynn. You're terrific."

"I'll remind you of that the first time I piss you off." Flynn grinned and walked Allie out to the hall, her arm still around Allie's waist. The door to the treatment room opposite them swung open and Tory halted when she saw them, holding the door open.

"Prefect timing. I was just about to deliver a status report," Tory said.

Allie looked past Tory to where Ash lay on the treatment table, a sheet pulled up to her chest. Her shoulders were bare and her left shoulder was mottled with the beginning of a huge bruise. Her cheek was scraped and still bleeding. Ash Walker's gaze skated over Allie's face before moving to Flynn. Then she slowly closed her eyes and turned her face away.

Tory said, "I can give you a minute, but that's about it right now."

"I don't want to interfere," Allie said softly. Ash didn't want to see her, that was clear enough. "I only wanted to be sure she would be all right."

"Everything looks good so far."

"That's all I needed to know," Allie said. "I won't keep you, then. We were just leaving."

❖

Rica stood back and admired the five new paintings she'd just hung on prominent display in the front of the gallery. She'd placed the main work, a 4 x 5 foot impressionistic rendering of a cityscape that appeared to be at once ethereal and ominous, on a half-wall in front of the street-level plate glass window where it would be eye-catching to passersby.

"What do you think?" she asked Caroline Clark.

"I think I should reconsider my choice of careers. God, she is so awesome." Caroline shook her head, her shoulder-length flaxen hair teasing around her cheeks and sweeping her neck, making her look innocent and sweetly seductive at the same time. In her tight black hip-hugger pants and red short-sleeved corset shirt, she'd been the object of admiring glances all day long. Rica had watched at least four people—women and men—trying to pick her up, but Caroline was completely oblivious. The thin silver band on her left ring finger was more than an ornament, and Rica found her complete lack of guile refreshing and heartbreakingly tender.

"Give up painting? Really?" Rica said, carrying the final canvas she intended to display to the side wall opposite the one showcasing the featured works. She hung the brilliantly hued landscape depicting a sliver of land, sweeping dunes, and several ramshackle dune shacks overlooking a stormy ocean, and stepped back to admire it. The scene, while a frequent one in works of local artists, was captivating in the purity of color and the wild, untamed brushstrokes. Rica felt the wind against her face and tasted the tang of salt water just looking at it. "Well then, I'm not sure I should sell this. In ten years, I might be able to retire on it."

Caroline gasped. "That's mine."

"It certainly is, and I hope there's more where this came from. I love it."

"You do? Really?"

Rica slipped her arm around Caroline's shoulders and gave her a hug. "Sweetheart, it's terrific. I know you just brought it over for me to see, but you don't mind if I show it, do you?"

"Mind? Oh my God! Oh, I can't wait to tell Bri!" Caroline threw her arms around Rica's neck and hugged her exuberantly. "You're the best. I love you. I love you."

Laughing, Rica hugged her back.

He leaned against the storefront opposite the gallery, sipping coffee from a paper cup and watching them through the front window. Watching them caress each other—their breasts molded together, their hips pressing, parting, pressing again—made him wish they were naked. Women together aroused him. He liked watching them in videos, their long hair sweeping over full breasts and soft bellies. He liked to imagine one of the women was *her*—just like now—and he would stroke himself, biding his time. In the end, she would turn to him, open her arms to him, and beg him to give her what she truly needed. The pictures in magazines weren't as satisfying as the videos, and the videos couldn't come close to exciting him the way watching her like this did. Smiling, he thought about following her home. Maybe she would leave the light on in her bedroom. He slid his hand into his pocket and fingered the square of red silk he'd cut from the shirt. He rubbed it up and down inside his pocket, over the ridge of his erection.

The first time he'd seen her after—after—he'd gotten so hard he'd almost taken her right then, not caring who might've seen or heard. He'd barely managed to restrain himself, but now he was so glad that he had. Watching her, envisioning all the different ways he would touch her and taste her, was proving to be so much more satisfying than having her just once. And there were all the others to amuse himself with—all the pretty women. Her friends. All for him.

Suddenly, a figure cut across his line of vision, striding rapidly toward the front door of the gallery. He stepped back into the shadows, his fingers stilling against his cock. Pressure built in his chest, his head pounded. One of them. He'd been so intent on *her*, he hadn't seen which one it was, but they were all the same. They defiled what was rightfully his. Maybe he didn't have to wait for his pleasure. Maybe it was time to take one of them.

❖

The chime above the door sounded, and Bri walked into the gallery. Stopping abruptly with her hands on her hips, she cocked her head and growled, "Hey! What am I missing here?"

Caroline looked over her shoulder, her arms still around Rica's waist. "Hi, baby." She tilted her head toward the wall. "Look!"

Bri followed her gaze and grinned. "Oh yeah. What did I tell you?" She opened her arms and Caroline threw herself at her. Laughing, Bri kissed her, sliding her hands down her back to cup her butt. Caroline wrapped her arms around Bri's neck and hooked her heel behind Bri's leg. Bri broke off the kiss after half a minute and whispered in her ear, "You're going to be famous, babe. Just wait and see."

"I don't care about that," Caroline said. "I just want you to be proud of me."

Bri nuzzled her neck. "Always, babe. Always."

Rica laughed, wondering if she should break them up or just charge admission. She settled for tapping Bri on the shoulder. "Hi, Bri."

"Hey, Rica." Reluctantly, Bri loosened her hold on Caroline, who eased away a few inches and pushed her hand into Bri's back pocket, gripping her ass. "She's really good, huh?"

"She really is."

"Okay, okay," Caroline protested. "Enough already. Where have you been, baby? I thought you were going to meet me for dinner."

"I would have, but Allie and Ash got caught in a building collapse this afternoon. I was at the clinic."

"Are they okay?" Caroline asked anxiously.

"Yeah. They're both going to be fine."

"Was anyone else with them?" Rica asked. "Is Carter all right? I haven't heard from her all afternoon."

"Carter's probably still there, securing the scene. She's good." Bri checked the time, then said apologetically, "We should go, babe. I, uh, need to talk to you before I get ready for work."

Caroline asked Rica, "Do you need me to help close up or anything?"

"No. You go ahead. Thanks for giving me a hand getting these paintings uncrated and hung." Rica dimmed the lights in the front of the gallery. "I'll be leaving soon myself."

Caroline kissed Rica's cheek. "Thanks again. You've made me so happy."

"You deserve it." Rica hugged Caroline. "Now go, before Bri busts something. From the way she's looking at you, I think you better go straight home."

"Oh, she always looks at me that way," Caroline confided with a tiny smirk.

"Lucky you." Rica laughed. "Get out of here, you two."

Rica held the door for them, still smiling as they sauntered off, arms around each other. She watched them, wondering what it would have been like if she'd met Carter when she was their age. Her father had made it clear before she was out of her teens that he expected her to marry, preferably the man of his choice. She shivered, wrapping her arms around herself when she thought of Lorenzo Brassi and his dark hungry eyes, undressing her, devouring her, as if she were already his. But Enzo was gone, and she had Carter. She would have fallen in love with Carter at any age, and that thought was enough to warm her all the way through. She closed the door and went in search of her phone, unsure why she suddenly felt so unsettled. All she knew was that she needed to hear Carter's voice.

❖

"He's out?" Caroline asked softly, dropping abruptly onto the side of the bed. She clasped her hands together in her lap and stared at Bri.

Bri nodded, hating the tremor of fear she heard in Carre's voice, even though Carre tried hard to hide it. "We don't know he's here, babe. Okay? You just need to be careful. Don't walk around alone at night. Make sure the doors are locked. Keep your phone with you all the time, even when you're in the house."

"What about you? Will you be all right?"

"Hey," Bri said, putting a swagger in her voice. "I'm a cop, babe. You don't have to worry about me."

Caroline laughed and shook her head. "You are so full of it." She patted the bed next to her. "Come here and hold me for a few minutes."

Bri covered the distance in one second flat. She stretched out on top of their platform bed and pulled Carre into her arms. "It's going to be okay, babe. Reese will find him, if he's here."

Caroline rubbed her hand back and forth over Bri's chest. "You'll be careful too, right? Even if you are a big tough cop?"

"Count on it."

"And like you said, he might not be here at all, right?"

"Right." Bri tightened her hold, wishing she could stay there for the rest of the night. She felt him. He was out there somewhere, she knew it.

Chapter Fourteen

Turn here," Allie told Flynn, pointing to a narrow one-way street near the center of town that ran between Commercial and Bradford. "I'm about halfway up on the right. I used to rent a place in Wellfleet, but I can walk to work from here."

"I know what you mean. One of the perks of small-town living." Flynn pulled her Jeep Wrangler into the small three-car parking lot in front of a six-foot wooden privacy fence. She'd hitched a ride with one of the EMTs at the clinic to pick up her Jeep earlier so she could take Allie home.

"I've got the apartment in the back." Allie led Flynn through the gate into a postage-stamp-sized yard. One of the things she loved about her apartment was that she had her own entrance and didn't have to see anyone coming or going. If she brought women home, she wasn't broadcasting her business. Not that there'd been very many. Come to think of it, there hadn't been *any* for the six months she'd lived there. During the summer she'd always gone to Deo's condo, and before Deo, she'd mostly been trysting with pickups in *their* rooms. Now she was bringing Flynn home, and she was nervous. She never got nervous with women. She unlocked the door that opened on her kitchen and held it open.

Flynn looked around after Allie turned on the light. "This is nice." She slid her hands in the back pockets of her navy blue uniform pants. "So can I fix you anything? Tea? A drink, maybe?"

"You know what?" Allie said. "I'm filthy and I could really use a shower. After that, a beer, I think. Do you mind helping yourself?" She pointed to the door opposite the one they came in. "Living room is right through there. It will only take me a few minutes."

"Hey. Take your time."

"Thanks." Allie kissed her cheek. "Be right back."

Allie showered and washed her hair, then dressed in loose tan drawstring pants and a white long-sleeved ribbed pullover. Barefoot, she padded into the living room. Flynn had stretched out on the couch and had a Victoria's Secret catalog propped on her chest. Allie laughed. "Looking for underwear?"

Flynn turned toward her, balancing her beer bottle on her thigh and marking her place in the catalog with a finger. She grinned lazily. "Just looking at the girls."

Allie sat on the edge of the sofa, her hip against Flynn's. She could see herself stretching out beside her, curling up into her. She could see herself unbuttoning Flynn's shirt with the EMT logo on the sleeve and slipping her hand inside. She could see herself doing a lot of things. The pictures in her mind made her body warm and liquid. But she didn't move. "How come you don't have a girlfriend? You're prime real estate, you know."

Flynn's grin flickered and disappeared.

"Sorry," Allie said instantly. "I didn't mean to get personal."

"Isn't that what we're doing?" Flynn said quietly. "Getting personal?"

"I don't know. I'm not sure what I'm doing tonight." She laughed shakily and pushed damp hair away from her face. "But I was serious about you being special."

Flynn sat up and patted the sofa next to her. "Lean back and relax. You're supposed to be taking it easy."

Allie made a face, but she settled back and curled her legs up under her. Flynn put her arm around her. It was comfortable. She was tired and sore and Flynn felt good. She rubbed Flynn's thigh, remembering how it felt to have those hard muscles pressed tight between her legs. "I don't have anything against girls who play the field, you know. I've pretty much always been that way myself."

"I haven't had a lot of time to get a girlfriend, not seriously," Flynn said after a while. "Before I became a paramedic, I went to school in Cambridge."

"What? They don't have girls at Harvard?" Allie teased.

Flynn smiled. "They had a few girls. None of them were interested in me, though."

Allie snorted. "I find that hard to believe."

"I didn't go to Harvard, I went to a place called EDS. Episcopal Divinity School. I'm a priest."

"Holy shit," Allie whispered, then clapped her hand over her mouth. "Oh—I'm sorry. I shouldn't have said—"

Flynn grasped Allie's wrist and pulled it away from her face. "You can see why I don't talk about it that much. It's kind of a mood killer on a date."

"Then what are you doing here? Why aren't you—in a church or something?"

"It's a long story. I am ordained, but I've never ministered. I realized that I didn't have the calling, and I think you need to. So I went another direction."

"Wow."

"I guess you don't think I'm so hot anymore," Flynn said softly.

Allie shifted on the sofa and grasped both of Flynn's hands. "Wrong. Totally wrong. In a perverted kind of way, I think you're even sexier now."

Flynn's face relaxed and she laughed. Carefully, she pulled Allie onto her lap and wrapped her arms around her. She kissed her neck. "You're not freaked out?"

"I'm not very religious, so no. I'm curious, though."

"I meant it when I said it's a long story. Some other time, maybe." Flynn lightly nibbled a spot below her ear.

"Okay," Allie agreed. She would have probed but Flynn didn't seem anxious to talk about it, and Flynn's mouth was doing dangerous things to her brain. Like melting it. Flynn's kisses turned to gentle bites, and Allie's nipples started to tingle. The next thing to start would be her clit, and she didn't want to go there. Not tonight. But she didn't want Flynn to think it was because of what she'd just told her. "In fact, I'm not religious at all. I'm not sure I get it, completely. Does that freak *you* out?"

"Uh-uh," Flynn murmured.

"You're not a virgin, are you?"

Flynn tilted her head back and stared into Allie's eyes. "Episcopal priests don't take a vow of celibacy. And I've had a few years to catch up to what I missed while I was in seminary."

"Oh good," Allie whispered, squirming in Flynn's lap as Flynn rubbed her cheek over Allie's breast, making her nipple harden beneath the thin cotton. "Oh fuck, that feels good. Sorry—sorry, I can't think when you do that."

"Don't apologize. Swearing doesn't bother me."

Flynn's warm breath teased her breast through her shirt. Her breasts were a huge trigger and she couldn't stop herself from pressing her nipple against Flynn's mouth. When Flynn obediently bit down, Allie whimpered softly. "God, Flynn, that turns me on so much."

With a groan, Flynn released Allie's nipple and let her head fall back against the couch. "All I have to do is kiss you and I totally forget everything. Like the fact that you're bruised and sore and I'm trying to maul you. I'm sorry."

"Any other time, believe me, maul away." Allie leaned down and kissed her, slowly and thoroughly. When she pulled back, she was panting and Flynn's eyes were glazed. "I hate to say this, but I really do think I need to go to bed. I'm just—I'm just a little strung out over everything, you know?"

"I know, and I'm good with that, really." Flynn hesitated. "If you wouldn't mind, I'd appreciate it if you didn't mention anything about what I told you."

"I won't. Promise." Allie sighed.

Flynn helped Allie get to her feet, then put her arms around her and whispered, "Anything I can do before I go?"

"Oh, you've done plenty. Gold star, Flynn." Allie walked Flynn to the door and gave her another serious good-night kiss. Flynn held her close, caressing her back and her ass, but not pushing for anything more than the kiss. Just the same, Allie throbbed in all the danger zones by the time she broke it off. "And I don't just think you're hot. I think you're blazing."

❖

"You need to get out of here," Nita said, leaning in the doorway of Tory's office. "You were only supposed to work half a day, remember?"

"Did Ash Walker get taken care of?" Tory asked wearily.

"Yes. One of Reese's officers came by to drive her home. Really, you look beat. I'll take care of the chart work."

"I appreciate it. Reese picked the baby up a little while ago, and I'd really like to get home before she goes to sleep. It's been a long couple of weeks without her."

"Go, go."

"Can you come in for a minute and close the door?" Tory dreaded asking, but she'd pushed everything out of her mind during the last few chaotic hours, taking care of two injured friends. She couldn't hold her worry off any longer. "What do you think about Reese?"

"You know the party line," Nita said gently, settling into one of the chairs in front of Tory's desk. She crossed her legs and draped one arm over her knee, leaning forward, her face serious and compassionate. "I told her I wanted to get a CAT scan just to be sure we aren't dealing with some small area of cortical scarring that's acting as a seizure focus. I had Sally draw blood for routine chemistry and also an endocrine panel. Until I get the results, anything I say would be premature and possibly inaccurate."

"All right. You've given me the safe answer," Tory said evenly. "Now tell me what your gut says."

"I think she's possibly the most amazing women I've ever met."

Tory laughed. "Flatterer."

"I mean it," Nita said, smiling, "and you know how I feel about Deo."

"Yes, I witnessed the courtship, remember."

"And I have no secrets left." Nita's smooth café au lait skin flushed. "In addition to all her obvious attributes, psychologically Reese is really remarkable. And unusual. You know that, right?"

"She's spoiled me," Tory said softly. "When I met her, I didn't believe in love anymore. Not the kind of love that changes your life. Not the kind that…well, you know." Tory took a breath. "And then, there she was. So…damn perfect. So strong, so clear minded, so utterly completely focused on me. She gave me everything I ever wanted and let me want more." Tory folded her hands on her desk and stared at her intertwined fingers. "And I've indulged myself in how wonderful that makes me feel. How wonderful she makes *me* feel. And maybe I've asked too much of her all this time."

"Oh boy," Nita murmured. "I'm going out on a limb here, because I've only known you two a relatively short time. But I think you're wrong. About indulging yourself and about taking advantage of her. That's what you're getting at, aren't you?"

"Maybe. I guess so." Tory was sick thinking that Reese needed her and had been afraid to tell her. Thinking that she hadn't given Reese what she needed when Reese came home so damaged. That she'd allowed herself to believe that Reese was strong enough to handle anything that came her way, because *she* needed her to be.

"Reese is about the most honest person I've ever met," Nita said. "I asked her some pretty pointed questions and we talked about some pretty frightening things. Or what would be frightening for most people. In my opinion, she's not frightened, she's not anxious, she's not psychologically fragile. She's every bit as strong as you think she is."

Tory straightened. "You don't think she has PTSD?"

"I think she's displaying completely normal, human reactions to a horrifying experience. Mild psychic trauma that's well on the way to mending. She said herself that her nightmares are getting better. You seem to think that she's improving."

"Yes. But if it's not that…" Tory's chest tightened as if a huge hand were squeezing around her heart. For a second, she couldn't catch her breath. "You think…you found something physical?"

"No, no," Nita said quickly, shaking her head. "God, I knew I should wait until we had the tests—"

"I'm sorry. I'm fine. Really. I want…I need to hear this. Please."

"Okay…bear with me while I try to put this into words. Reese is really complicated, and she's also really simple. She functions on two levels, as far as I can tell. You said yourself she's a Marine, and that goes far beyond just a job description. It's part of her psyche—an ingrained need to take responsibility for others, to see that good wins out, if you will. It's the soldier mentality. She needs to be the sheriff now just as much as she needed to be a Marine before. It's her purpose."

"I know. I realized that soon after we met, and as hard as it is, I would never ask her to change."

Nita nodded. "And then there's the bigger part of her. That part you're too close to see. The part where she's vulnerable. And that's you."

"Me."

"The only time I got a response out of her that was anything other than totally calm and controlled was when we were talking about you. Anything that affects you—your mental or physical comfort—that's her Achilles' heel." Nita hesitated.

"What? What aren't you telling me?"

"Her blood pressure spiked to two-thirty systolic at one point. We happened to be talking about you."

"Two-thirty," Tory whispered. "God, Nita. She could stroke at that level."

"If she weren't in such superb physical condition, I'd be a lot more worried." Nita kept her gaze steady on Tory's. "I'm not saying it's not something to worry about, but we need more information before we panic."

"What do you recommend?" At that moment, Tory couldn't even begin to think like a physician. All she could envision was something happening to Reese. She saw her hands trembling, but she couldn't feel them. Her lips tingled but when she ran her tongue over them they felt like wood. The room dimmed and she wondered if someone had turned the lights off in the clinic.

"Tory." Nita's voice came from far away. "Tory, put your head down."

Tory felt fingers on the back of her neck, gently kneading. She took a deep breath and slowly became aware of her cheek resting against her desk. She pushed herself upright. "I'm sorry. I don't know what happened."

Nita sat back down, her expression sympathetic. "You know, Reese isn't the only one susceptible to PTSD. You've been under almost as much stress as she has. And you're exhausted."

"I'm all right," Tory said quickly. "I haven't been sleeping that well and my leg's bothering me." She saw Nita's eyebrows lift almost imperceptibly. "And, all right, I'm terrified of something happening to her."

"Well, then I would say the two of you are perfectly matched. As far as Reese is concerned, I'm recommending that she wear a cardiac monitor and a transdermal blood-pressure sensor twenty-four hours a day for a week." She pointed her finger at Tory. "And you need to let me be responsible for her. Let me take care of her. And trust me."

"All right." Tory smiled faintly. "I'll try. I really will."

"Have her come by tomorrow and I'll get her set up. Now you go home and remember your promise."

"Yes ma'am."

Tory looked at the pile of charts and lab reports on her desk that she still needed to review, and decided that nothing was more important at that moment than Reese. She repeated her promise to let Nita handle things all the way home, and when she walked in the house, the first thing she saw was Reese lying on the couch with Reggie perched on her chest. Jedi, his paws twitching in his sleep, snored on the floor beside the sofa. Tory vowed that for the rest of the night the only thing she would do was enjoy her family.

"Hi, love," Reese said, a wide smile chasing the shadows from her eyes. "Look what I found."

Reggie squealed and held up her arms. Tory dumped her blazer and briefcase unceremoniously in a pile on the floor and scooped up her daughter. She breathed in the faint odor of baby shampoo and apricots and thought she had never smelled anything so beautiful. She spun slowly in a circle. "Hello hello hello. Look who's home!"

Reese made room on the sofa and Tory sat next to her. Reggie immediately demanded to get down, and Tory set her on the floor. Watching Reggie out of one eye, she scooted closer to Reese, looped her arm around her waist, and kissed her. "Hello, darling. I missed you."

"I'm glad you're home," Reese murmured against her ear. "Are you hungry? We're having hot dogs."

"It's almost nine o'clock," Tory chided. "She should be in bed."

"But we're hungry."

"Hungry," Reggie confirmed with a happy shout.

Laughing, feeling her weariness drop away like an unwanted coat on an early spring morning, Tory rose and pulled Reese up with her. "Then you're cooking."

Reese leaned down and plucked Reggie up with an arm around her middle, then slung the other arm around Tory's shoulders. "Grab a seat at the counter, put your leg up, and prepare to be feasted."

"I love you," Tory laughed, amazed at how easy it was to live just in this moment, when she had everything she needed.

❖

Allie rolled over and looked at the clock. Ten thirty. She couldn't sleep even though she was tired. Every muscle and bone in her body ached. She closed her eyes and concentrated on the softness of Flynn's lips, the heat of her mouth, the gentle tug of fingertips on her breasts. When she started to get excited, she touched herself and instantly, the images shattered.

Cursing inwardly, she flopped onto her back and stared at the ceiling, so wide-eyed she was vibrating. Patchy moonlight cast leafy shadows across her ceiling. She thought of the flowers she'd seen along the path to Ash's room that afternoon. The afternoon felt so long ago. An image of the blossoming bruise on Ash's shoulder as she lay on the treatment table clicked into sharp focus. Allie recalled the hot glint of Ash's eyes when she'd looked at her in the burned-out building, just before she'd fallen. Just before she'd fallen and disappeared.

Allie lurched up straight in bed, clutching the sheet so tightly in her fists her fingers ached. Ash's eyes had looked so empty when she'd stared at her and Flynn together in the clinic. God, Flynn. She couldn't think about Flynn right now.

Grabbing her phone from the nightstand, she punched in Ash's number from memory. A few seconds later her call went to voicemail. Ash should be home by now. What if something had gone wrong? What if she was still at the clinic? Hurriedly, she dialed the clinic number. She took injured tourists and townspeople there so frequently, she knew the number by heart. Three rings. Four rings. The answering machine picked up.

Tossing the covers aside, she vaulted from bed and dressed hurriedly in jeans and a cotton pullover sweater, not even bothering with underwear. She grabbed her keys and was in her car before she had time to talk sense to herself. Five minutes later, she pulled up in front of the Crown. A minute after that she knocked on Ash's door.

"Ash?" she called softly. "Ash, it's Allie. Are you there? Ash?" She tried the knob. The door was locked. The room was dark. Maybe Ash was with a woman. The one from last night. Maybe she was inside, hurt. Maybe…

The door opened and Ash stared out at her. She was barefoot in a white V-neck T-shirt and loose navy blue sweatpants. The only light came from a series of muted floods situated near the eaves of the buildings surrounding the courtyard, but even in the dim illumination,

Allie could see the blank futility in Ash's eyes. She looked hurt. She looked beaten.

"I couldn't sleep," Allie whispered. "Damn you, Ash. I couldn't sleep."

Ash opened the door wider. "Neither could I."

Chapter Fifteen

Allie followed Ash inside and stood in the dark wondering what to do next. After a few seconds, Ash turned on a table lamp in the sitting area. She looked at Allie questioningly, as if waiting for some explanation. Allie didn't have one. Ash was pale, gaunt looking, as if she'd been ill for a long time. She stood awkwardly, clearly favoring her left hip. Allie could barely stand to see her hurting so much.

"I don't know why I'm here, exactly," Allie said softly. "I guess... I'm worried about you."

"I'm okay," Ash said hoarsely.

"You look horrible."

Ash grinned lopsidedly. "Your pickup lines could use some polish."

"Bullshit," Allie protested, smiling back. "My plays are legend."

"True."

Allie was grateful for the little bit of banter that defused some of the tension that filled the distance between them with a heaviness that made her ache inside. She'd been disappointed by women plenty of times in her life. She'd been crazy in love with Bri, and probably still was a little bit, somewhere deep inside. But Bri had been in love with Caroline, always and forever. She could have fallen for Deo—she'd been in a place where she'd *wanted* to fall for her, but that hadn't worked out. And then another girl too, right after high school, who'd been special and who'd moved on. She hurt still, a little bit, for all of them and what might have been, but none of them had ever left with a piece of her heart. Ash had walked away with a huge chunk of it and maybe that was all this was about. Just trying to get back that piece of her heart that she needed to feel whole. Maybe she just had to sever whatever invisible connections still kept them tethered to one another, despite time and distance and hurt. But not now, not tonight.

"Go back to bed, Ash. I shouldn't have come over here in the middle of the night."

"I wasn't sleeping," Ash said. She'd been lying awake thinking about Allie. Half worried and half crazy. Worried that Allie might be more hurt than she appeared, and half crazy thinking about someone else taking care of her. No matter how many times she reminded herself that Allie didn't need her anymore, she couldn't stop the desire to see her, be near her, care for her.

"Can I get you anything?" Allie asked gently. "Medicine or something?"

Ash wiped the sweat that had suddenly surfaced on her forehead, even though the room was cool. "I took some aspirin. Earlier."

"Okay, fine." Allie couldn't stand by and watch Ash struggle to stay upright any longer. She shot across the room and put her arm around Ash's waist. "Then you need to go to bed. Now."

Ash stiffened, her flesh burning beneath Allie's fingers. The soft curve of Allie's breast pressed against her side, and despite being sick at heart and battered physically, she was instantly aroused. She tried to pull away, but Allie held her more tightly.

"You can't be here, Allie," Ash whispered.

"I *am* here. Let me just help you and then I'll go."

Ash relented because she wasn't strong enough to resist. Because Allie smelled so good, felt so good. They walked into the adjoining bedroom together, and Ash slowly lowered herself into bed. Allie disappeared and Ash thought she was leaving. She waited to hear the sound of the door closing. Waited for the night to yawn long and empty before her. Then Allie reappeared with a fresh glass of water and set it beside her.

"Did Tory give you any pills?"

"A prescription," Ash admitted. "But I didn't fill it."

Allie jammed her hands on her hips. "Really, Ash. Do you have to be such a hardheaded ass all the time?"

"Apparently." Ash shrugged, but cut the motion short when her shoulder screamed in protest. "I don't want to take that kind of medication. I know what's wrong, and it's not going to kill me. I look worse than I am."

"That's really not saying very much."

Allie spun around and stomped into the bathroom. A few seconds later she came back and placed four aspirin next to the glass of water. "Two if you wake up tonight, and two in the morning. Okay?"

"How are you feeling?"

Allie took stock and to her surprise, felt better than she had all night. The stitches in her leg twinged every time she moved, and her hands burned from the many small cuts on her palms, but the horrible sick tension that had plagued her since the moment of the accident was gone. She knew Ash was going to be all right, and that's what she'd needed to know all along. "I'm not the one who fell through the floor."

"Please don't remind me."

"I'm sorry," Allie said softly. "It was my fault."

"That's not true." Ash started to push herself up on her elbows, but groaned and fell back against the pillows.

"Would you please relax?" Allie snapped.

"Yes, all right, fine...but understand this. The situation could have just as easily been reversed. I could've put my foot down in the wrong place at any time this afternoon and you would have been the one falling ten feet into a hole. I shouldn't have let you come with me. It was all my mistake."

"Look, Walker, I can take responsibility for myself. I insisted on coming along. I was there to do my job, just like you. I just...messed up." Allie looked away, horrified to feel tears forming beneath her lashes. She blinked rapidly until she forced them back. "I let personal stuff get in the way of doing my job. I'm so sorry."

Ignoring her protesting body, Ash sat up, unwilling to appear like a victim when Allie was taking all the blame for her injury. "No one can just turn off the things that matter to them, even when they're working. Everyone carries personal baggage around with them all the time."

Allie shook her head vigorously. "Reese doesn't."

Ash rolled her eyes. "Oh, for Christ's sake. None of us will ever be Reese Conlon."

"Yeah, true," Allie said, laughing despite her misery. "Okay, bad example. But I should've done better."

"So next time you will. Next time I'll keep a better eye on where you're stepping too."

"Next time?"

Ash dropped back on the pillows, unable to support herself any longer. She sighed. "I've still got a dozen major scenes to evaluate. Are you planning on letting me do it by myself?"

"No," Allie said vehemently, secretly hoping Reese wasn't going to pull her from the assignment. She wanted to see it through. She really liked the work. And she really liked working with Ash. Maybe they could even end up friends, someday.

"So we'll do better next time," Ash said.

"I guess we can work on it." Allie saw that Ash was fading. Her eyelids flickered and her words had begun to slur. Allie wanted to stay. She just wanted to be there if Ash woke up. If she needed anything. If she hurt. She bit the inside of her lip and reminded herself of all the many reasons that was a really bad idea.

"I'm going to go now," Allie said softly. "Will you go to sleep?"

"I'll try."

"Not good enough, Walker. Promise."

"Promise," Ash whispered.

Allie reached to turn the light out and as she leaned over, made the mistake of looking into Ash's eyes. The dark pupils were cavernous and her irises had turned smoky, the way they did when Ash craved her. Want surged in the pit of her stomach and she quickly extinguished the light before Ash could see it. She backed away, retreating by memory to the door.

"Good night, Ash." She let herself out quickly, not waiting for an answer.

❖

"Tell me she's asleep," Tory said as Reese came into the bedroom, undressing as she walked.

"The perks of a full stomach." Reese grinned. "Down for the count."

Tory leaned back against the pillows with a sigh. "I'm really glad she's home, and I'm really glad she's asleep."

Nude, Reese pulled back the covers and slid under next to Tory. She turned on her side and propped her head on her elbow. Skating her fingers lightly up and down Tory's arm, she said, "Tired?"

"Darling," Tory murmured, "the heart is willing but the body…"

Reese laughed. "I wasn't talking about that. I was actually talking about talking."

"Why? Is something wrong?" Tory rolled over to face her, draping one arm around Reese's middle.

"Nothing's wrong at all. But we never finished talking about the baby thing this morning."

"Oh. That."

"Uh-huh." Reese wasn't exactly sure what she was going to say, but she couldn't ignore something that she knew was important to Tory. "You took me by surprise. I kind of thought that we were done."

"I guess it did seem to come out of nowhere," Tory said quietly. A lot had changed in the course of a day. Right now, the foremost thing on her mind was determining if Reese had any serious physical illness, and helping her through whatever residual remained from her recent trauma. Baby-making was suddenly low down on her list. "My timing was bad, and maybe that's an omen. Let's talk about it some other time, when life is less hectic."

"Our life is no more hectic now than it ever is." Reese frowned. "What's got you backpedaling?"

"Nothing," Tory said, knowing she was evading. She didn't want to frighten Reese with her own fears.

"You talked to Nita," Reese said flatly. "I asked her not to discuss anything with you until I was with you."

"No...I mean, yes, we talked, but she didn't go behind your back. She doesn't have any of the results yet. We only talked in generalities."

Reese snorted and sat up in bed, her hands tightening on her thighs. "You're a doctor, Tory. There is no such thing as generalities with you."

"I'm sorry. I didn't mean to invade your privacy."

"I don't care about my privacy. This affects you as well as me. It's just that..."

"What?" Tory asked softly, curling closer and resting her hand in the center of Reese's chest. "It's just what, darling?"

Reese covered Tory's hand and ran her thumb slowly over Tory's wrist. "I didn't want you worrying."

"Sweetheart. I love you. I'm going to worry...a little...about anything that hurts or troubles you."

"What did Nita say?"

"That's just it," Tory said. "Nothing. She has to wait until the tests come back."

"Something came up to make you decide it's not the right time to get pregnant."

"I just want to deal with one thing at a time."

Reese knew she should be relieved that the subject was tabled temporarily, but she wasn't. She didn't want Tory to sacrifice anything in her life because of her, and she didn't want to use an excuse not to be honest with her. She took Tory's hand. "I need to tell you something."

"Okay."

"I don't know if I want another baby."

"Okay," Tory said slowly. "That's really important information."

Reese sighed. "It's not what you think. I'm crazy about Reggie. I think Reggie would probably like a sibling, but—"

"That's all right, darling. You don't need to explain yourself. It's enough—"

"Tory." Reese gently drew Tory into her arms. "Love. Listen. It's not that I don't like the idea. But last time, you almost died. I can't..." Reese remembered the ambulance ride so clearly—the blood, the EMTs shouting Tory's vital signs over the radio, Tory whispering for her to choose the baby, if a choice had to be made. She felt the ambulance careening around the curves, heard the wail of sirens, felt the earth tilt. Bombs burst, men screamed, and she was helpless, helpless...helpless to help them. She groaned softly.

Tory felt Reese's heart pound wildly beneath her cheek, so fast she couldn't count the beats. Reese's body shuddered lightly all over, as if an electric current were coursing beneath her skin. Tory didn't doubt if she took her blood pressure right then it would be in the stratosphere. She sat up, her own heart racing, and took both of Reese's hands in hers. "Reese. Reese, darling, look at me. I'm fine. You're home with me, and we're both fine."

"Sorry," Reese said thickly. "I drifted there for a minute."

"I know." Tory skimmed her fingers through Reese's hair. "I know. It's all right."

"I'm sorry."

"You have nothing to be sorry for. Nothing at all." Tory pushed up higher on the bed and reversed their positions, drawing Reese's head to her shoulder. She stroked her back, waiting for Reese's breathing to quiet and her heart rate to steady. "All right now?"

"Yes." Reese closed her eyes. "You know, when Ash went down today, I was fine. Worried, but fine."

"Why don't you try to get some sleep? We'll talk about this tomorrow."

"You're not going to pull the plug on me? Declare me unfit for duty?"

"No, absolutely not." Tory tightened her hold. Nita had said that *she* was Reese's Achilles' heel, and she thought Nita might be right. She wasn't certain what she was going to do about that, but she wasn't going to compound the problem by taking away something that meant so much to Reese. "You haven't shown any evidence that your command abilities are compromised. And if you did, I know that you would put yourself behind a desk."

Reese relaxed. "I'll work this out, Tory. I promise."

"Oh, sweetheart. I know." Tory kissed her. "We'll work it out together."

❖

The town was small enough, only three miles from one end to the other, that he could walk or take the bus for a dollar and complete his circuit in an hour. He enjoyed making the rounds, watching the lights go on and off in a downstairs living room, in an upstairs bedroom. It hadn't taken him long, just a few days of observing, to discover who was important to her. Who her friends were. Now he visited them regularly.

Since he'd arrived right after the storm had passed through, he'd come to realize that the residents were all focused on disaster relief and the law officers were spread thin and overworked. He'd gotten tired of breaking into empty houses, and rented a room in a bed and breakfast on a small quiet street north of Bradford. Clean sheets and breakfast in the morning. No one paid him any attention at all.

So he was surprised when he realized that he was being followed. At first, he thought the man was just another man like him, walking aimlessly down empty streets after midnight. It wasn't until he'd started walking toward *her* house that he sensed the man somewhere in the shadows, behind him. Then he began to wonder how long he'd been there. Long enough to see him watching her through the window? Long enough to suspect? Abruptly, he changed directions, skirting down a narrow gravel alley barely wide enough for a car. When he reached the most shadowed spot, he stepped off and pressed against the side of a wooden fence. He waited, listening to the silence.

Then he heard the quiet, nearly inaudible crunch of careful footsteps on stone. The man was good. A professional. A cop, maybe? But his survival instincts were better. As the man drew nearer, his anger escalated. He would never again be the hunted. He was the hunter.

So when the figure glided into view, he took down his prey with a single long slice of the blade.

CHAPTER SIXTEEN

T his is Conlon," Reese said when her cell phone rang sometime
in the middle of the night. She felt Tory come awake next to
her and automatically put a hand on her shoulder to urge her back to
sleep.

"It's Carter. We've got a homicide."

Reese got out of bed and headed toward the closet for a fresh
uniform. "Where?"

"An alley between Franklin and Creek—Clover."

"Who do you have on the scene?"

"I assigned Smith and Chang to secure the scene. Bri's canvassing
witnesses. We're starting to draw a little bit of a crowd."

"Suspects?"

"Nothing yet."

"ETA five minutes."

"You'll tell the coroner?"

Reese glanced at the bed where Tory was now sitting up. "I'll tell
her."

"What is it?" Tory said as she got out of bed and Reese ended the
call.

"Carter has a homicide. I don't have the details." Since Tory was
also the county coroner, Reese didn't have to elaborate. Tory would
need to examine the body, not only to declare death, but to document
the evidence. She gave her the location as she pulled on her pants.

"I'll call Kate and see if she wants to come here," Tory said. "I
hate to wake the baby up now."

"Okay. Thanks."

"Homicide. Unusual for here." Tory grabbed a pair of comfortable jeans, hoping she'd actually get home before she had to go back to the office.

"Yes," Reese said. Bar brawls, muggings, vehicular manslaughter— those were the violent crimes she usually dealt with. Homicide in their small seaside village, even during the height of the tourist season, was very unusual. "You should probably take your own car. I'll be out there the rest of the night."

"Good idea." Tory paused while buttoning her shirt. "Reese, Nita will probably want to see you in the morning. She wants you to wear some monitoring devices for a few days."

"Why?"

"Your blood pressure was erratic and quite high at times. She wants to see how it fluctuates over the course of your normal activities."

Reese shook her head. "I'm going to be really busy tomorrow. Can't it wait?"

"No," Tory said evenly. "It can't wait."

"Monitoring devices. All the time?"

"Not in the shower."

"What about when we're having sex?"

Tory smiled. "You know you have a one-track mind?"

"I'll take that as a yes." With a sigh, Reese started for the door. "I'll find time, if she calls. I'll see you at the scene."

❖

Reese parked behind a cruiser, with its light bar flashing, blocking the alley generously called Clover Street. Carter had already rigged a portable floodlight, and Reese could make out figures moving within a cone of bright light halfway down the narrow gravel pathway. Fluorescent yellow crime scene tape marked a generous perimeter all around the area. Civilians, probably awakened by the lights and activity, milled around. Chang, one of the part-time officers, was talking to the onlookers, taking notes.

Ducking under the plastic tape, Reese played her Maglite over the ground in front of her, taking care not to tread on footprints, tire tracks, or anything else that might be evidence. Carter stood in the circle of light, alternately regarding the body at her feet and scrawling in a palm-sized spiral notebook. Her face was all sharp angles and shadowed hollows in the flat, harsh glare. She looked up when Reese stopped a few feet away. A man lay on the ground on his back, a black puddle beneath his head and shoulders. The source of the puddle appeared to be a wide gash that bisected his neck halfway between his chin and the collar of his blazer.

"ID?" Reese asked.

"None yet," Carter said. "I didn't want to turn the body until Tory gets here. I patted his front jacket and pants pockets. Nothing in them." She stepped closer to Reese and said quietly, "He's packing a Glock."

"Witnesses?"

"None. A young tourist couple on their way home from a party almost tripped over him. They're giving their statements to Bri right now. I don't think they've got anything useful for us. They didn't see anyone in the vicinity, didn't hear anything. Just taking a shortcut back to their B-and-B."

"Someone going door-to-door?"

"Smith."

"Nice work. Thanks."

"Not exactly what I expected my second night on the job." Carter regarded the dead man. "Fast and clean. Looks like one slice—the doc will have to tell us for sure, but whoever did this—it wasn't his first time."

Reese squatted down and shone her light over the man's face. She didn't know him. Light sandy hair, cut short on the sides and back; no facial hair; clean, even features. His eyes were closed. His clothes were business casual. Tan chinos, navy blazer, a dark polo shirt—new, upper end of the price spectrum, suitcase wrinkles in the pants. His shoes were dark brown loafers, polished, well soled. His skin appeared waxy white. Matching two-inch-wide trails of black coagulated blood ribboned down either side of his neck, ending in an irregular pool beneath his head and shoulders. The wound itself gaped open several inches with the severed ends of muscles, tendons, and a circular ring of tracheal cartilage visible. Carter was right—this was a deep, killing cut. A practiced cut. Most amateurs involved in a knife fight stabbed or slashed at their opponents, generally inflicting superficial damage or shallow punctures. This wound took strength, intention, and cold calculation. She lifted the edge of his blazer with a pen and noted the holstered weapon on his hip. A Glock 22 or 23.

Reese rose and regarded Carter. "He looks like a cop."

"That's what I'm thinking too." Carter regarded Reese with a puzzled expression. "But what the hell? If he was, why don't we know about him? And what's he doing out here in the middle of the night?"

"I don't know." Reese fought down her anger. If he was a law enforcement agent and there was some kind of official investigation going on, she should have been notified. If he'd had backup, or if she'd known there was a potentially dangerous situation brewing, he might not be dead. If it turned out he was a civilian and not a LEO, which she doubted, his murder was still in her territory. Her town. "But I intend to find out."

"Looks like the coroner has arrived," Carter said. "If you don't mind, I'll wait to see what she has to say and then give Bri a hand checking the area." She eyed the crowd, which had grown in the last few minutes. "He could still be here."

"This might be a revenge killing," Reese said. "Someone recognizes this guy and decides to take him out in retribution for something that went down in the past."

"It might," Carter said carefully.

Reese appreciated both Carter's expertise in handling the scene and her diplomacy in not expressing her disagreement with Reese's theory. Carter was not only a good cop, she was also a good team player, despite the reputation she had gained as a loner and a rebel. Reese suspected Carter's rep was more about doing what had to be done to complete her assignment, rather than an inherent desire to buck authority. "But it doesn't smell like revenge. For one thing, this guy was probably taken from behind. When you kill someone for revenge, you want them to see your face. You also want to see them suffer for the injustice done to you, so there tends to be overkill. Multiple stab wounds, not one quick one. If the kill is over too fast, there's no time to enjoy the revenge."

"I agree," Carter said, nodding to Tory as she joined them. "This looks like an ambush."

"Or an execution." Reese turned to Tory. "He's wearing a weapon. We don't have an ID yet, so I'd like to turn him as soon as possible to check for a wallet."

"I understand. Can you get the lights focused on him a little more?" Tory looked at Carter. "Do you have a video camera in your squad car?"

"We've got a dash mount. I can get that."

"Good. I want you to walk the perimeter and video his position from three hundred and sixty degrees."

Reese added, "See if you can get the crowd too."

"Got it," Carter said, moving away.

Tory opened her emergency kit, removed a camera, and handed it to Reese. "Photograph the body. I'm going to have to move his clothing to get a core temperature. It's getting colder out here by the minute and I don't want to wait until we finish the scene photos." As she spoke, she withdrew a twelve-inch temperature probe. While she was doing that, Reese took several shots of the undisturbed corpse and then Tory carefully pulled his shirt from beneath the waistband of his trousers, palpated the lower edge of his anterior rib cage, and inserted the sharp stainless steel probe through the skin and into the core of the liver. The digital readout when compared to the ambient temperature would give her a very good approximation of the time of death. However, she could tell when she touched him that he had not been dead very long. His skin was still pliable, and even through her gloves, she could feel that his body was not cold.

"He hasn't been here very long," she murmured.

"Any doubt that he was killed here?"

"None. I'll take some soil samples and see if we can extrapolate the volume of blood underneath him, but from the looks of the extent of spread, I'd say he bled out here and very quickly."

As she spoke, Tory removed paper bags from her kit and secured them around the victim's hands to preserve any evidence that might have resulted from an altercation. "There's no indication of trauma on his hands—no scrapes, lacerations, or bruises. It doesn't look like he fought back. It's probable he never saw his attacker."

"Came up behind him?"

"That will have to wait until I have him on the table where I can examine the wound more carefully. It's too dark out here and the wound itself is too deep for me to tell the direction of the slice. This kind of injury, though, is almost always inflicted from behind." Tory shook her head. "But you don't need me to tell you that."

"Your observations are more important than mine at this point," Reese reminded her quietly.

Tory reached into her kit one more time and took out a small recorder. She quickly recited the date, the time, the location, her name, and the general appearance of the body, the surrounding ground, and other facts that would help her to write a report that might at some later date be crucial to convicting a killer. While she spoke, she concentrated on being thorough and accurate. She did not allow herself to wonder about the victim or the fact that Reese thought he might be a law enforcement agent. She especially did not let her mind veer toward the dangerous territory of imagining that the body on the ground might have been her lover's. Although this man was dead and she could not help him, her job was critical to ensuring that his killer was brought to justice—that was all she could allow herself to think about right now.

"Let's turn him." Tory crouched down, wincing as pain shot up her leg.

"Carter and I can do that," Reese said quickly.

Tory smiled faintly and slid her hands under the victim's shoulders. "Remember our talk earlier about putting yourself on desk duty if necessary? Same goes for me. I'm fine."

Reese nodded and gripped his legs. On Tory's count, they turned him. Tory felt his back pockets and extracted a slim leather folder that she handed to Reese.

Carter, a small portable video camera in her hand, came over and craned her neck as Reese flipped open the holder and focused her Mag on it.

"Son of a bitch," Carter murmured. "What the hell is going on?"

Tory stood and moved closer. When she saw the picture of their victim beneath the laminated overlay of letters spelling out FBI, she caught her breath.

Reese clenched her jaw, carefully closed the badge holder, and slid it into the inside pocket of her short uniform jacket. "Carter, you're lead on this case. We don't cede jurisdiction, no matter what."

"You got it."

"Tory, they're going to want the body. Let's get everything we can as quickly as we can. He was killed here for a reason, and whatever that reason is, it affects this town. That makes it my business. My responsibility."

"Yes. I understand." Tory waved over the EMS techs who had been waiting to help transport the body. "We'll take him to the clinic and get started now."

"I'm sorry to rush you."

Tory regarded the man on the ground. "You're not rushing me at all. He deserves all the attention we can give him."

❖

He lingered in the crowd of onlookers, comfortable that no one was paying any attention to him, until they took the body away. When the officers videoed the bystanders, he ducked his head and stepped behind several other people. Everyone was focused on the comings and goings of the investigators, so he hadn't been concerned that anyone would notice the few spots of blood on his shirt. He'd been careful, but it was nearly impossible to avoid a little bit of cast-off when the big arteries in a man's throat were slashed.

He hadn't planned on staying around, but when he heard the sirens, he couldn't help but backtrack to see the reaction to his handiwork. Then when he recognized the first responders, it felt like poetic justice. Earlier in the evening he'd been contemplating making one of them his victim, and now here they were, players on the stage that he had set. He felt powerful and superior, watching all of them scurrying about.

The kill had been unexpectedly pleasurable. The exhilaration of feeling the body stiffen as he slashed the neck, then the almost instantaneous death tremor, had given him the kind of satisfaction he usually got from dominating a woman sexually. His body had responded in the same way, and the gratification had left him euphoric, very much as if he'd actually had an orgasm. But now that the scene had played out and everyone was leaving, he felt oddly deflated. Empty. Suddenly, he wanted, needed, to get that high back again. He wasn't ready for another kill. But he was ready for a woman, and he knew just the one he wanted. He'd made his choice. His first, but not his last.

CHAPTER SEVENTEEN

Caroline woke up with a start, her senses on high alert and her heart racing. The room was cold. She was cold. She'd gone to bed in only a T-shirt and hadn't thought to close the window. The air blowing through the six-inch opening felt more like November than September. She jumped out of bed, raced across the room, and slammed the window closed. On her way back, she grabbed a pair of Bri's sweatpants from a chair, dove into bed, and pulled on the sweats under the covers. Then she curled into a small ball and wrapped her arms around herself, hoping to get warm. She loved the new apartment they'd rented from Carter when Carter had moved in with Rica, but when she was there alone in the middle of the night it seemed a lot bigger and a lot emptier than the studio they'd had before.

She shivered. That was another big reason why she hated it when Bri worked nights. Not only didn't they get to go to bed together and have sex before falling asleep—or when waking up, or both—she missed Bri's warmth during the night. Not just the heat of her body, and Bri always radiated like a furnace, but being wrapped up in Bri's arms as she slept, sheltered and secure. She missed the way Bri cuddled and stroked her when they were both half asleep. Bri never let her doubt for a second that she was wanted.

Wide awake now, Caroline started thinking about the morning and what she'd do when Bri got home. Bri always came home wired, and when Bri was wired she always wanted sex. Caroline laughed inwardly and rubbed her arms, starting to feel warm all through. Maybe she'd give Bri a massage, work her up nice and high and make her wait for the payoff. Teasing her was so much fun because Bri didn't have a whole lot in the way of self-control. Of course if she did that, she'd end up suffering too, because just touching Bri always got her so hot.

Caroline glanced at the clock. Almost 3:45 in the morning. Nothing happened in this town at this hour. Bri was probably sitting in her cruiser somewhere drinking coffee and bullshitting with Carter. Maybe she ought to call her and tease her a little bit right now. She reached for her cell phone. She could masturbate and then call her right when she was getting ready to come. That would be quick, she wouldn't take Bri away from work for more than a few seconds, and hearing her come would make Bri totally crazy. By the time Bri got home, she'd be a wild woman. Caroline slipped her hand inside her sweatpants. She knew she'd already be wet. Thinking about Bri did that to her. She tapped a fingertip on her clitoris and caught her breath. Not just wet. Really hard too. She put her thumb on the number on her speed dial—she wasn't going to have very long before she needed to call.

She held her breath, preparing for the pleasure, and that's when she heard it. A rattle. Different than the night noises she'd grown accustomed to—tree branches creaking in the wind, distant shouts, engines revving. The thump of the radiator kicking on in the middle of the night. This was something different, something foreign. Metal scraping on metal. She looked at the window, but of course there was nothing there. She was two stories up at the back of the building and there was nothing outside except the parking lot. One thing she'd learned a long time ago was to trust her instincts. She got out of bed and walked carefully to the doorway that separated the bedroom from the kitchen, living room, and dining area. The rattle came again, louder this time, and she knew what it was. Someone was jiggling the doorknob on the front door.

❖

Reese sat halfway in her cruiser at the end of Clover while Carter and Bri wrapped up the scene. Tory had already taken the body back to the clinic. Reese figured they'd have an hour or two at most once she notified the FBI before the feds demanded jurisdiction. She could fight them for investigative control, but they weren't going to let them keep the body. Still, she couldn't put off contacting them—a man was dead and his family as well as his superiors needed to be notified. She pulled up the number for the Boston field office and punched it in.

A minute later, a man said in a bored, flat voice, "Federal Bureau of Investigation, Special Agent McCoy, how may I help you?"

Reese introduced herself, gave her rank and location, and said, "I'd like to speak to Special Agent Robert Lloyd's supervisor, please."

"What's this in reference to, Sheriff?"

"Just get his supervisor and I'll be happy to explain. Here's my number." Reese gave him her cell phone number. "I wouldn't be calling in the middle of the night if it weren't important."

"Well, the office opens at seven, so if you'll tell me the nature of your problem I'll pass it on."

Reese had spent a lot of years in the military police, most of it as a senior investigator. She knew how carefully the rank-and-file guarded the peace and privacy of senior agents, especially in the middle of the night. She also knew the agent on the phone was obligated to relay her message now—it was an official request, with or without further details. He was just trying to impress her with how busy they all were at the FBI.

She wasn't about to tell him that a fellow agent had been killed in the field. If there was an ongoing investigation, she couldn't risk compromising it. In addition, the Bureau would want to put a cover story in place before news of the agent's death became public. If it ever became public. "Thanks for your help, Agent. Have a nice night."

Reese checked her watch. Ten minutes to four. At least the supervisory agent who was about to be awakened had had almost a full night's sleep. She climbed out of the cruiser and started back down the alley to see where things stood with Carter before heading over to the clinic. Suddenly, she heard a shout and then someone came barreling toward her, a flashlight swinging crazily back and forth like a light-saber cutting a swath. She sidestepped quickly as Bri raced past, yelling something into her phone as she ran.

Reese didn't bother asking questions—she just took off after Bri. She managed to make it to the cruiser and yank open the passenger side door just as Bri slammed it into Drive. Reese dragged her door shut, punched the lights and sirens, and grabbed the ceiling grip as they rocketed forward.

"What's going on?" Reese said.

"Caroline. Somebody's trying to break in."

Reese radioed for backup.

"Where are you?" Bri yelled into her phone as she drove one-handed. "No! Don't try to leave." Bri fishtailed around the corner onto Bradford and floored the accelerator. "We'll be there in one minute. One minute. Where is he? Can you see him?"

Reese reached across the space between them and gripped Bri's forearm. "Angle the cruiser into the alley at the bottom of the staircase. If he's inside, he's got to come down that way."

Bri nodded grimly and jammed the cruiser nose first into the gravel walkway that led to the outside staircase and their second floor apartment. She was out of the car with her weapon in her hand before the vehicle had rocked to a stop but, following procedure, she waited at the bottom of the stairs for Reese.

"Bri?" a voice called down from somewhere above. "Baby, I'm out here."

Reese tapped Bri on the shoulder, indicating she should wait, and after scanning the alley, stepped back and looked up. Caroline was leaning over the second floor deck staring down at them.

"Did he get inside?" Reese asked.

"I don't think so. I'm not sure."

"Stay right there. Do not go back inside." Reese returned to Bri, pointed to the staircase, and they both started up, Bri covering the door in case an intruder should bolt from the apartment, and Reese scanning the street and alley below them for any sign of a suspect.

Bri pulled her shirttail out with her left hand and used it to turn the knob, keeping her weapon up and ready. She shook her head. Locked.

"Use your key," Reese whispered. An intruder could have jimmied the lock and slipped inside, and then let the door lock again behind him.

Bri used her left hand to insert the key and slowly turned the lock. She glanced at Reese, who silently mouthed a countdown, and on three, Bri twisted the knob and pushed open the door. Bri went in fast and low to her left and Reese went high and right.

"Clear," Reese shouted after surveying the small room. To her right, sliding glass doors opened onto the front deck. She and Bri moved quickly to the rear, each taking a bedroom.

"Clear," Bri shouted.

"Clear." Reese holstered her weapon, radioed backup to stand by, and strode through the apartment to the front deck. By the time she got there, Bri already had Caroline wrapped tight in her arms.

"Let's go inside so you can tell us what happened," Reese said.

"Okay, babe?" Bri kissed Caroline's forehead.

"Uh-huh. I'm okay." Caroline patted Bri's chest and eased out of her arms.

Inside, Bri sat on the futon sofa with Caroline curled against her side.

"What happened?" Reese asked.

"I woke up and I heard something strange—after a while I realized it was the doorknob rattling. When I went to check, I saw someone standing on the landing. I knew it wasn't Bri, because she would've used her key, and he was bigger than Bri." Caroline's voice cracked and she shivered. "I called Bri. I didn't think to call nine-one-one."

Stony faced, Bri rubbed Caroline's arm and murmured, "You did good, babe. Real good. Don't be scared."

"Did you recognize him?" Reese asked evenly, needing to get the facts while they were still fresh in Caroline's mind. When Caroline had time to think about what might have happened, her fear could cloud her memory. As difficult as it was for the victim to talk about the details of a crime, it was critical that they do so as soon as possible. And Reese needed to be the one asking the questions. Bri had done well outside, had handled herself with a clear head. But right now, Bri was completely focused on Caroline, as she should be. "Did he say anything?"

Caroline shook her head, staring at her fingers entwined with Bri's. "I couldn't see his face. I think I screamed when I saw him." She lifted her eyes to Reese. "He laughed. He laughed like he was having a good time."

"Fucker," Bri muttered.

"Then I pushed speed dial for Bri and ran toward the deck. I didn't know where else to go and I didn't want to be stuck in the back of the apartment. I thought I could maybe jump off the deck if he got in."

Bri made a low sound in her throat, like an animal in pain, and turned her face into Caroline's hair.

"You did well, Caroline," Reese said. "When you were outside, did you hear him run away? Did you hear what direction he might've gone?"

Caroline frowned. "It's funny, I can always hear Bri on the stairs. They're kind of creaky and noisy and she usually runs up them." She smiled and rubbed Bri's leg. "I didn't hear him go down, and I would have if he was running. I think he just took his time walking away."

"What about a car door slamming? A motor starting? Motorcycle, maybe?"

"No, nothing. And I didn't see anyone on the street out front, so he must have gone down the alley to the back."

"That leads to Center Street, and from there to Cemetery Road," Reese said. "Plenty of places to disappear back there." She radioed the backup officers and instructed them to cruise through the streets directly behind Bri and Caroline's apartment. "It's a little early yet for recreational walkers," she told the officers, "so take a good look at any single males who don't seem like they're on their way to work. Make sure you have the description of William Everly I circulated earlier."

Caroline gripped Bri's leg tighter. "You think it was him?"

Reese was aware of both Bri and Caroline staring at her, waiting for her to announce that a nightmare had re-entered their lives. "I don't know. I'm going to swing by his mother's place right now, just to check. You two went to school with him—or not that far behind him, at least. If he was coming home, but didn't want to stay with his mother, who might he crash with?"

Bri looked at Caroline. "Ned Phelps? They were pretty tight all through high school. Who was the girl he was dating right before..."

"Um, Suzy Silva, I think." Caroline grimaced. "I never paid that much attention to him."

"And I don't want you to waste a lot of energy on him now, either," Reese said, standing up. "I want you to be cautious. I want you to be aware of your surroundings. All the things Bri has probably already told you and that you know anyhow." Reese leaned down and kissed Caroline's cheek. "I'll see you tomorrow."

Bri started to get up, but Reese waved her back. "It's almost end of shift for you. Stay here. Anything you need to write up, you can do tomorrow sometime."

"No," Caroline said instantly. "Bri, you go back to work."

"How about this," Reese suggested to Caroline. "How about we take you over to Rica's—she won't mind if we wake her up. In fact, it might be a good idea if you stayed over there the next few nights while Bri's on the night shift."

Caroline looked at Bri. "You okay with that, baby?"

"Absolutely. Come on." Bri rose and put her arm around Caroline's waist, her gaze on Reese. "Reese and I have to check on Everly's potential locations. Right, Sheriff?"

Reese studied Bri, silently taking her measure. Bri's eyes were hot, but steady. Things had changed since the morning, when she'd told Bri she didn't want her involved in the hunt for Everly. This morning he was just a potential problem. Tonight, someone had threatened Caroline. She knew what she would do if Tory were threatened. She couldn't deny Bri the same right, not until Bri showed she couldn't handle it.

"Right," Reese said. "Let's get to it."

❖

An hour later, Reese and Bri had cruised past Everly's mother's house as well as the addresses of the high school friends Bri and Caroline had remembered. His mother's house was still dark. The garage door was open, and his truck didn't look as if it had been moved. At five thirty a.m., some of the other residences showed lights inside—people getting ready for work.

"What now?" Bri asked, her voice flat.

"I'll send someone by the school this morning to talk to his teachers, the guidance counselors, and the principal. See if we can draw up a more comprehensive list of Everly's previous associates. Then we'll question all of them." Reese pulled into the parking lot at headquarters. "We'll step up patrols in his old neighborhood and watch his friends. This is a small village. If he's here, we'll find him."

"What about Caroline? What about during the day?" Bri scrubbed her face vigorously. "Jesus, I don't want her to feel like she can't go out, you know. She shouldn't be the victim here."

"You're right, she shouldn't be treated like one. Caroline is smart. She'll be careful." Reese gripped Bri's shoulder. "Trust her. She needs that from you."

Bri swung her head around and stared at Reese. "I do trust her. But *I* couldn't take him, and I'm tougher and stronger than Carre."

"He's not going to get that close to her."

"How do you—"

Reese's phone rang. She looked at the readout and took the call. "Conlon."

"Sheriff?" a woman said with a hint of irritation.

"That's right."

"This is Supervisory Special Agent Marilyn Allen. You have some sort of problem that can't wait for proper channels?"

"Is Agent Robert Lloyd under your command?"

"Sheriff, I realize that in little towns like yours protocol is, shall we say, not really all that necessary," Agent Allen said without bothering to hide her condescension, "but we don't discuss Bureau affairs with just anyone who happens to call."

"Agent Lloyd was murdered in my town last night. I thought you might like to know. But I certainly don't want to interfere with your protocol, so when I find out who did it, I'll be sure to call during business hours." Reese disconnected.

"Did you just hang up on the FBI?" Bri tried to stifle a grin.

Reese glanced at her and half smiled. "I'd prefer you pretend you didn't hear that, Officer."

"Yes ma'am. I mean, no ma'am, I didn't hear a thing."

Reese's phone rang.

"That will be the supervisory special agent calling back, I imagine," Reese said. "Conlon."

"I'll be there in thirty minutes," Marilyn Allen snapped. "And I'll expect a full report upon my arrival."

"Give me a call when you land," Reese said. "I'll brief you."

"Where's the body?"

"With our coroner."

"I know something of your reputation, Sheriff," Marilyn Allen said. "You may have made a name for yourself busting drug dealers and arsonists, but you don't want to get in the Bureau's way on one of our operations."

"Agent Allen," Reese said quietly, "my town, my case. Call me when you arrive." Then she disconnected and put the phone back on her belt. "Well. This is going to be an interesting day."

"Can I stay and watch?"

Reese laughed. "Don't worry, we'll be crawling with feds before we're done. You won't miss anything. When you've finished reports, check that Carter doesn't need you. Then go collect your girlfriend, take her home, and get some sleep."

"Do you know this FBI agent?"

"Not half as well as Carter does," Reese said softly.

CHAPTER EIGHTEEN

Reese let herself into the clinic with her key. The reception area was dark. The first time she'd entered the clinic, it had been dark too. She'd been answering a call from Tory, who had come upon a burglary in progress. That was the first time she'd seen Tory, and at that moment, everything in her life had changed.

She threaded her way through the rows of chairs and walked down the hall to the one room with a light shining under the door. She tapped on it and pushed through. Tory, wearing scrubs, gloves, and a mask, glanced over at her. Deep shadows underscored her eyes. The body on the table beneath the round surgical light was nude, skin tinted the faint bluish gray of death. His clothes rested in plastic evidence bags on the counter behind Tory. His holstered weapon sat in the center of metal tray on a stand next to her. Apparently he'd had nothing else in his pockets, which wasn't unusual if he was on the job. Loose change could rattle. A wallet was unnecessary. A badge and a gun were all that was needed, and Reese had his badge in her pocket.

"Hi, love," Reese said softly. "How's it going?"

"I've just started the external exam. We need to make a decision about whether I do a full post. Ordinarily I would, but considering the circumstances…"

"Is there any doubt as to cause of death?" Reese walked to the opposite side of the table as Tory went back to work.

Tory shook her head. "None whatsoever."

"Can you get everything you need without cutting him open?"

"If he'd been shot and we needed the bullet to identify the weapon, or there were any question as to COD, I'd insist on doing the internal part myself—jurisdictional issues be damned. But that's really not the case here." Tory tipped her head toward the counter where a row of blood-filled test tubes sat next to a line of small plastic containers, each labeled and filled with a clear solution. Pieces of tissue floated inside. "I've taken blood and tissue samples for tox. I already have specimens from his hands and under his nails for possible foreign DNA, but I'm doubtful you'll find anything. I'd want to have his clothes checked independently for trace anyhow—the FBI should handle that."

"If we turn over the body to the feds without a fuss, that might buy me some leverage in keeping them at arm's length in the investigation. At least for a little while," Reese said. "But that's totally your call."

"I'll have everything I need if I can have another hour with him, without opening him up," Tory said.

"You'll have it. Can you tell anything more about the manner of death?"

"Your assailant was right-handed. No help there, I'm afraid. A single cut, almost exactly as deep on the left as the right, which tells me that he's not only ruthless, he's trained. He understands the importance of severing both carotids and the trachea to produce nearly instantaneous death." Tory looked up. "I'm thinking military—special forces probably. Or a terrorist-trained assassin. Or just your garden variety home-grown hitman who's had lots of practice. Whoever he is, he kills for a living."

"That narrows it down some." Reese slid her hands into her pockets, thinking about all the men in prison who learned to be highly effective killers with only homemade shivs to work with. Knives made from toothbrushes, razor blades, and rubber bands. Food utensils honed on the chipped edges of bathroom tile until they were sharper than any conventional blade. Once released, with real weapons in their hands, these men were proficient and deadly. "Type of weapon?"

"A relatively short, thin blade. Probably a switchblade."

"Double edged?" Reese asked, thinking a special forces member would more likely carry a standard single-edged combat knife.

"Possible. The slice in the trachea, which is in the deepest part of the wound, appears to be the same width as that in the skin. Nothing distinguishing, however."

"Could it be a garrote?"

"Not as likely. Even the sharpest garrote requires some amount of sawing—and back-and-forth movement tears up the edges of the skin. I don't see that here."

"Okay," Reese mused. "So our suspect probably didn't go out hunting, but killed on impulse. You don't set out to kill someone with a switchblade. That's usually a defensive weapon. Something about this guy set him off."

"It could be random," Tory suggested. "Maybe your suspect is just psychotic and he didn't like the color of this man's jacket."

"Anything is possible, but once a cop is involved, we have to assume a link. I have to believe this agent was murdered because our suspect made him or the agent stumbled into something he wasn't prepared for."

"Still, killing a cop." Tory forced herself to think through the problem dispassionately. Ultimately, Reese's life or the life of any other member of the department could be in the balance. "Even if your suspect recognized this man, why kill him? Why call attention to himself that way? Wouldn't he be more likely to want to keep a low profile?"

Reese nodded. "Ordinarily, yes. And that worries me. Because a cop killer who's also crazy is going to be completely unpredictable."

"You keep saying he—couldn't this be the work of a woman?"

"Possible. Women can be trained to kill with the same efficiency as men—the hardest hitmen to track down are female, precisely because they aren't on most people's radar. A female soldier could do this, sure." Reese stared at the gaping wound in the neck. "She'd have to be tall, and damn fast to kill up close and personal like this. Most female assassins prefer guns—the great equalizer."

"True." Tory examined the wound through a dinner plate–sized magnifying glass that she swung over the table. "When do you expect the FBI?"

"Unfortunately, in about fifteen minutes. I won't be able to put off briefing them, but I'll try to keep them out of your hair as long as I can."

Tory smiled over at her. "Thank you. I'm not feeling particularly diplomatic at the moment."

"We had another incident just before I came over here." At Tory's look of alarm, Reese hastened to add, "Everything's okay now. But someone tried to break into Bri and Caroline's place. Caroline heard him working on the door and called us. He was gone by the time we got there."

Tory straightened. "Oh, damn. Is she all right?"

"She seemed to be. A little scared, the way you'd expect. But she kept her head. Bri and I took her over to Rica's."

"Darling, what's going on? Our house, Rica's car, now Caroline? Can these really all be coincidences?"

"I'll admit, I don't like it. But I don't have anything at the moment that ties them all together." Reese frowned, frustrated that she couldn't get a handle on what was happening. She hated feeling that she was missing some critical piece of the puzzle, and if she could just find it, everything would make sense. What worried her was that she wouldn't find it in time and someone she cared about would pay the price. She clenched her fists. Impotence was not a feeling she was familiar with.

"Talk it out, darling," Tory said gently.

"I wish I could. It makes sense Everly would go after Caroline— classic stalker behavior. I can even see him going after Bri first, not only to get her out of the way, but to make Caroline suffer. He has reason to be angry at me too, which would explain him breaking into our house. That would tie two of the three together."

"And Rica's car would just be coincidence?"

"That could easily be simple vandalism. Or Everly again, targeting Caroline's friends."

"But you don't like it."

"Not with this too," Reese said, indicating the body on the table.

Tory handed Reese a pair of gloves. "Help me turn him."

Reese pulled on the gloves and, together, they slid the body to the edge of the table with Reese supporting most of the weight, then tilted him up on his side and finally over onto his abdomen. Tory resumed her microscopic examination, starting with his hair. She sifted through it with a wide-toothed stainless steel comb, then visually examined his scalp for tears, blunt injury, or lacerations.

"Nothing here," Tory murmured. "And if it's not Everly?"

"Then we have a much bigger problem," Reese said grimly.

❖

When Reese arrived back at the station, Carter was waiting for her. She motioned Carter into the office and closed the door.

"Sit down. Long night and it's not over yet." Reese settled behind her desk and Carter sprawled in a chair in front of it. "Where are we?"

"In a nutshell?" Carter said. "Nowhere. No wits to speak of, no suspects. Anything from the post?"

"Not much more than we already knew. The guy's a pro." Reese sighed and leaned back in her chair. "The one thing we have going for us is that nothing goes unnoticed in a place like this for very long. We'll ask around—check with shopkeepers and bartenders. See if we can put together a victim profile, since we don't know anything about the suspect. If we know where the FBI agent was right before he was killed, we might have some idea what he was doing or who he might've gotten tangled up with."

"A lot of legwork and a lot of luck."

"That's about it," Reese agreed.

"Rica called me about what happened with Caroline. Any ideas about that?"

"If I was betting the odds, I'd have Everly at the top of my list."

Carter nodded. "Mine too. But it doesn't set completely right with me."

"No," Reese said. "Me neither. Unless he's changed, he likes to ambush girls outdoors away from people. He's a coward. Breaking into someone's apartment, running the risk of their being able to get a call out—doesn't feel like him."

"Anything I can do to help there, let me know."

"With Tremont out on sick leave today, I may need you to run some known associates down later."

"No problem." Carter leaned forward, her shoulders tense. "What about the feds?"

Reese looked at her watch. "I expect they'll be here any—"

Someone knocked sharply on the door to her office. When Reese had arrived, the outer room had been empty except for one officer manning the phones and handling dispatch. Everyone else was out in the field. It was still too early for Gladys to arrive. Reese stood up as the knock was repeated with an impatient cadence.

"I'd say the FBI is here." Reese opened the door and nodded to the thin, cool blonde in a severely cut black jacket and tailored pants. In her low heels, she was only an inch shorter than Reese.

"Supervisory Special Agent Marilyn Allen," the blonde said.

"Reese Conlon, Agent Allen." Reese held out her hand while behind her, the chair scraped back as Carter bolted to her feet. Reese stepped aside and watched Marilyn Allen's face register first surprise, then a sharp predatory gleam. "And I believe you already know Officer Wayne."

"I didn't realize you'd returned to law enforcement, Carter," Marilyn said as she walked in.

"I guess your sources aren't as good as you thought," Carter said.

The FBI agent laughed lightly. "Oh, they're quite good. Perhaps when I'm done with the sheriff, you and I can catch up."

Carter glanced at Reese, who said, "Carter is the lead in the investigation into your agent's death. She'll be staying during the briefing."

"I hardly see where that's necessary," Marilyn said smoothly, taking the chair next to the one Carter had abandoned. She sat down and crossed her legs with cool precision. "Since there won't be any local investigation."

"We don't want to waste any of your time," Reese said, "and I'm sure you don't want to waste ours. So let's cut through all the posturing and get right to it. We are not going to cede this investigation to you. We'll work with you because we all want this killer found. But we're not going to sit back while you run your own investigation in our town."

"A federal agent was murdered," Marilyn said.

"Yes, and I'd very much like to know what he was doing here," Reese said. "What was he working on?"

"I'm afraid that's highly confidential."

"That's not what I would call cooperation."

"Very well," Marilyn said, pursing her lips as if carefully considering her next words. As if she hadn't already decided exactly how much she would give them before she'd set foot on the landing strip at Race Point. "Agent Lloyd is part of a much larger ongoing operation and he was here doing routine surveillance."

"Alone?" Reese asked, knowing that federal agents rarely undertook solo assignments.

"He was checking out a lead from an intelligence source we did not believe to be particularly credible. He was supposed to be in and out in a few hours." Marilyn smiled at Reese. "Otherwise, of course I would have notified you."

"Of course," Reese said. "Who was he following?"

"No one to concern you." Marilyn shrugged. "A midlevel drug dealer who we were hoping would lead us to his connection, someone much higher up."

Reese didn't have any reason to believe or disbelieve her, but her instincts told her that the federal agent was blowing smoke. At the moment, however, challenging her would lead nowhere. "We have to assume that this suspect of yours recognized Lloyd and killed him. I'll need a name and description."

"I'll see that the information is faxed to you."

"This morning. You and your team can work out of here."

"As soon as possible, Sheriff." Marilyn rose and smoothed down her jacket. It bulged almost imperceptibly over her left hip where her weapon was holstered. "I've booked several rooms at the Driftwood Inn. We wouldn't want to trouble you any more than necessary."

"When we get your information, I'll send you the crime scene photos and reports. Do you want to go to the scene?"

Marilyn cast Carter a speculative look. "I'm sure *Officer* Carter was thorough. If I have any questions after reading her report, I'll let you know."

"Fine." Reese watched her walk out, then looked at Carter. "How much of her promise to provide information did you believe?"

"Try none. First of all, Marilyn Allen is the head of the regional anti-organized crime unit working out of Boston, at least she was the last time I heard. She's probably got dozens of agents keeping tabs on midlevel dealers and above. She's not likely to send one agent anywhere to check out one possible sighting."

"Sounds thin to me too," Reese mused. "For now the best we can do is watch them. Sooner or later, they'll tip their hand."

"Let's hope it's before someone else gets killed."

❖

Ash woke up aching, inside and out. She took a long hot shower— her mind a careful blank—dried off, and dressed in jeans and a collarless pale blue shirt. She walked four blocks to a coffee shop and ordered coffee and chocolate croissants. While she waited, she asked if she could see a phonebook. The barista, who looked barely awake, shot her an annoyed glance and then dug around under the counter and came up with a dog-eared local phonebook a half inch thick. Ash thumbed through it quickly, then pushed it back across the counter. She took out a twenty, paid, and left the change as a tip.

"Hey, thanks," the punked-out young woman behind the counter said in surprise.

"You're welcome," Ash said and left.

The early morning sky was hazy bright, the sun hidden behind clouds. Commercial Street was almost empty except for delivery vans and dog walkers. Ash strode quickly, knowing what she was doing was crazy. *She* was crazy. She'd been crazy for months and pretending otherwise. She couldn't keep it up anymore. She just couldn't. Maybe she would have been able to keep going, working around the clock, losing herself in strange bedrooms with strange women or at the bottom of a shot glass, if she hadn't come here. But she was too close now, too close to escape. So she didn't slow down long enough to think.

Turning up one of the many narrow side streets, she found the address and checked the mailboxes until she located the one she was looking for. She didn't pause, but opened the wooden gate and followed the flagstone path through a small patio to the only door. She knocked and waited, nothing rehearsed, nothing planned. Only knowing she had no choice.

After a minute or two, the door opened and Allie stood in the doorway, wearing a loose ribbed tank that came just to the top of her thighs. A white bandage covered the outside of one leg. Her skin was damp and flushed, and the tendrils of dark hair at her temples moist, as if she'd just splashed water on her face.

"How did you find me?" Allie asked.

"Phonebook." Ash held up the cardboard tray holding the cups and take-out bag. "Coffee and croissants."

Allie hesitated. She'd been so amped after leaving Ash the night before, she'd had a hard time getting to sleep. She'd tossed and turned for a long time, angry and agitated because she'd wanted to stay with her. She'd wanted her. Dumb. Dumb. Dumb dumb dumb. She ought to close the door.

"Chocolate croissants?" she asked instead.

Ash nodded, holding her breath, wanting to beg, knowing she didn't have the right.

Allie moved aside to let Ash enter. "Come on in the living room."

"Thanks." Ash sat next to Allie on the sofa and handed her the café au lait she'd ordered for her. Then she took out the croissants and put them on napkins on the coffee table. Allie's naked thigh was an inch from hers. Her skin was smooth and still tanned from the summer. A dark purple bruise extended from beneath the white bandage. "How's your leg?"

Allie sipped her cafe au lait and murmured with pleasure. Just the way she liked it. Ash had gotten her favorite croissants and remembered exactly how she took her coffee. Stupid to care about something like that, but she did. "Not too bad. Achy, but not enough to set me behind a desk." She sighed. "I think Reese is going to, though. I guess I don't blame her, since I fucked up yesterday."

Ash set down her coffee. "We've been through this. You didn't fuck up. These things happen. Reese knows that. Quit beating yourself up."

"Yeah. Okay," Allie said quietly. It helped, talking with Ash. Knowing that Ash wouldn't say something just to make her feel better. Ash was like Bri that way, always supportive but also always totally honest—at least about stuff like this. If she'd fucked up yesterday, Ash would've told her, if only so she would be safe the next time. She trusted Ash that way. She'd trusted her about everything once. Remembering that, the pain came flooding back. Turning, she stared at Ash. "What are you doing here?"

"I need you to know something," Ash said, her throat feeling dry and tight. The hurt was so clear in Allie's eyes. "You said something yesterday. Something that wasn't true."

"What?" Allie whispered.

Ash knew she shouldn't touch her, but she couldn't help it. She traced her fingers over Allie's cheek. Her hand shook and she steadied it by cupping Allie's jaw, her thumb gently tracing the corner of Allie's mouth. "You said I only cared about your body. That's not true. It was never true." She grinned wryly. "I do think you're beautiful. I love your body. I can't stop thinking about it. But that's not why I… You're so much more, Allie. So much more. You're tender and warm and brave and daring. You're like a beacon in the dark, baby—I'm sorry, I know I'm not supposed to call you that...I just...Just being near you always made me feel so alive."

"Jesus," Allie whispered. She could barely absorb what Ash was saying. Ash's hand was so hot, almost as hot as Ash's eyes, roving over her face as if Ash wanted to devour her. Her stomach tightened. Her breasts flushed and her sex gave a warning pulse. "Ash, what are you doing?"

"I know it's too late, but I needed you to know." Ash groaned and slowly, with infinite tenderness, raised her other hand and cradled Allie's face. She brushed her mouth over Allie's, then rested her forehead against Allie's and closed her eyes.

"You know what your problem is," Allie murmured against Ash's mouth as she stroked the back of her neck.

Eyes still closed, Ash shook her head, insanely on fire just from the sensation of Allie's fingers on her neck.

"You always think you know what I feel." Allie reached up for Ash's hand and drew it down to her breast. Instantly her nipple tightened against Ash's palm and she shuddered. "And you're always wrong."

CHAPTER NINETEEN

At a little before eight, Carter finished typing in the last line of her report on the findings at the murder scene. Aware of Bri standing quietly just behind her chair, she pushed Save, then Print, and swung around in her chair. "What's up?"

Bri rocked back on her heels, her hands bunched in her pockets. "Reese told me to make sure you didn't need anything."

"We're good here. Why don't you head on out." Carter cocked her head when Bri didn't move. For such an honest kid, Bri wasn't all that easy to read, and something was clearly bothering her now. Playing back recent events in her mind, Carter thought it might have been how she'd handled things when she and Bri had responded to the DB call. She'd automatically kicked into investigative mode as soon as she saw the body, and had pretty much taken over. Then Reese had shown up and made *her* the lead in the murder investigation. She'd been too busy getting a jump on the early facts of the case to consider how all that might appear, but Bri was probably feeling pushed aside by someone who hadn't earned her stripes yet. Justifiably so, too. "Problem?"

"No. Are you leaving now?"

"I thought I'd stick with things for a while," Carter said carefully. "Find out where Agent Lloyd was staying in town. Maybe get a lead on where he was last night. You can bet the feds won't tell us."

"You're going to go door-to-door?"

Carter lifted her shoulder. "This is a small town. Someone will have seen this guy."

"What's she like, the agent in charge?" Bri asked.

"Not someone you want to cross." Carter had spent a couple of days behind bars because Supervisory Special Agent Marilyn Allen had thought she could browbeat Carter into turning state's evidence against Rica and her father. Come to think of it, she hadn't heard anything through her considerable sources that the agent was still actively pursuing Alfonse Pareto, but she couldn't believe Marilyn Allen would give up. Which made her all the more dangerous. Of course, Bri didn't know any of that history. "Sometimes agents like her have an agenda that supersedes solving an individual case, if it doesn't suit their long-term purpose. That's why Reese is right in insisting that we keep control of this case. Our only agenda is to solve this murder."

"So can I stick with you this morning?" Bri hurried on before Carter could respond. "I want to check and make sure Caroline's okay, but you know…the first day in a murder investigation is critical, right? So I figured I should work it with you. I've never had the chance before."

"You okay with me taking lead?"

Bri's eyebrows rose, then she grinned. "First of all, Reese wants it that way, so it's fine by me. Secondly, next to Reese and my dad, you're the most senior person here. I want to learn. And I want to solve the case."

"Jesus, I wish I knew how Reese learned to walk on water."

"Born that way," Bri said seriously.

"I believe it." Laughing, Carter stood up and stretched the kinks out of her shoulders. She hated typing. One of the great things about being undercover was that she almost never had to file formal reports. Now that, along with almost everything else she knew about policing, had changed. Somehow, she'd become the senior partner, and a rabbi on top of it from the looks of things. She was surprised at just how good that felt. "I want to stop home and see Rica too. Why don't we swing by my place, grab something to eat and maybe a shower." She looked Bri up and down and shook her head. "I don't have anything that will fit you, String Bean, but you're welcome to the hot water."

"Sounds good," Bri said enthusiastically. "I've got a change of clothes in my locker."

"You know if you plan on working this case, you won't be getting any sleep until we break it."

"I know that."

Bri's smooth, clear features hardened, reminding Carter that she was young but she wasn't green. Reese had told her about Everly's attack and how Bri, just a kid then, had fought him off. Bri wasn't a kid anymore and she'd been tested more than once.

"How did you get that scar on your neck?" Carter asked quietly.

"Knife," Bri said neutrally. "Reese put me undercover and I walked right into a drug bust gone bad."

Carter nodded. "Yeah, been there. Looks like you handled that okay."

"How do you know?" Bri asked.

"Easy. You're not dead." Carter clapped her on the shoulder. "Let's go, partner."

❖

"Allie, what are you doing?" Ash's fingers trembled on Allie's breast.

"You know." Allie bit her lip as Ash's hand tightened on her, chafing her T-shirt over her nipple and sending shock waves through her core. She was tired of fighting the warning voices in her head cautioning her to stay far away from Ash Walker. Surrendering to every instinct she had, Allie slicked the tip of her tongue back and forth over Ash's lower lip, darting inside and back out, taunting her. *I wanted to do this from the moment I saw you in the parking lot. I wanted to do this when I saw you in the bar. I wanted to do this in the middle of a dark abandoned building. I wanted to do this last night. I've wanted and wanted and wanted and I can't stop wanting.*

"Allie," Ash groaned.

"You know what I'm doing, what I want," Allie murmured. "And you want this too."

"You're right." Ash sank back on the sofa and pulled Allie with her. She skimmed a hand under the back of Allie's ribbed tank and caressed the length of her spine while she chased Allie's tongue with hers. She couldn't touch her enough, couldn't taste her enough, couldn't get deep enough inside her. She wanted her so much she was afraid to touch her, afraid she would rip her clothes off, force herself on her, in her. So she feathered her fingertips lightly over the delicate curves of her shoulder blades, the muscles along her spine, the rise of her ass. The lightest of touches, the gentlest of kisses. Careful, reverent, fearful that in the next breath, the next heartbeat, Allie would be gone and she would be alone again. Desolate. Lost. So empty all she could hear was herself screaming in the silence.

"Ash," Allie whimpered. She was coming apart under Ash's hands. Ash had been a considerate lover, but always a demanding one. One of the things Allie had always loved about being with Ash was how much Ash wanted her, and how powerfully she made that clear. Allie was used to fast and hard with Ash, used to being taken, used to being driven relentlessly, breathlessly over the edge. She'd missed the wild ride, the out-of-control abandon, the reckless surrender. The first touch of Ash's hand on her breast had primed her, and now, now these slow, teasing kisses and delicate strokes were driving her completely out of her mind. She was poised on the peak of an enormous roller coaster and she wanted, needed, to careen down the slope, faster and faster and faster until she flew off the rails into screaming oblivion. She couldn't rein in her excitement, dial it down, find the brakes—she was just helpless, mindless need. She climbed onto Ash's lap, straddling her, her T-shirt riding up, her damp panties rubbing on Ash's fly.

"God I want you, Al," Ash gasped.

"Baby," Allie moaned, "baby, don't hold back." She pushed her tongue into Ash's mouth and gripped her wrist, dragging Ash's hand between them. She lifted her hips and pressed herself into Ash's palm. "God, feel me. I'm so hot. If you don't touch me I'll die."

When Ash gently circled the firm ridge beneath the wet silk panties with a fingertip, echoing the movement with her thumb on Allie's nipple, Allie gasped and dropped her head onto Ash's shoulder. So good, so good but not enough.

"Oh my God." Allie squeezed her eyes closed and squirmed against Ash's hand. "Oh my God, I want to come so bad. Ash, *please. Help me, baby.*"

"Shh," Ash soothed, flicking the silk aside and sliding one finger into the warm slick groove. Allie's hips bucked and she made a strangled sound in her throat. Ash kissed her jaw, felt her quiver all over. She eased farther inside, one finger, two. Her thumb brushed Allie's rigid clitoris. She stroked gently over the top. Any harder, any faster, and Allie would come, and she didn't want her to, not yet. She wanted to be inside her, this close, with no anger or hurt or disappointment between them, forever. "Pull your shirt up, honey. Let me suck you."

The muscles in Allie's stomach danced and rolled as she sat upright, forcing Ash's fingers deeper between her legs. Gripping the lower edge of her tank, she pulled it off, every movement adding to the pressure pulsing low in her belly. She kept her eyes on Ash as she braced one arm against the sofa next to Ash's head and cupped her own breast in her hand. She leaned forward, brushing her nipple over Ash's mouth. "Fuck me, goddamn you."

Ash's eyes turned to midnight and she flipped Allie onto her back so fast that Allie cried out. Then she cried out again as Ash knelt between her legs and filled her hard with one thrust. Allie's vision went dark and stars danced against the inside of her eyelids. She drove her hips up, forcing Ash even deeper, and came on her hand in sharp, hard bursts of pleasure.

"Is that what you need?" Ash cried. "Is that what you need, Al?"

"Oh, *yesss!*" Allie dug her nails into Ash's forearm as she held her inside. When Allie finally slumped back, her arms and legs shaking, Ash collapsed on top of her. Allie's lids flickered open and she blinked until she could focus on Ash's face. This was always the time, when they had dropped all their shields, surrendered all their defenses, when Ash was most open, most unable to hide what she was feeling. Right now, her eyes were hazy and twilight blue with a combination of desire and uncertainty. Allie marshaled her strength and traced Ash's lower lip with her thumb. Ash's tongue darted out and licked at her.

"Did you let that blonde from the bar go down on you?" Allie whispered.

"No," Ash said, her voice gravelly and low.

"Why not?" Allie pushed her thumb into Ash's mouth and Ash sucked on it. She felt herself getting hard again. She would come again fast if Ash touched her just a little, but what she ached for now wasn't another orgasm. She slid her thumb in and out, sweeping over the inner surface of Ash's lower lip. "You fucked her, didn't you?"

"Allie."

"You must have, from the looks of your neck the next morning." Allie kept up the rhythmic in and out with her thumb, watching Ash's eyes glaze over. "Didn't fucking her make you want to come?"

"No," Ash gasped when Allie pulled her thumb out. "Fucking *you* makes me want to come."

"Good. Now stand up."

Looking dazed, Ash climbed unsteadily to her feet and stood next to the couch. Allie sat up, pushed her knees between Ash's legs, and unbuttoned her jeans. "Get these off."

Ash kicked off her boots, shoved her jeans down, and stepped out of them. When Allie framed her sex with both hands and took her into her mouth, Ash braced her legs against the sofa to keep from falling. Her head swirled wildly as Allie licked and sucked and nibbled at her. Distantly, she heard Allie tell her not to come, or maybe telling her to ask permission first, but she couldn't make out the words and it wouldn't matter if she could. All that mattered was the silky heat of Allie's mouth and the pull of her lips and the rhythmic sweep of her tongue. Pleasure mushroomed out of her depths and she jerked.

"I'm going to come," she whispered, and Allie's fingers dug into her ass, pulling her closer. Teeth teased over her, light and sharp, and she jerked again and came in Allie's mouth. Her thighs trembled and she struggled to stay upright and Allie kept sucking and she came again. Allie wouldn't let go of her, wouldn't let up on her, wouldn't give her time to breathe and she kept coming until she dropped, sagging forward into Allie's arms.

"So easy," Ash gasped. "So easy with you."

Laughing, feeling perversely triumphant to have fucked Ash to her knees, Allie ran her fingers through Ash's sweat-soaked hair until she realized that her shoulder was wet underneath Ash's face. Wet with tears, and she instantly feared she had pushed her too far. "Ash? Baby, did I hurt you?"

"No." Ash kissed the side of Allie's neck, just below her jaw, and whispered, "I hurt you."

"I don't want to talk about that now." Allie held Ash against her, continuing to stroke the back of her head and neck, the rhythmic motion soothing her own inner turmoil. She was too raw and open to talk right now, to think about what they'd done. What it meant. Where she would put these feelings later. How she would go on without Ash, knowing that what lay between them, despite all that stood between them, was everything she wanted. She pushed back on the sofa. "Come hold me."

Wordlessly, with infinite care, Ash did.

Chapter Twenty

Tory opened her eyes at the sound of movement at her office door. Reese leaned against the doorjamb, observing her with a whimsical smile. She imagined how she must look, clothes wrinkled and hair disheveled, slumped in her chair with her feet propped up on her desk, sound asleep. She hadn't meant to fall asleep. She'd only retreated to her office for a few minutes' downtime—she checked her watch—an hour ago.

"Was I snoring?" Tory asked Reese.

"I'm not sure," Reese said seriously. "Your mouth was open, though."

"It was not," Tory protested as she carefully shifted her feet to the floor, favoring her damaged leg as she stood.

Reese came in and closed the door. "Nita called. I stopped by to get wired up."

"Thanks for making the time." Tory kissed her. "Is there any way you can stop by Kate's and check on Reggie when you get a break?"

"Already did. In fact, I did airplane cereal with her." Reese pointed to several damp spots on her uniform shirt. "Missed deliveries."

Tory smiled. "Sorry I wasn't there to witness that. I was hoping I could see her before my hours started, but there's just not enough time. Especially considering my unplanned nap."

Reese rubbed her back. "I'm sorry."

"Not your fault." Tory sighed and rested her cheek against Reese's shoulder. "I'll grab a quick shower here and be good as new. You missed Supervisory Special Agent Allen, by the way. Accent on *supervisory*."

"Now I'm really sorry," Reese muttered.

Tory laughed softly. "Yes, I can imagine. She's already arranged to pick up the body."

"What about the evidence?"

"She made me sign over the blood and tissue specimens." When Reese grimaced, Tory added, "One set of them."

"One set?"

"I've seen too many specimens get lost or end up improperly catalogued. It's always good to have a backup. I'll be running my own set of reports."

Reese grinned. "You're good."

Tory tapped Reese's chin with a fingertip. "You've mentioned that."

"I guess I better go find Nita," Reese said quietly.

Tory kissed Reese, then took her hand. "Let's go find her together."

Ten minutes later Reese perched on the examination table, staring at the flat two-by-one-inch plastic case attached with a flexible band around her left bicep. She looked up, her gaze shifting from Tory to Nita. "How does this work?"

"It's a remote wireless system—using technology a lot like Bluetooth, the device records pulse and BP and transmits it to me," Nita explained. "My laptop is the base station, and depending on how I program your particular unit, you may feel the cuff inflate regularly or intermittently. The results will be graphically recorded in a file that I can review."

"And I don't have to do anything?"

"I will set the upper limit parameters and if the device registers a reading above that, you'll hear a faint beep." At Reese's frown, Nita said, "It will be a very faint five-second pulse. Unless someone is very close to you, they're not likely to hear it. If possible, you should take note of what's happening at that moment. Your level of activity, perceived stress, physical symptoms."

"Okay. If I can, I will."

"That's perfect, then." Nita made a note in the chart. "I'll call you tonight after I review today's data, Reese." Then she smiled at Tory and Reese and left them alone.

Tory handed Reese her shirt. She was glad Nita was being so

thorough, but just the sight of the device on Reese's arm made her anxious. Irrational, she knew. Diagnosis was the first step toward averting more serious problems, but she wasn't thinking like a physician. She was thinking like a woman who desperately did not want anything to threaten her partner. "I love you."

Reese stopped buttoning her shirt and opened her arms. Tory pressed close and Reese wrapped her in an embrace. "I'm okay."

"You know," Tory said softly, "it's okay for you not to be a rock all the time."

"A rock." Reese lifted Tory's chin and studied her eyes. "We both know I'm not."

Tory stroked Reese's cheek. "I just don't want you to think you need to be—for me."

"You have it backwards, Tor." Reese cupped her face and kissed her softly. "You are my strength. You're the foundation of my whole world." She carried Tory's hand to her chest and pressed it over her heart. "As long as my heart beats, I'll live for you. You and Reggie." She skimmed her hand over Tory's abdomen. "And maybe one more before too long."

Tory's eyes flooded with tears. She knew she was tired, a little bit scared, but mostly, amazed. She wrapped her arms around Reese's neck and kissed her back. "You make me so happy."

Reese grinned. "Love?"

"Hmm?"

"If you keep it up, the thingamabob on my arm is going to start beeping."

Tory laughed. "Well, we'll know just what to tell Nita, won't we?"

"Why don't we try some serious testing tonight?"

"It's a date."

❖

Bri found Caroline on Rica's back deck, curled up in a lounge chair, an untouched cup of coffee on the low table next to her. She looked fragile and pale in the bright sunlight. Tenderness, mixed with near-blinding rage, sluiced through her. Some low-life bastard had tried to hurt her, and Bri wanted to find the fucker and tear him apart. She had to be cool, though, stay steady for Caroline. Leaning down, she kissed Caroline gently on the mouth. "Hi, babe. How are you doing?"

Caroline wrapped her arms around Bri's neck and arched up to kiss her harder. Then she slumped back and dragged Bri down next to her. "Mostly okay."

"Mostly?" Bri traced Caroline's eyebrow with a fingertip, marveling at her delicate beauty.

"I don't want this to be happening again."

"I know, babe. I'm sorry." Bri remembered how helpless she'd been to stop Everly's harassment the first time, and how the impotent fury had become a barrier between her and Caroline. She wasn't going to let that happen this time. "We'll get him and send him away again. Until then we'll just be careful."

"I wish I could be the one to find him. I want to kick his ass myself."

Bri grinned, loving the way Caroline's eyes sparkled with righteous anger. For all her sweet softness, Caroline was tough and strong. More than her, sometimes. A lot more than her. "If I get the chance, I'll kick his ass for you."

Caroline cuddled closer, fitting her head below Bri's chin. "You think you will? Find him?"

"Carter and I will be questioning a lot of people today, about another case. I'll be asking about Everly too. It won't take long to track him down."

"Good. Because I really like Rica, and I don't mind staying here for a night or two." She kissed Bri's neck and then sucked lightly until Bri squirmed. "But being company really cramps my style. I had big plans for you this morning."

"Yeah?" Bri twisted to check the kitchen through the glass doors behind them. It was empty. She found Caroline's hand and drew it to her fly. "Want to demonstrate?"

"Can you be quiet?" Caroline murmured as she pulled on Bri's belt.

"Babe," Bri said hoarsely, lifting her hips. "You oughta know by now. I can be anything you want."

❖

"So what do we do now?" Ash murmured when Allie stirred in her arms. They'd fallen asleep together on the couch, and judging from the light outside, it was late morning. She still wore her shirt and nothing else. Allie was naked. Despite the stiffness and pain in her injured shoulder, and considering she hadn't had much to eat or hardly any sleep for a couple of days, she couldn't remember the last time she'd felt this good. This right. She was terrified to walk out the door, terrified that when she did, the rightness would disappear and she'd never get it back again.

"You know this was a bad idea," Allie said softly.

"Why?" Ash asked, her breath catching in her throat.

"Breakup sex is always a bad idea. Great while it's happening but then it just confuses everything."

"Is that what this is?"

"This is way past breakup sex." Allie leaned up on her elbow, her thigh resting over Ash's. Her breasts swayed gently and Ash's stomach tightened.

"Maybe it's something else," Ash whispered.

"Like what? You *left*, remember? You said you didn't want to get involved with someone so much younger. *You* told *me* I wasn't ready for a serious relationship."

"I remember."

"So we're over. We've been over for a long time." Allie smiled wryly and cast her eyes over their joined bodies. "Except for this part, I guess. Or maybe this is really all there ever was."

"No. It was more than just this." Ash needed Allie to know that. No matter what happened, she needed her to know that there had always been more than just this. That's why she'd come that morning, not expecting anything at all. Just needing her to know. "We were always about more than this, baby."

"Really?" Allie asked, sorrow in her eyes. "Then explain to me what happened, Ash, because I just don't get it."

"I was scared," Ash said softly. "I knew I was falling for you in a big way, and I panicked."

"What?" Allie couldn't believe she was just hearing this now. They'd argued. She'd cried. Ash had stonewalled. She'd sworn at Ash, railed at her, practically begged her for a chance to prove her wrong— all to no avail. Finally—to preserve her pride and her dignity—she'd done exactly what Ash had insisted she do. She'd let Ash walk away, she'd dated other women, she'd slept with other women. She tried to convince herself that she hadn't been in love with Ash. If Ash had once said that it'd been about her fears, and not about Allie's age or Allie's lack of experience or *something* Allie was lacking, then everything might have been different. "What are you saying?"

"I wanted you so much that I was afraid. Afraid that if I fell in love with you I wouldn't make it if you left me."

Allie sat up abruptly, furious and confused. "You broke up with me—you broke my fucking *heart*—because you cared about me too much? Is that what you're trying to tell me now?"

"Something like that."

"You need to go." Allie jumped up, snatched her tank top off the floor, and pulled it over her head. Her panties were nowhere to be found, but at least now she didn't feel so vulnerable. She just felt mad. Raging mad, and she needed to stay that way—especially now, when Ash looked so fragile, so damn wounded. At least when she was angry at Ash, she could bear the pain of losing her. Ash's confession had flayed her heart open, and if she lost her anger, she'd be left with nothing but tears. "You fucking coward. How could you have done this?"

Ash sat up and reached for her pants. She pulled them on and found her boots and socks. "It wasn't about you. It never was." She finished dressing and finally met Allie's eyes. "It was always me."

"That doesn't help me right now," Allie whispered.

"I know." Ash feathered her fingers over Allie's cheek and kissed her lightly on the mouth. "I love you, Allie. And I'm so sorry."

Ash walked to the door and Allie let her go. When she was sure she was alone, she sat on the sofa, rested her hand on the spot that was still warm from Ash's body, and cried.

❖

He slept well, despite his missed opportunity the night before. He hadn't expected her to be awake, and definitely not so feisty. Most prey ran. They never confronted the hunter. She'd taken him by surprise when she'd appeared, a small shadowy figure through the glass. He'd barely had time to back into the shadows so she couldn't see his face. He heard her scream, but she stood her ground. The suddenness of her confronting him, the shock, had been so exciting he'd almost been satisfied with that. Almost. But it hadn't been her face or her scream he'd returned to over and over in his mind, lying in his rented room with his hard, throbbing cock in his hand. It had been the sensation of the blade severing tissue, the sound of life escaping on a wheeze, the convulsion of death that felt so much like coming. He knew the next time he hunted down his prey, he'd experience it all.

So he was feeling confident, invincible, as he strolled casually to the coffee shop after awakening around noon. The midday crowds were thin, and after a few blocks he became aware of more officers on foot and in patrol cars then he'd noticed before. He slowed and moved closer to the buildings, studying the activity, ready to duck up one of the side streets if he needed to. Then he saw the two officers standing in the doorway of the bar he'd been in the night before, talking to someone who was probably the manager. One of them had a photo in her hand. He recognized her and she would recognize him, if she saw him.

Quickly he slipped down a narrow passageway between two buildings, unnoticed. He almost laughed out loud. He'd always been so much better than her. Stronger. More clever. He'd remind her of that, before very long. When he took what belonged to him. When he took the woman she thought was hers and reminded her just how wrong she was.

❖

Carter got into the passenger side of the cruiser and said to Bri, "So what do you think?"

"I think Agent Lloyd was looking for someone last night," Bri said carefully, thinking this might be a test. "So far we can put him at the Governor Bradford, the Gifford House, and the Atlantic House. Chronologically, it looks like his last stop was Good Times—that was only half an hour before the estimated time of death."

"The timeline works, I agree," Carter said as Bri drove down Commercial Street. "So what do we do with this information?"

"We go back tonight and talk to the night bartender and the regulars. Find out who else was there. Ask if anything unusual happened." Bri shot Carter a glance. "Maybe someone noticed Lloyd leave with someone or right after someone?"

Carter nodded her approval. "Sounds like a plan. In the meantime, let's start on the B-and-Bs. We still don't know where he was sta—"

The radio crackled to life.

"All units. Code five at Bayberry and Pilgrim Heights. Approach with caution, code two."

"Felony fugitive," Bri exclaimed. "Everly!"

"That's right around the corner from my house!" Carter hit the lights but not the siren to avoid alerting the suspect to their arrival. "Go. Go!"

CHAPTER TWENTY-ONE

Allie zipped her jeans, pulled on a sleeveless dark blue tee, and debated flip-flops versus running shoes. She opted for running shoes because she was going to work. She might be on sick leave, but she could be "sick" at the station. Reese hadn't actually told her to stay home. So she'd have to sit at her desk. That was a lot more appealing than what she was doing now—staring at the walls and replaying every word that Ash had said, being alternately angry and hurt. Trying *not* to replay every moment of making love with her—burning one second, shivering the next, switching from hot to cold so fast her skin ached. Even the idea of paperwork was looking good. If she sat around here thinking about Ash, or trying not to think about her—

Her police scanner blared, "All units. Code five at Bayberry and Pilgrim Heights. Approach with caution, code two."

Allie shoved her badge into her back pocket, grabbed her weapon in one hand and her keys in the other, and raced out the door. "All Units" as far as she was concerned meant every able-bodied officer. She was not going to let the scumbag who'd almost raped Bri get away. She backed out of her parking space in a hail of gravel and sped toward Bradford. She made the turn right behind a cruiser and followed close on its tail as its flashing light bar cleared the road ahead of them. When the patrol car turned onto Pilgrim Heights and angled across the intersection, she pulled onto the shoulder next to it and jumped out.

Reese climbed out of the cruiser, took one look at her, and waved her over. Allie hurried forward and said quickly, "I know I'm supposed to be off—"

"Rica and Caroline are in the house. We know where he is. I want you with them until we catch this guy."

Allie knew better than to protest, even though she wanted to be in on the pursuit. She wasn't even supposed to be working, so she was grateful that Reese didn't sideline her. And if Caroline was a target, she needed to be protected. "Yes ma'am."

Reese got on the radio and Allie ran across the street and sprinted up the hill toward Rica and Carter's cliff-top home. Rica answered the door, looking worried. Caroline was right behind her.

"What's going on?" Rica asked.

Allie glanced at Caroline, then realized there was no reason to keep anything from these women. "William Everly might be in the area. Reese wanted me to stay with you until they catch him."

"Is Bri with Reese?" Caroline asked quickly.

"No, probably with Carter." She smiled at Caroline. "Don't worry. Bri can handle herself."

"Sure, I know."

Caroline still looked worried, probably afraid that Bri would go off on Everly if she caught him. Allie wasn't so sure she wouldn't, and couldn't blame Bri if she did. No one could really blame Bri for exorcising her demons in her own way. Just like all of them.

"There's no reason to think he's coming here, but until they clear the street or run him down, why don't you two stay together, maybe in the kitchen." Allie checked the front door to make sure it was locked and closed the drapes on the front windows. "I'm going to take a quick walk around outside. Do you have an extra key?"

Rica found one in the desk drawer in the living room and handed it to Allie. "Let me give you my cell phone number." Rica repeated it and Allie plugged it into her phone, then gave Rica her cell number.

"Okay," Allie said. "I'll be right back. Any problems, call me or nine-one-one."

❖

Reese radioed Carter and Bri to confirm their locations, then did the same with Smith and his partner. All were on foot, scouring yards and footpaths around the area where Smith had apparently sighted

Everly approaching the house of one of his old high school football buddies. Reese ordered the remaining officers in squad cars to block Bradford in case Everly tried to come down off the Heights in a vehicle. They had no description of what he might be driving, but he wouldn't be difficult to spot. Then she set out on foot to triangulate with the two teams moving through the neighborhood. Hopefully, they could converge and force him out into the open.

Every now and then she was aware of the cuff on her arm inflating, but she'd quickly become acclimated to it and now she just ignored it. It hadn't beeped, and she wondered if it was working. Considering she was running uphill and charged with adrenaline, she suspected it was malfunctioning, because her blood pressure had to be elevated. Probably just as well. Tory was already worried enough.

Then she heard a shout from somewhere up ahead, followed by a shot, and the only thing on her mind was securing the safety of her officers. She pulled her weapon and ran.

The sharp crack that rifled through the air might have been a tree falling. Allie had heard plenty of those during the storm. But the sun was shining and the sky was clear and she knew a gunshot when she heard it. Her heart leapt and she reflexively pulled her weapon. She couldn't judge the distance of the shot, but suddenly the stakes had changed. She wanted to run toward the sound, to help protect her fellow officers. But she couldn't leave Rica and Caroline unprotected. She moved carefully to the rear right corner of the house. The deck from the kitchen was cantilevered over her head, the brush- and scrub-covered hillside dropping away steeply below her. The nearest house was fifty yards away and separated from Rica's by dense foliage. Anyone approaching the house from the rear was in for an arduous climb, and she doubted someone on the run would try it. Nevertheless, she waited a full minute, scanning the drop-off below the deck. Nothing moving. Skirting along the rear of the house, she climbed back up to the front. She didn't see anyone in the street. She considered going back inside, but thought she'd have a better chance of spotting Everly if she took cover outside. She called Rica's cell phone.

"Hello," Rica said.

"Everything looks clear out here, but I'm going to stay outside. Don't leave the house."

"We're fine," Rica said coolly. "You should also know that I'm armed."

"Ah…" Allie said. "Maybe you'd better leave that to me."

"It's legal. And I know how to use it."

"All right. Be careful."

"Was that a shot?" Rica asked, lowering her voice to a whisper.

"I think so."

There was a long silence, then Rica said, "You be careful too."

"Will do. Just sit tight." Allie disconnected and took cover near the front of the house behind a dense, chest-high shrub that gave her a vantage point of the street. If he came this way, she'd see him.

❖

"Can you turn up the scanner?" Ash asked Gladys Martin, the sheriff's department dispatcher, as she got to her feet. After leaving Allie, she'd walked aimlessly for an hour, unaware of the throbbing pain in her shoulder and hip. The pain in her heart had been all-consuming. She couldn't believe how many times she'd made the wrong decision where Allie was concerned. She'd let her fear of being hurt and, yes, her arrogance in thinking that she knew what Allie would do convince her that she and Allie had no future together. She'd pushed Allie away, pushed her at other women, just to prove that she was right. What an idiot. No, Allie had been right. What a coward.

And then she tried some half-assed apology when it was way too late—she was lucky Allie had even let her in the door. And then…God, and then she just stopped thinking completely and went to bed with her. Being with Allie again had been like tasting cool clear water when she was dying of thirst—after she'd finally accepted that the arid wasteland in front of her stretched forever and she'd given up hoping for a drop of rain. Now, having tasted her again, her soul would never survive another drought. And she had no one to blame but herself.

So she'd finally just walked to the station house and sat down at an empty desk with her files. Working. The only thing short of chemical oblivion that would blunt the pain for a while. When the call for All

Units came in, the two officers in the station ran out, leaving her alone with Gladys and the intermittent radio chatter on the scanner.

"Who is that? Is that Reese?" Ash asked again, working hard to quell her panic as she listened to the scattered reports from the officers in pursuit of William Everly. She stared at the scanner as if that would force it to divulge more news. When she glanced at the duty board behind Gladys and saw that Allie's name wasn't on it, some of her anxiety eased.

"That's the sheriff," Gladys said with a worried frown. "Everybody's out there. I imagine all our off duty people are headed that way too. They've all got scanners, and if they were anywhere near enough to hear that All Units call, they'll respond."

Then Allie was probably out there. Ash had seen the scanner on the kitchen counter on her way out that morning. She told herself to relax. Allie was a trained officer and good at her job. But Everly had to know he was going back to jail if apprehended, and the very nature of his original crime suggested he was unstable. Who knew what he was likely to do when cornered.

The scanner crackled and Reese's voice filled the room.

"Shots fired. Suspect is armed and dangerous. Do not approach without backup."

"Shit," Ash muttered. She ran a hand through her hair for the hundredth time that morning, but this time she wasn't frustrated or angry at herself, she was scared down to her toes. And she couldn't just stand by waiting for word. She spun around and raced for the door.

❖

"Jesus," Bri yelled when a car window ten feet from her shattered, showering glass all over the street. "That maniac is shooting at us!" She dove behind a shiny new Mercedes and peered around into the street, searching for some sign of Everly. Carter was crouched next to a dusty pickup truck just opposite her. "You okay?"

"Yes. Did you see where he went?"

"He ran behind a house up at the corner of Pilgrim." Bri's uniform shirt was stuck to her back with cold sweat. She was too pumped to be scared, but her skin was tingling like she was high, except her mind wasn't cloudy. It was crystal sharp. The whole world stood out in 3-D relief, every angle and shape shimmering, almost vibrating. God, she hoped that was normal, because she didn't want to make a mistake. Carter was depending on her. Caroline was depending on her. Reese trusted her to make the right call. She checked Carter again, and the calm resolve in Carter's eyes steadied her. Carter trusted her, she could read it in her face. And that's all it took to settle her down.

"Let's go get him, yeah?" Bri called to Carter.

"Damn right. Keep your eye out for any civilians and make sure they get to cover."

"Roger that."

Bri rose and ran. The thud of Carter's footsteps next to her was almost as good as Reese's hand on her shoulder, reminding her she was not alone.

Allie caught a flicker of movement across the street. Reese was ducking cautiously from one yard to the next, checking up and down the street and scanning driveways. Allie wanted to go with her to cover her back, but she stayed at her post. She couldn't see all the way down the street to the intersection with Bayberry, but that's where Everly had first been spotted. The shot sounded like it came from down there—where Bri and Carter were. She didn't let herself think about that. She just kept watch, waiting, preparing. Reese was out of sight now, and she suddenly felt very much alone. Every second felt like an hour. Her bare arms were covered with goose bumps even though she was sweating. Two houses up and diagonally across the street from her, a young woman with long blond hair and a short clingy dress came out her front door, beeped her car remote at a dark blue Honda Accord in the driveway, and hurried toward the driver's side door. A second later, a bearded man in a dark T-shirt and blue jeans appeared out of nowhere and sprinted across the street on an intercept course with the blonde. *Everly.* He was going to carjack the young woman. Allie didn't even question her next move. She couldn't let him take a hostage. She bolted into the street, her arms extended in front of her, her weapon two-fisted and trained on Everly.

"Stop, police! Down on the ground. Down on the ground!"

Without breaking stride, he half turned in her direction and fired.

The air around her vibrated with heat and her ears rang with the report of the shot. She couldn't return fire because now he was directly between her and the civilian. If she missed him, she could hit the woman or someone in the house. Hoping to draw his fire again, anything to distract him from the woman, who was now crouched next to her car and trying to scramble away, Allie ran toward him. Carter and Bri materialized at the end of the block and raced up the street, weapons out. Reese bolted from between two houses and grabbed the civilian, dragging the young woman behind the front of the Accord. Then Reese just stood up, tall and solid, and aimed her weapon at Everly.

"You're done, Everly," Reese shouted. "It's over, drop the weapon."

Everly's head swiveled between Allie, who was blocking the street in one direction, and Bri and Carter, who cut off his retreat in the other direction. Smith and Chang vaulted out into the street from between two houses and took up a position behind him. Reese walked forward slowly, her face completely impassive, her weapon never wavering from his center mass. After another quick look around, Everly raised his free hand, knelt, and slowly placed his weapon on the ground. Then everyone converged on him. Bri got to him first and jammed her knee into the middle of his back while she cuffed him.

Allie couldn't hear what Bri was shouting at him. She was still running, but she didn't seem able to reach them. Her weapon was shaking in her hand, but when she tried to holster it, she couldn't seem to do it. Then she saw the blood running down her left arm. That probably explained why she was moving in slow motion. In fact, she wasn't really moving at all. She was kneeling in the middle of the street. That wasn't what she wanted to do, but she was having trouble getting up.

"Officer down, officer down! Medics. We need medics, *now*," Reese shouted into her radio as she knelt next to Allie. "Take it easy, Allie. The medics will be here in a minute."

"I don't know why I'm bleeding," Allie said quietly, confused. "He didn't hit me."

Reese holstered her weapon and put an arm around Allie's shoulders. She eased Allie back against her chest and, using her fingers, pressed closed the wound in Allie's upper arm that pumped blood at a steady cadence. "Looks like he winged you. You'll be fine. Medics will be here in a second."

Allie tilted her head back on Reese's shoulder. "You have the most gorgeous eyes. I mean, like smoking sexy hot eyes."

"Thank you," Reese murmured.

"Is Bri okay?" Allie wondered why she sounded drunk.

"She's good. Everybody's good. You did fine today, Tremont."

"I didn't. I so didn't," Allie slurred. "I really fucked things up with Ash."

"You can sort that out later," Reese said.

"You think?" Allie whispered.

"Yeah, I'm sure of it. Just take it easy now."

"That's good. That's good because I really..." Allie sighed and closed her eyes. "You'll tell her, won't you?"

"You bet."

With Reese to keep her safe, Allie drifted off.

CHAPTER TWENTY-TWO

Tory heard the approaching sirens and hurried out the clinic door. When she saw Reese climb out of the patrol car ahead of the EMS vehicle in the clinic parking lot, she faltered, her legs suddenly weak. Reese's shirt was soaked with blood. "Oh my God! Reese!"

"I'm okay," Reese called, "it's Allie's. GSW—left arm."

The back doors of the EMS rig flew open and two medics jumped out with Allie on a gurney. One held an IV bag in the air as he ran alongside the stretcher.

"Vital signs?" Tory asked as she stepped aside for them to get through the clinic door.

"Pulse ninety, BP one thirty. She's in and out. Better since we got some fluid into her."

Allie turned her head and her eyes fluttered open. "I want to go home."

"Oh, I love cops," Tory muttered, assessing the bandage on Allie's arm as she followed the medics into the clinic. A three-inch splotch of bright red marked the center of the white gauze. Fresh bleeding. "Treatment room two." She glanced at Reese as they went back together. "You're all right?"

"Fine."

"Everyone else?"

"All good." Reese grasped Tory's arm to slow her down as they approached the treatment room. "I have to get to the station to take care of booking Everly. Let me know as soon as you've checked her out, okay?"

"I will. Has anyone called her mother?"

"Sorry. Not yet."

"I'll do it after I evaluate her. We may need to send her to Hyannis for a surgical evaluation."

Reese nodded, her jaw tightening. "Call me. I'll arrange an escort."

"You're sure you're all right?"

"I'd rather it was me than one of mine on that stretcher."

Tory skimmed her fingers along Reese's jaw. "I know that. So do they. And that's what matters."

Reese smiled wryly. "Thanks for the reminder."

"Happy to do it." Tory kissed her cheek. "I've got to go. I'll call you as soon as I know."

❖

Reese crossed to the small knot of officers congregated in one corner of the reception area. "She's stable. Dr. King's evaluating her now. It will be a while before we know anything, but I need volunteers to drive escort if she has to go to Hyannis."

Three men and a woman immediately stepped forward. Reese smiled. "Two of you will be enough." She pointed to two of the officers who were supposed to be off duty but who had answered the All Units call. She knew none of the officers were going to leave until Allie's condition was known. "You two, stand by."

"Yes ma'am," they said in unison.

"I'm headed back to the station. Good job today, all of you."

Ash Walker intercepted Reese just as she reached the door.

"Is it bad?" Ash asked quietly.

"I don't know," Reese said truthfully. Ash looked like hell— pale, hollow-eyed, shaky. Recalling Allie's somewhat incoherent conversation about Ash after she'd been shot, Reese surmised their relationship was in some kind of flux. She wasn't absolutely certain that Allie really wanted her to say anything to Ash, and thinking back to Allie's disjointed ramblings, she thought Allie might change her mind when she was awake. Just the same, Allie had wanted her to send *some* kind of message. "It looked to me like a flesh wound, but it was bleeding pretty good."

Ash raked a hand through her hair and cast a wild look toward the doors leading to the rear of the clinic and the treatment areas. "Jesus. I wouldn't ordinarily ask, but is there any way you can get me back there?" She let out a shaky breath and fixed Reese with tortured eyes. "I'm pretty much going crazy out here."

Reese took her arm and pulled her farther away from the officers, some of whom were regarding them quizzically. "I can't right now. Tory's working on her. You know Tory won't let anything happen to her. When Tory calls me with an update, I'll tell her that you're out here. If Allie is ready to see you and Tory clears it, I'm sure Tory will take you back."

"Okay. Yeah. I get it." Ash looked away. "I don't even have the right to be here."

"Look," Reese said quietly. "Allie wanted me to tell you that... well, I don't know what she wanted me to say, really. She was rambling a little. But she asked for you."

Ash jerked her gaze back to Reese's. "Yeah?"

"Yeah. So just try to hang in there, okay?"

"I fucked things up, Reese."

"Funny, that's exactly what Allie said." Reese squeezed Ash's arm. "Look, I've got to go. And I'm not the best person to be giving relationship advice. But if Allie's got a hold of you, inside where it counts, don't let her go easy. Not unless she tells you straight out you're done."

"Okay," Ash whispered, looking as if Reese had just thrown her a lifeline. "Okay."

❖

Ash followed Reese outside and sat down on the top step of the small landing in front of the clinic. She really needed to get some air and clear her head. Reese said it didn't look too bad. Her arm. Thank God it hadn't been a body shot. Christ, she hadn't even been wearing a vest. What was she thinking? Young and crazy and brave. Ash tried to put the thought of losing Allie out of her mind as she half focused on an EMS vehicle pulling into the gravel parking lot. At this rate, Tory was going to need more doctors to staff this place. She stiffened when the blonde from the bar—no, Allie's girlfriend, not just some bar pickup—jumped down from the driver's side and sprinted toward the clinic.

"Tory's with her now," Ash said as she shifted over to make room when the blonde vaulted up the steps. "She's stable. It's an arm wound. Not sure how bad. Everyone's waiting for word from Tory."

"Thanks." The blonde pushed open the door, perused the crowd inside, and stepped back out. She extended her hand. "I'm Flynn. We met briefly the other day, but never got introduced. You're Ash, Allie's friend."

"Yes," Ash said tightly, shaking the offered hand.

"Someone's going to let us know?"

"Tory will be out as soon as she knows anything."

"I can't believe Allie is back here again, after what happened yesterday. She was supposed to be home resting." Flynn sat down next to her. "She was really worried about you when that building collapsed. You doing okay now?"

"Nothing a few days and some aspirin won't cure. Doesn't even register compared to what Allie's going through right now." Ash wondered if Flynn was as torn up inside as she was right now—as helpless and sick at heart.

Flynn glanced back at the clinic door, looking as if she wanted to storm the place too. "Arm wound, you said?"

"That's what Reese told me. I couldn't get to her to see for myself." Ash's throat felt gravelly as she relived the panic of hearing the shot, hearing *officer down*, hearing Reese shouting for a medic. She rubbed her face. Her hands were shaking. Her whole body was trembling. "Christ. I wish Tory would tell us something. If anything happens to her, I don't know…" She clamped her jaws together, remembering who she was talking to.

"She was frantic about you yesterday. Couldn't rest until she knew you were okay." Flynn regarded Ash pensively. "There's something more than friendship going on, isn't there?"

Ash held her gaze. "I don't know. That's for Allie to say."

"You're right." Flynn paused. "We've had a couple of dates. I like her a lot."

"There's a lot to like."

"Uh-huh."

"We used to be involved," Ash said quietly. "I'm still crazy about her, but I…ah…I don't think she…" She shook her head. "I don't know anything right now."

"Well, now probably isn't the time to expect her to make choices."

"I think she already has." Ash closed her eyes, took a deep breath, then faced Flynn head-on. "But you're right, now's not the time. So I'm just going to wait, because I care about her and I can't do anything else."

"Same here."

"You want some coffee?" Ash stood up. "There's a pot going in the reception area."

Flynn rose to join her. "Yeah, I could use some. I'll come with you."

❖

"Everything okay?" Carter asked when Bri got off the phone with Caroline.

Bri slid down in her desk chair and stretched her lanky legs out in front of her. Her expression was studied casual. "Carre's good. So is Rica. Everything should get back to normal now."

"Uh-huh." Carter couldn't really disagree, even though something kept tugging at her gut. Telling her something wasn't right.

"Everly says it wasn't him, you know," Bri said. "At our house last night. He says he never followed Caroline. Never went near her."

"I heard him." Carter shrugged. "You didn't really expect him to confess, did you?"

"I don't know. He seems pretty much the same as he was back in school. He called me a fucking dyke. Told me if he'd had a shot at Carre, she'd never be with me." Bri's blue eyes turned winter cold. "If he'd gone after her again yesterday, I think he would have wanted to taunt me with it. Maybe get me to take a shot at him."

"Yeah. I heard him baiting you." Carter had seen Bri practically vibrating with rage when she was escorting Everly to the cruiser. Everly had been going on about how if he'd had a chance to fuck Caroline, Caroline would never have turned out to be a pervert. She had to give Bri credit for keeping her temper. She wasn't sure she could've done the same if someone had been talking about Rica that way. "You handled yourself fine out there."

"I wanted to kill him."

"I don't blame you."

"I'm not just saying that. I really really wanted to do it. He was talking about *raping* my girlfriend." Bri looked hard at Carter. "You don't think that's bad, me feeling that way and being a cop?"

"You're a human being first," Carter said gently. "Family comes before everything, and you protected your family today. What you're feeling—I'd be feeling the same. *Exactly* the same."

"Thanks," Bri whispered.

Reese returned from the holding area and motioned them toward her office. When they were inside, she closed the door.

"Any word on Allie?" Bri asked immediately.

"Not yet," Reese said.

"What about the scumbag who shot her?" Carter added.

"The state boys are on their way down to pick him up. His parole violation is small time now. He shot a cop. He's going away for a long time."

"What's your take on his claim he didn't try to break into our place last night?" Bri asked.

"He swears he was with Randy Thompson, his old football buddy, all night." Reese shrugged. "Thompson corroborates it, but I don't put a lot of stock in his word."

"There's still the issue of the dead FBI agent," Carter said. "Do you see any way he'd be involved in that?"

"I can't see him for that," Reese said. "The feds would have no reason to be looking for him. And he would have no reason to take out a federal agent. It doesn't play."

"What about the break-ins at your place and mine? And Rica's car?" Carter added.

"Everly admits to being in town for the last three days, so the timeline works for him being good for all of them. Of course, he denies that he did anything other than hide out at his buddy's place." Reese rested her hip against her desk and thought back over the sequence of events—the intruder at her home, Rica's car being vandalized, the burglary at Rica and Carter's, the attempted break-in at Caroline and Bri's. Everly was directly tied to her and Bri and Caroline, and Rica was Caroline's close friend. In a town this small it wasn't difficult to track anyone's movements, and Everly could easily have seen Caroline with Rica. Perps didn't always follow a logic that made sense to others, and a pretty solid case could be made for him being responsible for everything. It was tempting to tie it all up in a neat package because more often than not, the simplest explanation was the right one. William Everly, like so many criminals, was not particularly smart, and with the instincts of a homing pigeon, he'd simply returned to familiar ground. Once here, he'd wanted to exact a little revenge on the people who had sent him to prison and those close to them. And most of all, he'd wanted another chance to prove to Caroline Clarke that all she needed was a good man.

"We're not going to be able to prove it was him," Reese finally said. "One thing that bothers me is that Everly is a hometown boy. My house is all the way out at the East End, your place is at the far West End, and Caroline and Bri's is right in the middle. He had to cover a lot of distance getting from one place to the other, and we've been asking about him around town for several days. But no one has admitted seeing him anywhere."

"Yeah," Carter said broodingly. "I don't like that much myself."

Bri looked from Carter to Reese. "Why would anyone except Everly go after Caroline?"

"I don't know." Reese blew out a breath. "And we've still got the murdered FBI agent, who doesn't seem related to any of it." She glanced at Carter. "I think we need to have a sit-down with Supervisory Special Agent Allen, don't you?"

"Unfortunately, I agree." Carter grimaced. "I've got history with her, and I think she's still got an ax to grind with Rica. Maybe I can piss her off enough that she'll actually tell us something useful."

"Give it your best shot," Reese said with a wry grin. "In the meantime, make sure everyone keeps their eyes open. Just in case we've missed something."

❖

He wasn't sure what was happening at the far end of town, but he'd heard sirens racing back and forth for close to an hour. All the extra police activity on the streets suddenly disappeared, and he took that as a sign to make his move. He had gotten used to working at night, but he didn't want to wait until nightfall. He'd been waiting for so long already. He kept thinking back to the night before, to the surge of excitement when the knife had parted flesh, to the rush of blood in his head and his groin. He craved the sensation. Nightfall wasn't for hours, and he needed to satisfy his craving now. He felt for the knife in his pants pocket, and let his fingers drift over its smooth surface onto the hard ridge of his cock. She'd be alone now. And all his.

CHAPTER TWENTY-THREE

"I really don't want to go to Hyannis," Allie pleaded. "Look, it isn't even bleeding anymore. The x-rays are okay, right?"

Tory smiled indulgently as she wrapped Allie's upper arm with a clean dressing. "You've had a little Demerol, sweetie. You're not totally capable of making a rational decision right now."

"Nobody has the time to cart me all the way up there. And believe me, the Demerol is totally busy working as a painkiller. I don't feel high at all."

"Are you hurting a lot?" Tory asked gently.

"I think I'm supposed to be tough and say it doesn't hurt much," Allie said with a shaky laugh. "But it really really hurts. Like, I don't think I want to get shot again. Ever."

Tory stroked her hair. "I hope you never do either." She pulled over one of the stainless steel stools and sat down next to the stretcher. "I think you were very very lucky and the bullet went through your triceps and missed the bone and all the major arteries and nerves."

Allie brightened. "Which means I can go home and I'll be good as new in a few days, right?"

"Not exactly," Tory said with another slight smile. "There are a lot of important structures in your upper arm, and you were bleeding heavily when you came in. There's only so much I can do to evaluate what's going on inside without actually opening up the wound and examining it internally."

"Like an operation."

"Exactly. But operations can damage tissue, and we don't like to do them unless they're absolutely necessary. How about we compromise."

Tory checked her watch. "You stay here for another four hours. If there's no further bleeding and no change in your neuro exam—the feeling and movement in your hand—I'll let you go home with someone who can watch you."

"Okay. Yes. Perfect." Allie started to sit up, but Tory pressed a hand against her shoulder.

"That means four hours of lying still, sleeping if you can," Tory admonished.

"I need to talk to my mother. Let her know I'm all right."

"I'll get your cell phone." Tory gestured to the hallway. "A lot of your friends are outside. I'll let them know that you're doing all right."

"Thanks."

"Allie, is there someone you want to see? You can have visitors back here, I just don't want a crowd. You really do need to rest."

Allie looked away for the first time. "Is Reese here?"

"She was, but she had to go back to the station to take care of the arrest procedure. I just called her a few minutes ago to let her know that you're doing all right. She said she'll be by later. Bri will be here too, as soon as she can."

"That's cool. That's good."

"Reese mentioned Ash is waiting outside, and she's pretty worried about you." Tory didn't want anything to upset her patient right now, but she couldn't keep things from her either. "Flynn has been asking for you too."

"Flynn's here?" Allie asked quickly.

"Mmm-hmm."

"Will you ask her to come back?"

Tory nodded. "Of course. I'll get her."

❖

Ash sat for a while after Flynn went inside, waiting for the strength to return to her legs and for the sharp, bright pain that lacerated her heart to lessen enough for her to walk away. Allie had asked for Flynn. She shouldn't have expected anything different. Allie had told her, more than once, that she had a girlfriend and was happy with her. Flynn was decent and cared about Allie. That was easy to see. So Ash finally had her answer and she wasn't really surprised. She hadn't trusted Allie when it mattered, and nothing killed love faster than distrust. Her greatest regret was not telling Allie how much she loved her, and how very much she needed and wanted her. Ash grasped the handrail and pulled herself to her feet, feeling inconsequential in the still, dusty air. After taking a few shaky breaths, she walked down the stairs and across the parking lot to her vehicle. Her mind was sluggish, her movements hesitant and uncoordinated as she searched for her keys. The days and weeks of forgotten meals, late-night binges, and transitory hookups were finally catching up to her. She climbed behind the wheel and after a few tries, got her key in the ignition.

"Ash! Ash, wait!" Flynn jogged down the steps from the clinic and over to the car. She braced the vehicle door open with her arm. "She wants to see you."

Ash shook her head. She was done. She didn't have anything left, not even anger. "I'll stop by and see her tomorrow. Tell her I said I hope she's feeling better."

Flynn leaned farther inside, blocking Ash from turning the wheel, and waited until Ash looked at her. Flynn's eyes were oddly soft and tender. "Allie is hurt and she wants to see you. Forget the past, forget your pride. Do right by her."

"Do right by her," Ash whispered, gripping the steering wheel like it was the only thing keeping her tethered to the earth. *Do right by her.* What did that mean? She'd told herself she was doing right by Allie in refusing to tie her down, to box her in, to limit her choices. She'd thought she was making a sacrifice, being noble. But she hadn't done it for Allie, she'd done it for herself. *Do right by her.* She looked at Flynn, desperately needing guidance. "How?"

Flynn's voice was gentle, filled with compassion, and unexpectedly encouraging. "I think you've already figured that out. Now let *her* know."

Ash wasn't so sure, but she slid out from behind the wheel and closed the door. "Thanks."

"You're welcome," Flynn said.

Ash started toward the building, then looked back. "You coming in?"

"In a few minutes," Flynn said. "You go ahead."

Ash waited, but Flynn walked over to the EMT van, sat down on the wide rear step, and closed her eyes. When Ash entered the clinic, Tory was talking on the phone behind the high counter in the reception area.

"Allie asked to see me," Ash said.

Tory gestured to the hallway behind her. "Treatment room two. She's tired. Don't stay too long."

"Is she all right?" Ash asked.

"She's stable, but she really needs to rest."

"Okay. Thanks." Ash hurried down the hall, then hesitated in front of the door. *Do right by her.* She knocked and stepped into the room. The head of the stretcher had been propped up to forty-five degrees, and Allie lay covered by a sheet, her shoulders bare, her eyes closed. She was very pale. Her skin, framed by her dark hair, was nearly translucent. She appeared fragile and ethereal, and Ash's heart twisted at the thought of how very close she had come to losing her. Right at that moment, all that mattered to her was that Allie was safe. The world without her would be a far darker place. Crossing as quietly as she could, Ash stopped by the side of the stretcher and clasped Allie's hand. She leaned forward to kiss Allie's forehead and stopped when Allie's eyes flickered open. Her deep brown eyes were slightly unfocused, but still endlessly beautiful.

"I didn't mean to wake you," Ash whispered.

"Hi, baby," Allie murmured. "I didn't mean to fall asleep."

"Close your eyes again." Ash brushed her lips over Allie's cheek. "Tory wants you to rest."

"She said I can go home soon."

Ash wasn't so certain that was a good idea, but she wasn't going to argue. "That's good. How are you feeling?"

"Loopy. Arm hurts." Allie slipped her hand from Ash's grasp and rested her palm against Ash's cheek. "I think I'm still mad at you."

"That's all right. I don't blame you." Ash's throat was so tight she could barely talk. She wanted to climb onto the stretcher and pull Allie into her arms. She wanted the bullet to have pierced her flesh, not Allie's. She wanted to erase the pain she'd seen in Allie's eyes that morning, the pain she'd put there. She wanted to go back and do everything over again, but she knew she couldn't. Sometimes there were no second chances. "Do you need anything?"

"I do," Allie whispered, clearly starting to drift. Her fingers fluttered against Ash's cheek and then her hand fell away, leaving Ash bereft. "I need…"

Ash swallowed her pride, buried her pain. "Do you want me to get Flynn?"

Allie's eyes opened wider, and a small frown formed between her brows. "I can't tell what it means when you look at me like that—with your eyes so shadowy and dark. Tell me."

"I feel…" Ash lost her voice and struggled to contain the tears that suddenly flooded her eyes. She turned her head and wiped her face quickly against her shirtsleeve. She lifted Allie's hand and kissed the back of her fingers. "I look at you and I want to laugh out loud I'm so happy you're part of my life. I look at you and I'm excited to be alive. I want to rush forward into a day, into a *lifetime*, filled with possibility. I look at you and I feel like I could do anything." She leaned down and kissed Allie gently. "I feel so damn lucky to have ever touched you, to have ever been touched by you. I cherish every second we shared. If I could have one wish, I'd wish to be with you forever. I love you. I love you so much."

"You know what I wish?"

"What, babe?" Ash asked, no longer trying to stem the tears that streaked her cheeks.

"I wish you would take me home and hold me tonight. And that in the morning you wouldn't say good-bye."

"I can do that," Ash whispered.

"Every night?"

"Every single one."

"I wanted to stop loving you," Allie murmured, "but I couldn't."

"Neither could I." Ash settled onto the stool, leaned her forehead against Allie's shoulder, and slipped her arm gently around Allie's waist. "And I never will."

"I told Flynn I couldn't date her anymore."

"You did?"

"Mmm-hmm." Allie played her fingers through Ash's hair.

"How come?"

"'Cause I really like her and my heart isn't available." Allie pulled on Ash's hair until Ash looked up. "I was so mad at you this morning—you were such an ass, deciding what I needed and what I would do. All on your own."

"I know."

"But after you left I thought about all the other things you said—about falling for me, and being scared. You never said those things to me before." Allie's eyes turned liquid. "I knew then you really loved me. And I still loved you."

"I do." Ash's heart did a slow roll. She was almost afraid to be so happy. Almost. "What did Flynn say?"

"She didn't seem surprised," Allie said softly. "I think she was maybe a little sad, but she won't be alone long. She's...um..."

"Pretty special," Ash said.

"Yeah. Gorgeous too."

Ash laughed. "Not my type."

Allie scowled. "You don't have a type anymore, remember?"

"Oh, I remember." Ash kissed Allie's cheek. "I love you."

"You said that already."

"Can I say it again?"

Allie nodded. "As much as you want."

"I want *you* a lot," Ash whispered.

"That's good. 'Cause you have a lot of lost time to make up for."

Ash smiled, listening to Allie's breathing grow softer and slower as she finally gave in to exhaustion and slept. Ash was content just to sit by her bedside. She couldn't go back, she couldn't undo the mistakes she'd made and the pain she'd caused. But she was home in Allie's arms again, and she'd do right by her this time. She'd love her the very best way she could.

No police cars. No foot patrol. No one watching at all. He stepped confidently onto the flagstone walkway and walked purposefully, but unhurriedly, to the door. He knocked and heard the familiar voice call "just a minute." Stepping carefully to one side so that his face wouldn't be visible to anyone looking out through the window in the upper portion of the door, he drew the knife from his pocket and flipped it open. He had a fifty-fifty chance that she would open the door without asking him to identify himself. Somehow, people were far less cautious in the middle of a bright sunny afternoon. They often opened the door without thinking, especially when they weren't expecting any kind of trouble. And after all, why should she be afraid? She had no idea what was coming. He wasn't disappointed. The door opened a few inches, she said, "yes?" and before she could react to his face, it was already too late.

She had a gun, but she had barely begun to raise it when he pushed the door wide, forced his way into the room, and buried the knife to the hilt between her breasts. Her eyes widened in shock and surprise, and as her deliciously warm blood cascaded over his hand, he smiled and whispered hello.

CHAPTER TWENTY-FOUR

Carter pulled the cruiser off the road onto the shoulder and radioed her location. She sat for a minute letting the warm afternoon breeze wash away some of the tension of the last few hours. When she'd realized how close Everly was to her house, to Rica, she'd had to exert every bit of her willpower to stay out on the street and do her job when what she wanted was to be by Rica's side, protecting her. As it turned out, Rica had never been a target. Feeling the dread lift from her shoulders, she stretched and got out of the cruiser, leaving the windows down to capture the last bit of afternoon heat in the stale interior. The radio chattered at her back as she walked up the path.

As she drew closer, she saw the door ajar. In an instant, her brief interlude of comfort was shattered and alarm bells rang. She jogged forward, her hand on the grip of her weapon. When she reached the door, she pushed it open carefully, squinting into the gloom. For half a second, her mind refused to register the sight of the body on the floor, and she stood frozen with the sun on her back and hell at her feet.

"Oh Jesus." Carter pulled her weapon and quickly scanned the room. No movement, no sound. She shouted into her shoulder mic, "Code eight. Officer down. *Officer down.*"

Then she dropped to her knees and pressed both hands over the red fountain that pumped and splashed into the widening pool on the floor.

"Hold on, hold on," Carter extolled desperately. How could there be so much blood on the floor and still so much gushing out? She heard a moan and looked up into terrified eyes. Bloodless lips, so pale they verged on blue, formed words she couldn't hear. She leaned down closer, never taking her eyes away from those dark wounded ones. "I'm here. I'm right here."

"…n…go."

"No, no, I won't," Carter half shouted, hearing the fear in her voice and trying to contain it. "I won't leave. Stay with me. I'm right here. I'm not leaving you, so you stay here. You hear me, Allen? *Marilyn*, goddamn it. You *stay* here."

Carter's hands were sticky with blood and it kept coming. But not as fast now. She didn't know if that was good or not. Jesus, God, where were the medics? Her arms shook, her vision dimmed, and sweat burned her eyes. *Please, someone, please.*

Sirens. Footsteps. Shouts. She couldn't move. If she moved, the fountain would gush again. She had to hold it in. Had to.

"Officer," Flynn shouted in her ear. "We've got her. Move. Let us take care of her."

An arm gripped her shoulder, pulled her back, and she lurched to her feet. Her legs were wooden, numb, and she stumbled, falling.

"Carter!" Bri grabbed her around the waist. "Carter, you hurt?"

"No," Carter gasped.

"Okay. We've got this. Come outside."

Carter blinked, trying to focus on Bri's face. "I can't. I told her I would stay."

"It's okay. We won't go far."

"I didn't clear the other rooms…I forgot…" Carter raised her hand to wipe the sweat from her face and Bri grabbed her arm, preventing her. Carter stared at a hand she didn't recognize, covered in blood. Her hand. "Oh Jesus, Bri."

Bri half dragged Carter over to a low stone wall and pushed her down onto it. "Stay here. Catch your breath. I need to check with Reese. I'll be right back."

"Okay." Carter nodded, still stunned. No amount of training could prepare someone for the sight of a fellow officer down in the line. If only she hadn't taken that extra minute to let the breeze play over her face and chase some of her ghosts away. Now she'd have new nightmares to take their place.

❖

The phone on Tory's desk rang and for half a second, she contemplated not answering it. She didn't want to hear about one more problem. Nita had come in early for her evening shift and together they had managed to clear most of the patients who had gotten backed up when Tory had been diverted by Allie's arrival. Now there was actually a chance that she would be able to get home in time to feed Reggie dinner and give her a bath. She couldn't think of a single thing she wanted to do more than that. The harsh shrill of the phone's insistent ringing interrupted her reverie, and with a sigh, she picked it up.

"This is Dr. King," Tory said.

"This is Flynn, Dr. King. We've got a stab wound to the chest in full arrest. ETA four minutes."

Tory straightened. "What's the situation?"

"Female, approximately thirty-five years old. No pulse, no BP. Massive blood loss. We intubated in the field and started CPR."

Tory could hear the siren now. "Bring her straight back. We'll be ready." Her fatigue dropped away as she stood and hurried into the hall. She rapped on the closed door where Nita was seeing a patient and pushed it open a few inches. "Nita, I'm sorry, I need you. An emergency coming in."

Nita's expression echoed what Tory was feeling. Déjà vu. Madness in the air. Tory let the door close and pivoted toward the last empty treatment room. Allie was still under observation in the other one. The double doors at the end of the hall opened and a tall, dark-haired woman in jeans, boots, and a blue blazer covering a navy scrub shirt walked through.

"Oh my God, I am so glad to see you," Tory exclaimed.

"Hi, beautiful," Dr. KT O'Bannon said with her trademark grin. "Miss me?"

"You have no idea. What are you doing here?"

"Reese called me a couple of hours ago and said you were swamped over here. I figured I needed a little easy work and caught one of the puddle jumpers over from Boston."

Tory didn't even have time to consider why Reese had called KT, a trauma surgeon and long-ago lover of Tory's. She was just glad she had. "We've got a stab wound arriving any second in full arrest."

KT's grin never wavered but her eyes took on the intensity Tory recognized. KT was ferocious when faced with a life-and-death challenge. There was no doctor she trusted more, and very few people she loved more.

"Guess I got my wish for something simple," KT said as she flicked a lock of dark hair out of her eyes and pulled off her blazer. "Just like old times."

❖

Carter didn't know what to do about the blood on her hands. As it dried, the crimson turned a dull, lusterless brown, caked and cracked like barren earth devoid of life. A figure blocked the sun and she squinted up, recognizing Reese's broad shoulders and tapering torso.

"Any word?" Carter asked.

Reese sat down on the wall next to her. "KT and Tory stabilized her—the helicopter should be here any minute to take her to Boston."

"What are her chances?"

"I don't know. It looked bad to me."

"I must have just missed him," Carter said hollowly. "One minute earlier and I might've saved her."

"One minute earlier and he might have cut her throat. Or yours," Reese said. "There was another door on the far side of her suite. He went out that way. So far, we don't have any witnesses."

"She was terrified," Carter said softly. "She knew I didn't like her, and I was all she had. I tried. I really tried."

"I'm sure Marilyn knows that."

Carter jumped up, suddenly too agitated to sit still. "What the fuck! What the fuck is going on here, Reese? Two federal agents down in two days? Jesus, what were the feds into over here?"

Reese shook her head angrily. "I don't know, but I intend to find out. Marilyn only brought one other agent with her and he's riding back to Boston with her on the medevac chopper. I doubt he would have told us anything even if I questioned him."

"I've still got contacts with the troopers who liaise with the feds. I'll make some calls. My old partner might know something." Carter knew the feds would not cut them in on the operation, especially not now when something had obviously gone very wrong. This chaos had all the markings of an investigation that had gone south, and the FBI did not acknowledge mistakes like that. None of the federal agencies did—especially not to the locals.

"Good. Check with your contacts. I'll be pounding on some doors too, for all the good it will do." Reese rose and signaled Bri to join them. "Bri, drive Carter home. Carter, go shower and change. Get something to eat. Take a few hours' downtime. Then I—"

"I'm okay," Carter insisted. "I'll change and head back to the station."

"We've still got interviews to finish out here," Reese said evenly. "I want you to take a few personal hours."

Carter gritted her teeth but nodded in acceptance of the order.

Reese put both hands on her hips and surveyed the bedlam in the courtyard of the Driftwood Inn—officers milled about, searching for evidence, documenting the scene, interviewing guests and potential witnesses. Detritus left behind by the hasty departure of the EMTs littered the ground. A battlefield. And she was losing. "We've got a long night ahead of us. I'm tired of coming in last because I don't know the terrain or the enemy. That's going to change, as of now."

❖

Tory removed her bloodstained shirt and bra and rolled them up to take home and launder. She opened her locker, tucked into the corner of the clinic staff lounge, and searched the top shelf for a clean scrub shirt. When the door opened and closed behind her, she said without turning around, "You were great, as usual. I don't know what I would have done without you."

"I take it KT arrived," Reese said.

Tory spun around, her scrub shirt in her hand. "Darling! What are you doing here?"

"I came to take you home." At Tory's perplexed expression, Reese took the shirt from her hands, shook it out, and held it above Tory's head. "Arms up."

Smiling wryly, Tory obeyed and Reese pulled her shirt down over her arms and head. Then she smoothed her broad palms over Tory's shoulders and down her arms before leaning forward to kiss her. Reese felt solid and warm, and as Tory relaxed into her embrace, the empty aching places inside her calmed. "You must have a million things to do. How did you get away?"

"It helps to be the boss," Reese murmured, rubbing Tory's back. "I took an hour to get you and Reggie and take you home. You've been here long enough today."

Tory sighed and shook her head. "I can't leave right—"

"Yes, you can. I just told KT you were leaving." Reese shrugged. "She said no problem, she had it covered."

"She would." Tory rolled her eyes. "Have you ever known her *not* to think she could handle anything?"

"Nope. That's why I called her." Reese released Tory and gestured to the open locker. "Did you get everything you need out of there?"

"You know that this is highly irregular."

Reese grinned. "You mean I can't make a habit of manhandling you?"

"I wouldn't put it exactly that way, but basically, yes."

"You could think of it as practice," Reese suggested agreeably.

Tory frowned. "Practice for what?"

"Being pregnant again."

"Sweetheart, that's blackmail."

"Might be. But I don't really care." Reese reached around Tory, closed the locker door, and took another step closer, corralling Tory against the lockers with an arm on either side of Tory's shoulders. "If Wendy says it's safe for you to be pregnant again, I'd like for us to have another baby. But there have to be some ground rules."

"Ground rules," Tory said softly. Reese was so close, looming over her, her eyes intent and unblinking. Tory knew Reese's body better than that of any person on earth. She knew her voice, her scent, the sound of her breathing in the dark. She knew her so well that sometimes she forgot how strong she was, how lethally powerful. Reese was more than a Marine, more than a cop. She was a warrior at her core, and just at that moment, Tory understood completely how men and women would follow her anywhere, into battle, into death and beyond.

Reese nodded slowly, her gaze so fierce Tory quickened deep inside.

"You come first," Reese said, her voice low and steady. "You and the baby come first—before your patients, before your colleagues, before even me and Reggie. I've got the Reggie show down pretty good now. We'll be fine while you concentrate on keeping yourself and the baby healthy."

Tory smoothed her hands over Reese's chest, then gripped her shoulders and pulled her closer, so their bodies touched. She forgot the stress and horror of the last few minutes when death hovered just over her shoulder, mocking her for her inadequacies. She forgot the fear of being too late, of being able to do too little. She forgot every demand on her heart and her time and her energy except one. Except the one critical force that guided her life. "Take me home. I need you."

Reese's mouth came down hard over hers, pulling the breath from her body, pulling her blood like the moon draws the tide, surging, crashing, roiling with wild ecstasy. She moaned and arched into Reese.

Reese released her mouth and rasped, "Does the door lock?"

"No." Tory laughed shakily and Reese grinned.

"Then we really need to go." Reese rolled up her sleeve, released the Velcro strap, and removed the monitor from around her biceps. "I don't need this. I just need your promise."

"Oh, darling. You have it. Always." Tory kissed her softly. "You can trust me. I am forever yours."

CHAPTER TWENTY-FIVE

Carter braced her arms against the shower wall and let the hot water drum on her neck and back. Steam rose to fill the enclosure, blurring the room beyond the glass door. She wished her mind would fog over as easily. She couldn't get the terrified look in Marilyn's eyes out of her mind. The agent must have known she was dying and that Carter was all the hope she had. Every cop lived with the possibility of a bullet or a blade waiting for them in a dark alley or a deserted hallway. In order to do the job, they locked the picture away, down deep inside. Carter had never had a partner or even a colleague mortally wounded in the line of duty. She knew for certain she never wanted to see that look in Bri's, or Reese's, or any of her fellow officers' eyes.

"Baby," Rica called softly from outside the shower, "are you okay?"

"Yeah. Be right out." Carter straightened and shoved the images back down where they belonged. When she was sure she had a handle on things, she twisted the knobs and stepped out of the shower.

Rica held up a large towel and wrapped it around Carter's shoulders. "You were in there a long time."

"Sorry," Carter murmured.

"For what?"

"Just…" Carter shook her head.

"It's all right. You don't have to say anything," Rica said gently. When Carter had come home, her uniform splattered with blood, her eyes blank and her expression carefully neutral, Rica hadn't asked what had happened. She'd just kissed her and asked her if she needed anything. Carter had said a shower, and immediately disappeared into the bathroom. As the minutes passed, Rica had grown more and more uneasy, and finally realized that whatever had happened, Carter shouldn't be alone with it. Now she grabbed another towel, handed it to Carter to dry her hair, and started to blot the water from Carter's body. When she bent to towel off Carter's legs, she felt Carter's fingers in her hair. Stroking, trembling. She rose and rested both hands on Carter's shoulders. "What happened?"

"Marilyn Allen was stabbed today," Carter said. "I found her. She might not make it."

Rica's stomach clutched. Three law enforcement officers injured in two days. "Is everyone else all right?"

"Yeah. Whoever did it was already gone—or heard me coming and took off." Carter briskly rubbed her hair and draped the damp towel on one of the hooks next to the shower.

"I hate her for what she did to you," Rica said, "but I would never wish anything like this on her."

Carter slid her arms around Rica's waist. "None of that mattered to me when I found her." She closed her eyes. "There was so much blood and I couldn't stop it. She had to know how bad things were. I hope she knew I wanted her to live, with everything that was in me."

"Oh baby," Rica murmured, stroking Carter's face. "If she was aware at all, she had to know. She might have had it in for you because of me and my family, but she knows what kind of cop you are."

"I hope so." Carter pressed a kiss into Rica's palm and shook her head when Rica handed her the sweatpants and T-shirt she'd brought in with her. "I need to get dressed. I have to go back to work."

"Now? You were up all night."

"I'm okay. None of us are going to be sleeping much until we get a handle on what's going on." Carter clasped Rica's hand and led her down the hall to the bedroom. "We've got a cop killer out there, and we're way behind the curve in this investigation."

Rica sat on the side of the bed and watched Carter pull a polo shirt and jeans out of the closet. "Do you think it's something personal— with Marilyn and the other agent? Payback of some kind?"

Carter tucked her shirt in and buttoned up her fly. "What do you mean?"

"Two federal agents in two days? Where's the gain? Anyone would know that kind of assault only brings dozens more agents into the picture. Why risk that kind of attention unless you're sending a message?"

Sending a message. Interesting phrase. Carter never forgot who Rica was, but sometimes she forgot that Rica had been groomed since childhood to assume her father's business. Rica might have turned her back on her father's legacy, but she couldn't undo the instincts he had instilled in her. And she was right. Marilyn Allen had been investigating the organized crime syndicate for months, probably years, and her quarry had to know that. The last thing anyone in the syndicate wanted was more federal eyes on them. And if the attacks on Marilyn Allen and her agent weren't mob related, then what the hell were they? "You've got a point."

"What is she doing here, Carter? Do you think it's me?"

"If she's still interested in you," Carter said, "and I'm not saying she isn't, I'd think the last place she'd want to be is here. Why telegraph her intentions?"

Rica rose and walked to the double glass doors that led out to the bedroom balcony. "Do you think one of her agents had something to do with my car?" She spun around, her arms folded beneath her breasts as if warding off the chill. "And the break-in here at the house?"

Carter strode to Rica and pulled her into her arms. "No. If they wanted to plant a bug or a camera in the house or the car, they wouldn't make it obvious. They wouldn't break the car window. They might be heavy-handed, but they're not that dumb."

"You're right." Rica laid her head against Carter's shoulder. "Just the same, I'm going to call my father. He might know something. Are you all right with that?"

"There's nothing you can tell him that he probably won't already know by the time you talk to him. The feds will try to cover this up, but you can bet he's got eyes and ears on them, just as they do on him." She tilted Rica's face up and kissed her. "But I'd rather you not get involved. It's not about not trusting you. It's about wanting to keep you far away from this."

"I would never do anything to compromise you professionally," Rica said. "Or put you in any kind of danger. But he's still my father.

If his *business* dealings eventually land him in legal difficulties, that's one thing. But these attacks—they're crazy. I don't want him to be ambushed, Carter."

"I know. Which is why if you do talk to him, it's okay. Like I said, there's no way to keep any of this quiet."

"Caroline went home after Bri called and said Everly had been picked up. Do you think she'll be all right by herself?"

"Everly says he wasn't the one who tried to break into her apartment, but he's the most likely suspect." Carter kissed her again, then went back to the dresser to gather her badge and gun. "I can't see any reason why she should be a target now."

"When will you be home?"

"I don't know. I'm going to arrange a meet with Kevin tonight. See if I can get some information on the feds through the back door."

"Will he talk to you?" Rica asked, referring to Kevin Shaughnessy, Carter's old partner in the state police. Kevin had been one of the few people who had stood up for Carter when Marilyn Allen had accused Carter of changing sides and joining the mob. Still, Rica knew that Carter's association with her, and by extension, with her father, had seriously strained all Carter's relationships with her former law enforcement colleagues.

"I don't know," Carter said quietly. "I don't want to jam him up, so if he turns me down, I won't push."

"You'll be careful, won't you?" Rica knew it was a senseless question, because Carter would do whatever her duty required. But she had to say it. On some irrational level, she believed that by wishing Carter to be safe, to be careful, she could help make it come true. A wave of foreboding washed through her, and she put her arms around Carter's neck, holding on to her tightly. "I love you. Please be careful."

"I will. I promise." Carter kissed her. "I love you too. I'll be home soon."

Rica walked her to the door, then turned back to the silent house and the long night ahead.

❖

Reese hung up the phone and swiveled on the stool at the breakfast bar to watch Tory finish reading a story to Reggie. Reggie had a favorite book now, one with a plethora of farm animals and buttons that she could push to make the book crow, or moo, or oink. When Tory got to the end, Reggie bounced on her lap and said *story* in a clear and demanding voice while banging on the cover. Reese laughed.

"Want me to take a turn?"

Tory raised an eyebrow. "I'd love it, but don't you have to go back to work?"

"That was Carter. She's got a meet set up with Kevin Shaughnessy in Yarmouth tonight. If she gets any kind of lead, we're going to want to move on it. Until then, we're in a holding pattern. I can't get anything about Marilyn or what she and her team were doing here from the FBI. Maybe in the morning I'll be able to call in some favors."

"I'll never understand why different branches of law enforcement can't get along. It doesn't make any sense. You're on the same side."

Reese joined Tory on the couch and lifted Reggie into her lap. "We would be on the same side, if upholding the law were our only goal. But law enforcement is politics too. And these days, it's also bureaucracy. If I knock on the right doors, I might get someone to talk to me. Right now, everyone is playing deaf, dumb, and blind."

"And if Marilyn Allen dies?" Tory asked quietly.

"We'll be in the midst of a deep freeze that won't thaw this century." Reese slid her arm around Tory's shoulders and pulled her close. "How about I give Reggie a bath and put her to bed before I read her the story. You might want to take a little nap while I do that."

Tory circled her palm over Reese's stomach, murmuring appreciatively when Reese sucked in a breath and her muscles tightened. "You have something in mind?"

"Several somethings," Reese whispered in Tory's ear. "Several times."

"Maybe we should put the monitor back on you if you're going to get fancy."

"It won't show anything. Nothing triggered out there today when we apprehended Everly."

"I know." Tory nipped at the edge of Reese's jaw. "When I heard what had happened, I asked Nita to check the telemetry readouts that downloaded to her computer. If I didn't know any better, and only had your pulse and blood pressure readings to go by, I would have thought you were sitting at your desk filling out reports."

"I won't pretend you don't make my heart race," Reese said with a grin, "but you haven't given me a panic attack. Yet."

"Is that what you think you experienced?" Tory leaned back to study her intently. "Panic attacks?"

"That may not be the right medical term for it, but I think so, yes." Reese rescued her tie from Reggie's clutches and handed her a toy to divert her for a few minutes. "I think I got what happened over there, losing some of my troops, mixed up with losing you. I just have to remind myself that the two are different." She tightened her hold on Tory and kissed her on the mouth, a long, slow, possessive kiss. "You're here and you're mine and I won't lose you."

"Oh God, Reese," Tory whispered. "I need you and those several things you have planned. Soon."

Reese got a hot, demanding glint in her eyes. "I'll meet you in our room in thirty minutes. Go close your eyes." She skimmed her mouth over Tory's ear. "If you can't sleep, you can start without me. Just don't finish without me."

Tory's lips parted and her eyes grew glassy. "I'll wait. I'll wait, but God, hurry."

Reese stood and settled Reggie on her shoulder. "Come on, Champ, time for bed."

Tory watched them until they disappeared out of sight upstairs. Then she closed her eyes and waited for her breathing to settle. Thirty minutes had never sounded so long.

❖

From the shadows just beyond the circle of light emanating from the window, he watched the woman on the sofa. He knew she would fight him, even with a knife at her throat. When he pinned her down, she would struggle. He would have to hurt her, cut her just a little, to prove he was in charge. His gaze drifted over her breasts and he imagined them pressed against his chest, imagined himself between her legs. He wondered what it would take to put that look in her eyes, the look that Marilyn Allen had had in hers when the knife struck home. He needed to put that look in *her* eyes, and he was done waiting.

CHAPTER TWENTY-SIX

Carter pulled off Route 6 and into the parking lot of the Seaside Diner a few minutes before ten p.m. The parking lot was full, as were most of the counter stools and booths when she walked in. The place smelled like fish and chips and a mouthwatering hint of hot apple pie. She scanned the length of the long narrow room and caught sight of a broad-shouldered redhead whose close-cropped hair was sprinkled with gray sitting in a far booth. She made her way down the aisle, dodging waitresses and customers, until she could slide in across from her old partner, Kevin Shaughnessy. When she'd been undercover, Kevin had been her contact in the state investigator's office, feeding her information, relaying her verbal reports, and pretty much keeping her tethered to the real world when there were times she thought she might go under from the pressure of maintaining all the lies in her life. Ten years her senior, Kevin hid a sharp intelligence and fierce loyalty to the badge behind his florid, open face. She trusted him and hoped he still trusted her, even though she'd walked away from her career and the battle they had fought side by side for more than a decade.

"Hi, Kev." She signaled to the waitress for a coffee. "Thanks for making the trip."

"I figured since you called, it must be important," he said while forking up a bite of apple pie. He made the word *called* sound like an insult.

Carter felt herself blush. She hadn't kept in contact with him even though they'd been more than partners. They'd been friends. She hadn't thought it would do Kevin's reputation in the department any good if people thought they were still tight. Plenty of her former colleagues believed that her involvement with Rica, the daughter of a mob boss, meant that she was on Alfonse Pareto's payroll now. She also knew if she tried to explain that to Kevin, he'd blow her off. So she'd just stayed away.

"So you're back policing," Kevin said when the silence stretched between them.

"Couple of days—I guess you must know that's why I'm here."

"You need something."

"Damn it, Kevin," Carter muttered. "You're lucky you didn't lose your badge when the feds went after me. I'm not exactly healthy to be around."

He put his fork down and nailed her with a hot stare. "So you're saying you dropped out of sight to protect me."

"Hardly out of sight. You know where—"

"Don't play your smart lawyer word games with me," Kevin growled. "Do I look like some kind of pussy, I need you to take my hits for me?"

Carter grinned. "Fortunately, not like any I've ever seen."

Kevin laughed. "You always were a dick."

"No argument." Carter gestured to his plate. "You going to eat the rest of that pie?"

"Damn right I am. Get your own pie." Kevin cleaned his plate in two fast bites and picked up his coffee cup. "So what's going on?"

"We've got a dead FBI agent—and another one in surgery right now who probably won't make it."

Kevin's brows drew down. "That's major."

"More than you know. The one in surgery is Marilyn Allen. Somebody put a knife in her chest late this afternoon."

"Holy shit. Who?"

"I was hoping you'd be able to tell me. According to Allen, the feds were in town chasing a source who might finger some drug dealers."

"I can't see Allen or any of her team running down that kind of intel personally," Kevin said, frowning. "That's the B-team kind of assignment."

"We figure the same thing." Carter pushed her coffee aside. Her stomach already felt like she'd been dining on battery acid. "Have you heard any noise about Allen gearing up to go after Pareto again?"

"I don't think she ever stopped," Kevin said, "but if she's moving on him, she's not sharing with us."

"What about Rica?"

"Same story. You always hear rumors, but nothing I can confirm."

Carter leaned forward. "Look, we're in the dark. Right about now, rumors sound pretty damn good." When Kevin didn't answer, Carter sighed. She and Kevin didn't play on the same team anymore. Maybe he didn't think she played on his side at all. "Okay. Sorry to put you on the spot." She started to rise. "Thanks for driving down—"

"Oh, for Christ's sake, sit down and get the stick out of your shorts."

"That's not a stick."

Kevin grinned. "Yeah, you wish." Then his expression grew serious. "I don't have anything that's going to help you. Since the joint task force tanked, we haven't really been in the loop. We bump into some of the feds now and then when our territories cross, and I'm pretty sure Allen is still set on nailing Pareto. Obsessed with it, really. I heard after she lost her inside man—Rizzo—she turned another one of Pareto's top guys. That's all very hush-hush. I don't know who it is."

Carter rubbed at the headache pounding in the middle of her forehead. She didn't really care if Marilyn Allen had another informant in Pareto's organization. That was all part of the game. Alfonse Pareto could take care of himself—he had to know he was always vulnerable to someone in his organization betraying him. She wouldn't lose any sleep, other than for the pain it would cause Rica, if Pareto went to jail. "Rica's name hasn't come up?"

"Not that I heard."

"I can't see a connection between the mob investigation and what's been going on over here," Carter finally said.

"I don't see it, either."

Carter took out a twenty for Kevin's pie and left it on the table. "If you hear anything, let me know."

"Same goes." Kevin grasped Carter's arm. "Watch your back."

"Always."

❖

He waited thirty minutes after the downstairs lights went out and another went on upstairs, then he slipped through the shadows to the corner of the rear deck. He climbed over the railing, pressed his back to the wall, and sidled next to the sliding glass doors, listening, waiting. Even though excitement rippled through him, he didn't mind waiting. Now that he was so close, he wanted to savor every second. The anticipation of touching her, of hearing her moan, of hearing her beg, was only going to make his ultimate pleasure all the more sweet. He slid the glass cutter from his pocket and, after applying a short strip of duct tape from the roll he carried in his other pocket, he cut out a circular section of glass large enough for his hand to fit through next to the lock. And then he was inside. The kitchen was dark. A faint glow emanated from somewhere in the front of the house. Slowly and carefully he made his way forward until he could scan the living and dining rooms. Empty. Off to his left, stairs led up to the second floor, and judging from his observations from the beach, she was in the bedroom at the rear corner of the house. Now he was only a minute away from her. He reached into his pocket one more time and came out with his pistol. He'd save the knife for later, when she was helpless. Silently, he started up the stairs.

❖

Carter drove home frustrated and tired. She'd been hoping Kevin would have something for her—a name, a connection, some kind of lead. But Marilyn had obviously decided she didn't need the assistance of the state police and had cut them out of whatever her team was doing. Carter wasn't surprised. Marilyn had never wanted to work with the locals—she only tolerated Carter and Kevin because Carter's cover was so solid she could get inside Pareto's organization when no one else could. Marilyn had needed her. Now the agent had apparently found another informant inside Pareto's organization.

From what Carter knew of Alfonse Pareto's security, that couldn't have been easy. The last Pareto captain who had been coerced by the feds into betraying Pareto had ended up dead while in protective custody. Carter thought back to the men closest to Pareto. They were all family or longtime friends. She couldn't think of a single one who could be turned, not even with the threat of imprisonment. Pareto was generous with money and took care of his men's families if they were imprisoned or disabled. He was also ruthless and completely unsentimental when it came to meting out punishment for transgressions. A man would have to be crazy or have a major death wish to betray him.

The clock on her dashboard registered ten fifty. She'd be home in twenty minutes, maybe less. She wanted another shower and then she wanted to crawl into bed next to Rica and lose herself for a few hours in Rica's arms. She should check in with Reese first and find out if there was any word on Marilyn's condition. She hoped when she closed her eyes, she wouldn't see Marilyn's face. Wouldn't hear her broken plea. But she didn't think she was going to get her wish. Even with her eyes open and riveted to the hypnotic ribbon of black that streamed beneath her headlights, she could still see the stark terror in Marilyn Allen's eyes and hear her desperate words. Even now, the agent's strangled voice echoed in her head.

...n...go...

She doubted she would ever stop hearing... Carter shivered as an icy hand gripped her insides and twisted. She jerked and the car veered dangerously toward the shoulder. Panic surging, she yanked the wheel and managed to steady the vehicle.

"Oh Jesus," she whispered, fumbling for her phone. "Oh Jesus, no."

❖

Rica smiled as she slipped on the peach, thigh-length silk nightgown and adjusted the thin straps. Carter loved to undress her, and even though Carter might not be home for hours, and she'd probably be dead tired when she was, a girl could hope. She snapped off the bathroom light, padded barefoot across the hardwood floor to the bed, and turned down the covers. She reached out to switch off the bedside lamp and stopped when she heard the faint swish of the bedroom door opening behind her. Slowly, her blood stilling in her veins, she turned.

"Hello, Rica." His mad black eyes swept over her body as he stepped into the room.

Rica saw the gun in his right hand and she lunged for the top drawer of the dresser. A fist in her hair yanked her back so violently, she lost her balance. She lashed backward with both hands, trying to find his face, his eyes, but his other arm came across her throat and squeezed. She kicked and flailed until her vision dimmed and her strength failed her.

CHAPTER TWENTY-SEVEN

O h God," Tory sighed, running her fingers through Reese's hair. "You have the most amazing, incredible mouth."

Laughing, Reese rubbed her cheek against Tory's stomach. "You inspire me to greatness."

"Are you sure about the baby?" Tory asked softly, still caressing Reese's face.

Reese kissed the soft skin on the inside of Tory's hip bone and traced the faint stretch marks that tracked over her lower abdomen, glimmering faintly in the muted lamplight, and the long, thin line left from the C-section. Battle scars. But these scars were badges of honor celebrating life, not death. She thought of Reggie sleeping innocently in the other room, and of all the promise and wonder awaiting their child in the future. All the joy that lay in store for them as a family. She wouldn't change anything about her life—not her solitary years in the service or the brutal time she'd spent in combat, or the nightmares that would probably never leave her. Darkness and evil were part of the life she had chosen, but this woman, this family—they were the power that shone the light into her darkest reaches and gave her the strength she could count on. Raising herself up on her arms so she could look into Tory's face, Reese said, "I'm positive I want another baby. If it's safe."

Tory's eyes grew solemn and she wrapped her arms tightly around Reese's shoulders. "I will never do anything to risk what we have. I promise."

"Same here." Reese kissed her, groaning as Tory swept a hand down her back and pushed a thigh between Reese's legs. Reese deepened the kiss and thrust against the velvet skin and hard muscle, letting the pressure she'd been holding back while she made love to Tory rise and carry her toward release.

Her cell phone on the bedside table rang, and Reese groaned louder. Arms trembling, she took a deep breath and forced the tide of pleasure to recede. Rolling over with a grunt, she fumbled for the phone. "Conlon."

A tumble of shouts, nearly incoherent at first, assaulted her, and when the words finally began to make sense, Reese jumped to her feet.

"I'll be there in three minutes. Carter," Reese said firmly but calmly. "Carter—when you arrive, park on Bradford and call me. You do not approach the house."

The line was silent.

"Carter," Reese barked, harsher this time. "Do you understand? That's an order."

"Yes," Carter said hoarsely. "Yes. But, Jesus, hurry. I'm still ten minutes away."

"I'll be there." Reese disconnected and grabbed her pants, yanking them on as Tory got out of bed, found her shirt, and handed it to her.

"What can I do?" Tory asked.

"Carter thinks someone's making a move on Rica right now. Call Bri—tell her I need backup at Rica and Carter's. Tell her to come silent and call my cell. Tell her I need her now."

"You're going in alone?"

"I'll put cars on the street in case the suspect gets by us, but I can't risk alerting him if he has Rica. A small coordinated entry team is better." Reese unlocked the gun case inside a corner closet and removed an M16 assault rifle along with her service sidearm, a 9mm Beretta.

Tory watched Reese clip the holster to her waistband as she had thousands of times before. In moments like this, it came home to her with stark clarity that when Reese left the house, she would be in mortal danger. She could walk out the door and never come back. Swiftly, ruthlessly, Tory forced the thoughts away.

"I'll get Bri," Tory said, already punching in Bri's number on the cell as she followed Reese downstairs.

Reese grabbed her keys off the kitchen counter and kissed Tory fast and hard. "I'll call you."

"I love you," Tory called as Reese bolted through the door into the night.

❖

Rica sensed the light through her closed eyelids and for an instant, the golden glow felt soothing. She remembered the man in the doorway at the same time as the bruising pain in her throat destroyed any illusion of comfort. Then she registered the weight on her hips, pinning her down, and knew he was straddling her. Like any cornered animal, she wanted to flee, wanted to thrash and struggle and scream, and she had to fight hard to stay still. Calling upon every ounce of strength and pride and stubbornness she owned, she let her hatred for him surge through her, submerging the blind panic in a powerful undertow. Rica opened her eyes and stared into his flat black pupils, purposely not looking at the gun in his right hand. "I thought you were dead."

Her voice was hoarse, and her eyes watered from the pain of forcing the words out. She grit her teeth to prevent the tears from escaping.

Lorenzo Brassi laughed. "You didn't go to my funeral."

"I take it you weren't…incinerated in the car explosion…as reported." Rica concentrated on keeping her breathing even. She knew what fear did to Enzo. He loved it, fed off it. He had always tried to trap and torment her, even when he still believed she would one day be his wife. What he enjoyed most about women was dominating them sexually and physically. Marriage to him would have been a lifelong sentence of abuse masquerading as affection. He'd dropped all pretense of caring for her in any way other than as a possession when he'd finally accepted that she did not want him, that she wanted Carter. The last time she'd seen Enzo, he had caught her alone in a deserted alcove in her father's house and nearly raped her.

"As you can see," Enzo said with a sardonic smile, "the reports of my death were exaggerated."

"Not easy to fool my father." Rica turned her head ever so slightly to glance out of the corner of her eye at the bedside table. The top drawer was still open a few inches. She hoped her gun was still inside and that Enzo had not seen it.

"You have your FBI friends to thank for that." Enzo shifted his weight so his crotch rested more tightly against Rica's stomach and traced the underside of her breast with the muzzle of his H&K. "They made me an offer I couldn't refuse. I provide information on your father and his associates, they make sure all the reports, including DNA, support my death."

"It worked. No one suspected." Rica pushed her hips into the bed, recoiling from the press of his erection. She had to find some way to distract him so she could get to her gun, and she didn't have much time. She didn't know when Carter would be home, but it would be soon. If Enzo was still here, Carter would walk in, unsuspecting, and Enzo would gun her down. Rica had to find a way to kill him first, or give him what he wanted so he would leave.

"And since everyone thought I was dead, all I had to do was slip away from my keepers. They couldn't very well tell anyone they'd lost me." Enzo chuckled and slid the pistol barrel higher, dragging it painfully back and forth across Rica's nipple. "You and I have unfinished business. I've watched her pretend to fuck you, you know. She can't give you what you really need. After I show you, you'll understand that. You won't ever want to think of *Carter* again."

Rica froze, the breath stilling in her chest. He was insane, and from the venomous way he spoke Carter's name, she understood why he had risked his freedom to come here. Carter, in his mind, had stolen her away from him. Carter had bested him. Carter had taken what he believed to be his. Enzo was going to rape her to reassert his claim on her, but that was never going to be enough. No matter what he did to her, no matter what she said to him, he would still need to destroy the invader who had dared violate his territory. He would kill Carter, and that was something she couldn't let happen. Her only hope was to catch him off guard. She just needed a second or two, even if she only managed to wound him enough to make him flee. Even if he killed her in the process. She wouldn't let him take everything that mattered to her—he would not take Carter. She only had to distract him for a few precious seconds. Rica ignored the pistol playing back and forth over her breasts and reached for the button on his pants.

"What are you waiting for?"

❖

Reese's phone vibrated and she pulled it out of her pants pocket. "Conlon."

"The deck door is open. The glass is cut out," Bri said. "He's inside."

"That light upstairs—that's the bedroom?"

"Yes, the master. I can get up there—"

"Negative. I need eyes in that room before we move in." Reese surveyed the street for a possible vantage point. The house next to Rica and Carter's was a large two-story with a wraparound deck on the second level. "Hold your position. Do you have your radio?"

"Yes."

"Go to Tac one. Smith and Chang are on Tac two in their cruiser."

"Roger."

Reese quickly cut across the street to the side of the residence adjacent to Carter and Rica's. She saw no car in the driveway but couldn't be certain the house was empty. If she rang the bell and ordered them to evacuate, they were likely to turn on the lights, including the one on the front porch. She didn't want to do anything that might alert the intruder to a police presence. At this point, the neighbors weren't going to be placed in any significant danger if she didn't alert them to what was going on. She didn't intend to engage in a firefight. If she fired, it would be a kill shot.

Securing her rifle diagonally across her back, Reese climbed up on the railing of the rear deck, stretched upward, jumped, and grasped the lower edge of the deck above. She pulled herself up and then carefully climbed over the railing and skirted low along the side of the house until she was opposite the lighted window forty feet away. The builders had been smart enough not to place facing windows directly opposite each other, and she had a wall at her back, affording further protection to any occupant of the house if the suspect should fire at her. Resting her rifle on the railing for support, she sighted through the scope into Rica and Carter's bedroom.

❖

"Why the change of heart?" Enzo said, automatically thrusting his hips forward as Rica inched down the zipper on his fly. His gaze drifted down, away from her face, to her hands.

"You're here. She's not." Rica watched his eyes lose focus just a little as she slid her fingers along the ridge of flesh she slowly exposed. Adding what she knew he believed would be true, she said, "Besides, I want to enjoy it."

He pressed the gun between her breasts and pushed up the peach silk nightgown with his free hand, exposing her bare stomach and the matching panties. He grunted as her fingers closed around him.

"And we are going to enjoy it," Rica whispered, aware that the automatic still pointed at her throat. Until he moved it to a position where he wouldn't kill her instantly if he fired, she couldn't do anything but keep on with the course she had plotted. Numbing her mind to everything except her ultimate goal, to keep Carter safe, she pretended to enjoy what she was doing.

❖

Carter punched in Reese's number as she rocketed down Bradford, swerved around the cruiser blocking the intersection closest to her street, and jammed to a halt on the shoulder. When Reese picked up, she shouted, "I'm just pulling up at the bottom of the hill. Is she all right?"

"We've got an intruder." Reese spoke softly into her phone, assessing what she could see through the window. Rica was not visible, but it wasn't difficult to decipher the scenario in front of her. She could make out the head and shoulders of a man who appeared to be kneeling on the bed. He was oddly motionless. She didn't see a weapon, and until she knew if he was armed, she couldn't risk moving in prematurely. Right now, surprise was on their side. If he knew they were out there, they'd have a hostage situation on their hands, or worst-case scenario, he'd kill Rica and opt for suicide by cop. "Late thirties, black hair, dark eyes, looks Mediterranean."

"It's Enzo. It's gotta be Enzo," Carter gasped, running full out up the street. There were no streetlights, so she didn't have to worry about being seen, but she kept to the shadows, slowing as she neared her house. Every instinct screamed at her to barge inside, to find Rica, to destroy whoever threatened her. But her cop instincts were just as strong, telling her to slow down, telling her to listen to Reese. Telling her to trust Reese. "Reese. He'll hurt her."

"No, he won't," Reese said quietly. "Bri is on your rear deck. Meet her, move inside and upstairs. Do not attempt to enter the bedroom until I give the order."

"Okay. Okay."

Carter shoved the phone in her pocket, pulled her weapon, and ran to join Bri. She had to get inside that house. She had to get to Rica, and then she was going to kill him.

CHAPTER TWENTY-EIGHT

Rica was running out of time. She despised Enzo and loathed touching him, but she made herself keep watching his face to judge when his focus started to dissolve. She couldn't think about what she saw in his smug expression—the victory and the pleasure. She gasped when he lifted himself a few inches off her body, wrapped her flimsy panties in his fist, and yanked. The material tore away, chafing roughly over her unprotected flesh, and he laughed when she couldn't stifle a small cry. The pistol in his right hand wavered, swinging back and forth in front of her face, as his eyes dropped back to her fingers clenched around him. She picked up speed, waiting for his control to falter and his reflexes to slow.

"You're not trying to make me come, are you," he panted, his thighs still clamped around her hips like a vise. He pushed and pulled himself through her fingers, his tempo fast and erratic. "That's right. You're good...at this."

"I'm ready," Rica whispered, praying she would be fast enough.

"Spread your legs and put me inside," he growled through gritted teeth. "Hurry up."

"I can't with you where you are," Rica said, trying to sound eager. "Move down, Enzo, so I can put you where you belong. Come on, baby, I want you—"

Enzo grunted and shoved himself down until he was no longer straddling her hips. When he shifted his leg to force it between hers, freeing her of his weight for just a second, Rica quickly jerked both knees up to her chest and rolled off the bed, scrambling for the drawer in the bedside table. She heard his furious roar, and even as her hand closed around the pistol grip, she knew she was too late. The gunshot, or maybe it was her scream, was deafening.

❖

At the sound of the shot, Carter elbowed Bri aside and shouldered through the door into the bedroom, panning the room with her weapon, her stomach clenched into a knot. Two bodies on the floor. Blood everywhere. Globs of maroon splattered on the bed, the dresser, the wall. Ribbons of crimson streaking down Rica's face and chest.

"Rica," Carter moaned, rushing forward. Bri was right beside her and grabbed the suspect's shoulder, jerked him over, and trained her gun on his body. Carter fell to her knees next to Rica. "Baby! Oh Jesus, Rica!"

Rica shuddered and opened her eyes. When she saw Carter, she cried out and threw herself into Carter's arms.

"Are you hurt?" Carter shouted, clutching Rica to her chest. She rocked her, searching her body with one hand, looking for injuries. "Baby, are you hit?"

Wordlessly, Rica shook her head and burrowed closer into Carter.

"Is he dead?" Carter rasped, her hot eyes on the man splayed on the floor.

"Yes," Bri said, removing the weapon from Enzo's hand. She radioed Reese. "We're code four here."

"Rica?" Reese's voice came back staticky over the radio.

"She's okay." Bri glanced over to the shattered window, then down to the man lying in a pool of blood at her feet. She couldn't see the entry wound that must be in the back of his head, but the exit wound had taken out most of his forehead. "We'll need the coroner."

"I'll call her and get officers out here for crowd control. You have the scene."

"Roger that." Bri knelt down beside Carter and Rica. Carter's eyes were closed now, her face pressed to Rica's hair. Bri gripped Carter's shoulder. "I think you can take her to another room. I'll make sure the scene is undisturbed until Reese gets here."

"Thanks," Carter said gruffly. She got to her knees and eased Rica up with her. "Come on, baby. Let me get you out of here."

❖

Tory tapped on the bedroom door next to the crime scene and eased into the room. Rica sat stiffly on the side of the bed, Carter next to her, holding her hand. Rica's nightgown was splotched with darkened patches of blood, as were her bare shoulders and neck. Tory set her equipment bag down in the center of the floor and took out her camera.

"Rica, I need to take some photos, gather a few samples, and then you can get into the shower." Tory smiled at Carter, who looked so wired she was about to fly apart. "Carter, maybe you could get things ready for her. Make sure the bathroom is nice and steamy and find a robe and lots of fluffy towels."

Carter looked uncertain, but Rica said in a low, flat voice, "Go ahead, sweetheart. It's okay."

"I'll just be in the other room if you need me," Carter said, brushing Rica's cheek with her fingertips.

Rica watched until Carter had closed the bathroom door behind her, then smiled wanly at Tory. "Thank you. She doesn't need to hear this."

"She probably does," Tory said casually, moving back and forth in front of Rica, getting the photos she needed for her report. "You'll probably want to tell her, too, but you'll know when the right time is." She finished and stowed the camera away. Then she donned gloves and assembled a number of specimen containers. Moving closer so she could speak softly, she said, "Tell me what happened."

After a pause, Rica recounted the events while Tory quickly and efficiently took scrapings from Rica's nails, collected flakes of blood from her skin, and plucked errant hairs from her nightgown and body. Rica's voice shook when she described what she had done to distract Enzo. She glanced toward the closed bathroom door. "I don't know how to tell her that."

Tory affixed labels to specimen envelopes and jars and stored them in her case. Then she sat next to Rica and took her hand. "What you did was incredibly brave." She laughed softly. "Maybe just a little bit crazy risky too. Carter knows you love her. And she loves you. She's not going to be upset about anything you had to do to survive." Tory slid her arm around Rica's shoulders and hugged her. "Trust me on this. Trust her."

"I was so afraid Carter would come back and Enzo would kill her." Rica felt the terror for the first time, really felt it deep inside, and she couldn't stop the tears. "I was afraid he would kill me and then her."

"You stopped that from happening. You did really well." Tory held Rica tightly as she sobbed, and when the bathroom door burst open and Carter vaulted into the room, her eyes wild with worry, Tory shook her head. "She's all right. She just needs to do this for a few minutes."

Carter leaned back against the wall and closed her eyes. "As long as she needs."

After a few minutes, Rica straightened and brushed trembling fingers over her face. "Did I shoot him?"

Tory glanced at Carter, who nodded for her to go ahead. "No, you didn't. Reese shot him. She told me if you hadn't done what you did, if you hadn't gotten him to move, she wouldn't have had a clear shot. She couldn't see the gun earlier."

"I would have shot him," Rica murmured. "I would have killed him and I don't think I would have felt a thing."

"The bastard deserved it." Carter strode across the room and squatted down in front of Rica, taking her hands. "Baby, he assaulted you. He killed an FBI agent and knifed another one. He would have hurt you, baby."

Rica smiled weakly and squeezed Carter's hands. "I'm all right. Really." She turned to Tory. "Can I get clean now?"

Her eyes steady on Rica, Tory asked, "Do I need to collect sexual forensic evidence?"

"No. He never touched me."

"Then I think Carter owes you a shower."

❖

Reese watched dispassionately as the two medics zipped up the black body bag and lifted it onto the stretcher for transport to the clinic. When the room had cleared, she picked up Tory's equipment bag while Tory disposed of her gloves and washed her hands in the bathroom.

"All set?" Reese asked when Tory emerged.

Tory took one last look around the room, then studied the shattered window. "That was quite a shot."

Reese looked over her shoulder to the house next door. Lights blazed in most of the windows now. She had sent officers to speak to the neighbors and assure everyone that there was no danger, but with three patrol cars and two ambulances outside in the street, the entire neighborhood was awake. From her vantage point on the opposite deck, she'd been pretty certain of what was happening in this room, although her view was obstructed most of the time. And there hadn't been any question in her mind when Rica had bolted upright and the suspect, after catching his balance, had swung his pistol in her direction. Reese had had a millisecond to determine that Rica was not in her line of fire and that Rica was in imminent danger. She'd shot him in the head because she couldn't risk a body shot that might not have completely and instantaneously disabled him. Head shots weren't usually recommended, because the target was so much smaller than a center mass shot, but she had to stop him in his tracks before his nervous system could telegraph a signal to his finger to pull the trigger. She couldn't risk him shooting Rica, so she aimed for the medulla at the back of his head.

"Short-range shot," Reese said. "Every Marine is a marksman."

"And thank God for that," Tory murmured, brushing her hand over Reese's chest. "Are you all right?"

Reese sighed and took in the room and the remains of a near tragedy. "About taking out the suspect? Yes. But I'm not happy he got to her. I think I should've seen this coming."

"Of course you should have," Tory said with an edge. "Because you're clairvoyant in addition to being indestructible and…"

"Hey," Reese said gently. "Everybody's fine."

Tory slid her arms around Reese's waist. "When I saw you leave the house with that rifle, I knew it was going to be bad. I was frightened."

"I'm sorry."

"No. No apologies." Tory leaned back and smiled wryly. "And I'm sorry for nagging you. Get some sleep, and in the morning you and the rest of your team can go over all of this. If you missed something, you'll find it. But Rica's all right, and that's what matters."

"Thanks." Reese kissed her. "Let's go home."

CHAPTER TWENTY-NINE

Allie's phone vibrated on the table next to the bed, and she stretched carefully for it with her good right arm, trying not to wake Ash. KT had finally given her permission to go home around midnight, stating she was satisfied that Allie's wound wasn't going to require surgery. Allie had taken the prescribed pain pill, and the minute she and Ash had climbed into bed, she'd cuddled up in Ash's arms and checked out. In the soft light of early morning, Ash still looked exhausted, her face drawn and pale with dark circles under her eyes. Allie figured she probably looked as bad, but she didn't feel too terrible. Her arm hurt like anything, but mostly, she was happy. She had a lot to be happy about. She'd helped catch a perp yesterday, and best of all, she'd just woken up next to Ash.

The text message was from Bri, and it was a whopper. She hurriedly sent a response and eased to the edge of the bed. Before she could try standing up, an arm snaked around her waist. Then she felt a soft kiss in the center of her back.

"Going somewhere?" Ash skated her hand higher, cradling Allie's breast in her palm.

Allie leaned back against Ash, closing her eyes and enjoying the play of Ash's fingers over her nipple. "You know just how to get me going, don't you?"

"Don't know what you mean." Ash sat up and put a leg on either side of Allie's body, pulling Allie back against her chest. She kissed the side of her neck and nuzzled her ear. "Who were you texting? Girlfriend?"

Allie leaned her head away and gave Ash a look. "You were sweet for twelve whole hours. Are you going to be a dick again now?"

"Probably." Ash nipped at Allie's earlobe.

"That was Bri. They got the guy that knifed the FBI agents. He broke in and assaulted Rica at her house."

Ash stiffened. "Is Rica all right?"

"Yes, but I want to go to the station and find out what's going on."

"Are you sure? How's your arm?"

"My arm is fine. I want to talk about you being a dick, so don't change the subject." Allie tried to sound stern, but the tingling in her nipple was spreading to her clit. Her mind was getting a little fuzzy. She pushed her hips back into Ash's crotch, pleased when Ash groaned softly. "I like you being all possessive and stuff."

"Good," Ash rumbled, her mouth against Allie's neck.

"But I don't like you being stupid jealous."

Ash brought her other arm around Allie's body so she could hold both breasts. "Is there a difference?"

"Yes." Allie sighed, resting her head back against Ash's shoulder. "That feels so good."

"Mmm, to me too." Ash went back to kissing Allie's neck, the edge of her jaw, the corner of her mouth. "Don't move, let me do everything."

"No argument." Allie shifted restlessly. She needed more. She needed Ash to stroke her clit. And she really needed to finish her thought before she couldn't think any more at all. "When you're possessive, it just means you want me real bad."

"I want you something fierce." Ash caressed Allie's stomach with one hand, sweeping her fingertips over the delta between her thighs but not entering. Allie whimpered and Ash struggled not to push lower, deeper, right away. She wanted to claim Allie as hers. She wanted to be the only one who ever touched her again.

"But when you're jealous," Allie gasped, clutching Ash's wrist and moving her fingers lower, onto her stiff, aching clit. "Then you don't trust me. I need you to trust...oh, God baby...you're going to make me come soon."

"Mmm, I am."

"Trust me?" Allie moaned and pressed Ash's fingers harder over the spot that pulsed and beat frantically, moving Ash's fingertips in quick, firm circles. "Please. Please I need you."

"I trust you, I do," Ash whispered. "I love you. I love you, Allie."

Allie pushed back hard in Ash's arms, her hips lifting as she came. She dug her nails into the top of Ash's hand, keeping Ash right on the spot as her orgasm pounded beneath Ash's fingertips. After her muscles unlocked, she sank back with a long sigh. "Oh my God. I love when you do that."

Ash laughed. "I love to do it."

Allie shifted sideways and rested her cheek against Ash's shoulder. "What are we going to do?"

Ash kissed her forehead. "What do you want to do?"

"I asked you first."

Allie's tone was playful but Ash heard the challenge in her voice. She'd been the one to walk away before. Now Allie wanted her to be the one to take the risk. She would. She'd do anything to make Allie feel secure. To have Allie trust *her* again. "You're the only woman in my heart, so here's what I want. I want to be the only woman in your life from now on. For forever." Ash studied Allie's face, but got no clue as to how Allie felt about what she was saying. She had no choice but to put it all on the line. "I want to live here with you."

"What about your job?" Allie asked.

"I already travel for work. I'll just travel a little farther."

"And what about when you're on the road and you get horny?"

Ash was naked and when Allie brushed her fingers over her chest, tracing the curve of her breast with a fingertip, the muscles in her thighs twitched. "I'll call you and we'll have phone sex."

Smiling faintly, Allie raked her nails down the center of Ash's stomach. "What about when *I* get horny?"

"You can make yourself come while you think about me touching you."

Allie lifted her eyes to Ash's, her expression serious. "That's it? You and me? No one else?"

"No one else," Ash whispered.

Allie settled her head back on Ash's shoulder and slid her hand lower, between Ash's legs. "That sounds good to me."

"To me too." Ash closed her eyes and rested her cheek against the top of Allie's head. The unbearable pleasure that was coming soon, taking her fast and hard, would be exquisite, and only a fraction of the joy that filled her heart.

❖

"You okay?" Bri asked when Allie settled into the chair next to her in Reese's office. Carter sat on the other side of Bri in plain clothes. She didn't look like she'd gotten a whole lot of sleep.

"Yeah," Allie whispered. "It really hurts a lot, though."

"I bet. Take it easy, all right?"

Allie leaned around Bri to Carter. "Is Rica all right?"

"She's shaken up, but she's solid," Carter replied, not certain who was more shaken up—Rica or her. Rica had finally fallen asleep around dawn, but she hadn't been able to. Every time she closed her eyes, she saw Rica on the floor covered in blood. When she'd left for the station, Rica had seemed calm and steady, a lot steadier than Carter felt. Every now and then a picture of what might have happened if Reese hadn't taken the shot when she did popped into her head and she got sick to her stomach.

"Tell her I'll call—"

Reese cut in. "Tremont. You're on sick leave. Go home."

"I will, Sheriff." Allie settled back and folded her arms across her chest. "After the debriefing."

"You called her in, Parker?" Reese said to Bri.

Bri straightened in her chair. "Yes ma'am. I knew she'd want to be here."

Reese worked at not smiling. The two were partners, and she could team them up with others as much as she wanted, but nothing was going to change that. "Okay, then. Let's run it."

Allie noticed Carter's hands ball into fists when Reese got to the part about Lorenzo Brassi breaking in and assaulting Rica. She didn't even want to imagine how she'd feel if something like that happened to Ash, so she concentrated on the facts and remembered that Rica was safe because all of them, including Rica, had done what needed to be done.

"So you think it was Brassi all along?" Allie asked when Reese finished. "Doing everything? Breaking into Rica's car and your house and…" She glanced at Bri. "What about the intruder at Caroline and Bri's the other night?"

"I questioned Everly again this morning before he was transferred back to the federal lockup," Reese said. "Pushed him hard. He still denies going after Caroline, and although his alibi is weak, I think it's probably legit. He said he just wanted to lay low until everyone forgot about him, which is why he went to his buddy's place and didn't even let his mother know he was around."

Bri snorted. "As if we would forget he'd skipped out on parole."

"Well, he's not too bright."

"What did the feds say about Brassi?" Carter asked, her dark eyes edgy and troubled.

"They said they can't comment on an ongoing operation." Reese knew what was going on in Carter's head, could imagine the pictures that tortured her. Carter would be tormented by those pictures for a long time, but she'd be okay. She still had Rica, and that was all she needed. That and knowing the man who had harmed Rica had paid. "I don't think we'll ever get the entire story from the feds. According to Rica, Brassi said the feds helped him disappear. My guess is that someone in Alfonse Pareto's organization leaked that Pareto intended to eliminate Brassi because he was unstable and a threat to Rica. The feds saw a chance to recruit him and gave him a choice—either he turns informer for them and in return they help fake his death, or Pareto has him killed. Not much of a choice."

"And then," Carter said, "he slips away from them and goes after Rica."

Reese nodded. "Once he got here, Brassi hid out and stalked Rica. It's not unusual for stalkers to work themselves up to attacking their primary target while terrorizing their target's friends and loved ones. It gives them a sense of power, and they derive pleasure from their target's fear and pain."

"But why didn't someone tell us when Special Agent Lynch tracked him here?" Bri asked. "If we'd known, we might've picked Brassi up sooner. Agent Lynch might not be dead and no one else would have been terrorized."

"I don't think Marilyn Allen wanted to advertise that her team had lost track of an informant, particularly one who was dangerously crazy.

I'm not even certain she informed her superiors. She was probably hoping they'd find him and get him back under wraps with no one the wiser."

"She was willing to put Rica's life at risk in order to nail Rica's father," Carter said bitterly.

"What *about* Agent Allen?" Allie asked. "What's the word on her condition?"

"She's out of surgery, but in a coma. The doctors don't give her much chance," Reese said.

The room was silent. Reese closed the folder on top of her desk and pushed it aside.

"I think we have all the answers we're ever going to get," Reese said. "Tremont, I don't want you back here without a medical release form in your hand. Carter, Bri—go home and get some rest. I've assigned officers to cover your shifts tonight."

Reese waited until the team filed out, then she called Tory. "I'm taking a personal day."

"Really," Tory said slowly. "And what are you going to do with all that free time?"

"Can you get away?"

"KT is still in town. She'll cover for me."

"I thought I'd make reservations for us to have lunch in Boston. We can fly over and maybe you could pull some doctor strings and get us in to see Wendy later this afternoon. We can talk to her about making babies."

"You don't waste any time, do you, Sheriff?"

"When you know what you want, why wait?"

"I know what I want," Tory murmured. "Come home now."

"On my way, Dr. King."

About the Author

Radclyffe is a retired surgeon and full-time award-winning author-publisher with over thirty novels and anthologies in print. Seven of her works have been Lambda Literary finalists including the Lambda Literary winners *Erotic Interludes 2: Stolen Moments* edited with Stacia Seaman; *In Deep Waters 2*; and *Distant Shores, Silent Thunder*. She is the editor of *Best Lesbian Romance* 2009 and 2010 (Cleis Press), *Erotic Interludes* 2 through 5 and *Romantic Interludes* 1 and 2 with Stacia Seaman (BSB), and has selections in multiple anthologies including *Best Lesbian Erotica* 2006–10; *After Midnight*; *Caught Looking: Erotic Tales of Voyeurs and Exhibitionists*; *First-Timers*; *Ultimate Undies: Erotic Stories About Lingerie and Underwear*; *Hide and Seek*; *A is for Amour*; *H is for Hardcore*; *L is for Leather*; *Rubber Sex*, *Tasting Him*, and *Cowboy Erotica*. She is the recipient of the 2003 and 2004 Alice B. Readers' award for her body of work and is also the president of Bold Strokes Books, one of the world's largest independent LGBTQ publishing companies.

Her latest releases are an all-Radclyffe erotica anthology, *Radical Encounters* (Feb. 2009) the romantic intrigue novel *Justice for All* (April 2009), and the romance *Secrets in the Stone* (July 2009). Her forthcoming works include *The Midnight Hunt* (writing as L.L. Raand, March 2010) and the first in the First Responder Series, *Trauma Alert* (July 2010).

Books Available From Bold Strokes Books

Power Play by Julie Cannon. Businesswomen Tate Monroe and Victoria Sosa are at odds in the boardroom, but not in the bedroom. (978-1-60282-125-5)

The Remarkable Journey of Miss Tranby Quirke by Elizabeth Ridley. When love enters Tranby's life in the form of a beautiful nineteen-year-old student, Lysette McDonald, she embarks on the most remarkable journey of all. (978-1-60282-126-2)

Returning Tides by Radclyffe. Insurance investigator Ashley Walker faces more than a dangerous opponent when she returns to the town, and the woman, she left behind. (978-1-60282-123-1)

Veritas by Anne Laughlin. When the hallowed halls of academia become the stage for murder, newly appointed Dean Beth Ellis's search for the truth leads her to unexpected discoveries about her own heart. (978-1-60282-124-8)

The Pleasure Planner by Larkin Rose. Pleasure purveyor Bree Hendricks treats love like a commodity until Logan Delaney makes Bree the client in her own game. (978-1-60282-121-7)

everafter by Nell Stark and Trinity Tam. Valentine Darrow is bitten by a vampire on her way to propose to her lover Alexa Newland, and their lives and love are placed in mortal jeopardy. (978-1-60282-119-4)

Summer Winds by Andrews & Austin. When Maggie Turner hires a ranch hand to help work her thousand acres, she never expects to be attracted to the very young, very female Cash Tate. (978-1-60282-120-0)

Beggar of Love by Lee Lynch. Jefferson is the lover every woman wants to be—or to have. A revealing saga of lesbian sexuality. (978-1-60282-122-4)